Cutting
Loose

NOVELS BY NADINE DAJANI

Fashionably Late

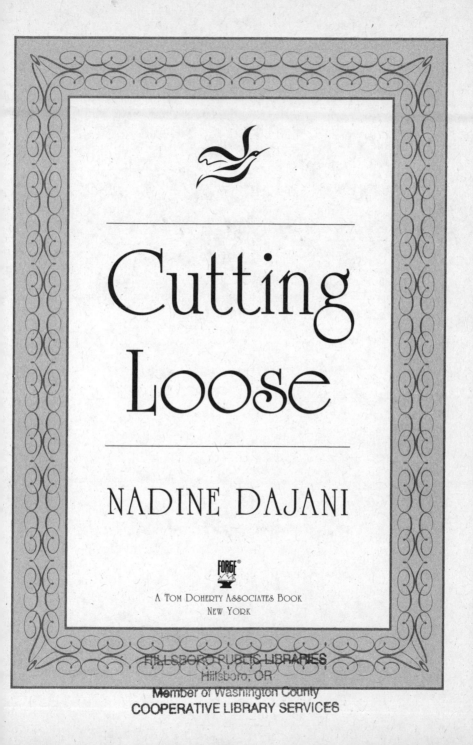

Cutting Loose

NADINE DAJANI

A Tom Doherty Associates Book
New York

CUTTING LOOSE

Copyright © 2008 by Nadine Dajani

A Forge Book
Published by Tom Doherty Associates, LLC
175 Fifth Avenue
New York, NY 10010

www.tor-forge.com

Forge® is a registered trademark of Tom Doherty Associates, LLC.

ISBN-13: 978-0-7653-1943-2
ISBN-10: 0-7653-1943-8

3754 4991 10/08

First Edition: October 2008

Printed in the United States of America

0 9 8 7 6 5 4 3 2 1

To my mother, for not being anything like the ones in this book

Acknowledgments

If writing your first novel is like driving through the fog with both headlights knocked out, then writing your second novel is like trying to get somewhere using the wrong map. You'd think you'd know where you were going, but you'd be tragically mistaken.

Thanks to the friends, family, and professionals who helped me through the sophomore-slump jitters with their encouragement, advice, and unwavering confidence.

Many thanks to Aryn, Wendy, Jenny, Kristin, and Dona for the priceless feedback and the lightning-speed reading. To Dara, Shirine, Basil, Carole, Christine, and Sharon for the pep talks (and yes, the occasional draft-proofing). To Jannyo for the support, the expertise, and teaching me to swear in Spanish with the best of them.

I am hugely grateful to Natasha for her relentless faith in my writing and to Paul for helping me bring out the best in this book.

And to Denis for always being there, no matter what.

London

Ranya

I didn't see it coming. They all say that, I know, but it's not like you wake up one morning and say to yourself: "This is the day it all falls apart; now, what should I wear?"

Dodi and I made sure everything would be as close to perfect as mere mortals could ever hope to get. From a Reem Acra confection of silk and organza so sweet and fluffy it could have been a meringue, to scheduling the big day to fall on Friday, that holiest of weekdays, our wedding day had been unequalled in pomp and over-the-top indulgence since Auntie Najla married off her fifth and final daughter to a lesser member of the Qatar royal family (much, *much* lesser).

Then, in less time than it takes to round off one lunar cycle, *kaboom*.

A mushroom cloud of unforeseen humiliation detonated in the halls of one of Montreal's finer department stores, and rose up with the dread of impending doom. The dust of public scandal has yet to settle on me, and already I have no idea what I'm going to do.

Snuggling deeper into my armchair, I surrender to the soothing aura of white linen tablecloths, tinkling stemware, and ebullient chatter of young women sitting in clusters around the hotel's private lounge, evidence of their morning jaunt to the shops stacked in brightly colored carrier bags at their feet. I try to channel a different time, when these things stood for all the wonder and delight of a five-year-old tagging along on a business trip with her indulgent father, or perhaps on a European shopping excursion with her mother. Instead I can only wonder if any one of those pretty girls with their flashy jewelry and bouncy giggles would ever have the misfortune of waking up one morning to the sucker-punch discovery that their husband of one month, the catch of the decade, the long-awaited award for obedient patience in the face of advancing time and mounting despair, was in fact, hopelessly and beyond any doubt, gay.

Probably not.

I pick up the cup of steaming amber liquid in front of

me, focusing on the mint particles huddled together at the bottom, and try to make like Julie Andrews and think about a few of my favorite things. Like Nutella straight from the jar and a lazy half-day at a spa.

"C'est payant, le terrorisme," I hear a woman next to me say, suddenly and without warning, to the man snuggled in a red velvet upholstered chair beside her. She tosses her wispy hair to the side and raises a glass of champagne to her lips, giggling.

I cradle my teacup back in its gold-rimmed saucer and square my shoulders.

Terrorism pays, she mouths again, surreptitiously jutting her chin at the groups of women sitting at tables around us.

Her eyes meet mine for half a second. She smiles, blissfully unaware the puffy-eyed woman in the belted Victor & Rolf shirtdress and cinnamon streaks happens to be one of *Them*—the Others. Girls who, if you were to take away their headscarves and have them show a little more leg, would look a lot like me.

"Them" being the veiled, coffee and mocha and olive-skinned versions of me.

There are lots of us filling the lounge, sitting around in gaggles, some conspicuous, some not, prattling in a thousand different variations of Gibberish, the official language of the Others—Urdu, Hindi, Farsi, and at least three different kinds of Arabic.

What I think has got the pointy-chinned blonde so miffed is that this particular set of Others isn't conforming to her general idea of what Others should be like—their headscarves are multicolored, some fringed, some sequined, some in solid, saturated hues and some patterned in plaid, or paisley, or Pucci. They're not bundled in shapeless black but rather swathed in longish boho skirts I recognize from the storefront windows lining Bond Street. Scattered throughout the room, flowing saris kiss the carpeted floors and pointy stiletto tips poke out from underneath the edges of structured wide-legged trousers while she, Miss Freckles, sits apart with her bored and listless companion. Worse—these Others seem contented, carefree, and positively unsubmissive.

I should say something.

I can embarrass her, bring a much-needed flush into those sallow cheeks. But I lower my head and stare into my own cup instead.

What would I say? Me, a grown woman who chose flight over fight when she had been wronged by a philandering husband?

"Excuse me, but I think you owe this lady an apology," a masculine voice booms in English.

What?

"What?" The blonde cradles her china cup back in its saucer and looks up at the man towering over her. Her face crumples up into a mask of loathing. Oh, no.

"I'm pretty sure you heard me the first time," says Mystery Man.

The blonde is just as frozen as I am. Her friend just sits

back and looks the other way, contempt dripping from every facial feature.

"Whatever." She shrugs.

" 'Whatever' isn't exactly an apology."

He doesn't budge. He has the build of an athlete, stuffed into a sleek (Italian? English?) single-breasted suit, and a sort of sunny informality about him that stands out in this somber crowd. I try not to stare, but that's hard to do when you're already frozen in place.

"Excuse me, Mr. Mallouk, can we help you with anything?" A hotel attendant with a shiny name tag that says "Katie" scurries up to us.

This should be my cue to leave. Now, before any more damage on my account is done. Still, I can't seem to budge.

"Yeah, actually, these guests were being rude to Miss . . . uh?"

He looks at me and smiles encouragingly. His teeth are too straight to be anything but American.

"Ranya." Should I give him my last name, too? Tell him I'm technically a "Mrs.," though I don't think that should count given the circumstances?

Again, probably not.

"I don't mean to cause a scene or anything, Katie," he turns to the attendant, who seems just as awestruck by this man as the rest of us are, "but I think Ranya is as entitled to a comfortable and respectful environment as the rest of us."

"Of course she is, Mr. Mallouk, may I ask exactly what happened?"

Katie looks back and forth from the American's relaxed face to the blonde's visible annoyance, then to my own mortification.

I came here to be invisible. This is the absolute last thing I wanted. To cause another scene, upset yet more people. But it seems Humiliation won't be releasing me from its clutches anytime soon.

"Well, this lady over here," the man Katie referred to as Mr. Mallouk nods toward the couple, "she made this joke—at least I think it was a joke—and I'm pretty sure I misunderstood. . . . Why don't you ask her to share it with us, you know, just in case I heard wrong," he says icily.

The culprit fidgets, scratches the back of her skull, and tucks a strand of yellow hair behind an ear, without once looking at any of us.

"Fine. I'm sorry." She exaggerates a bow of her head in my direction. "Are you happy now?"

"Not really, but you've wasted enough of our time." He turns to Katie, thanks her, and then stops in front of my table.

"Look—I'm really sorry about that. It was totally uncalled for. You really should have said something."

"How did you even know?"

He shakes his head and laughs. "Trust me, I know."

"Mallouk . . . Lebanese, right? You don't look it, though." I can feel myself blushing again. I'm not exactly prone to striking up conversations with perfect strangers in hotel lounges.

"Well . . . they taught us to say 'Phoenician' at Bible school, but yeah, Lebanese. I guess." He laughs. "Fourth generation. If it hadn't been for my dad's near-maniacal obsession of making sure we spoke Arabic in the house, I don't think I would've been any more Lebanese than this English muffin over here. I'm Georges, by the way." He looks flustered, as if not sure whether to shake my hand or not.

He settles on shoving both hands into his pockets instead and nodding in my direction.

"Well, uh, it was nice meeting you, Ranya. I'm sure I'll see you around."

"Mmm-hmm." I try to convey my gratitude by flapping my curled and tinted eyelashes at him. It's the best I can do. Where, I wonder, did the sparkling social graces I was bred to exhibit go? The au courant remarks designed to hint at a political science major, minor in French literature? An offhand reference or two to semesters at a Belgian lycée, summers at the family flat in Cyprus where beautiful Cypriots would slow their scooters to a near halt on dusty narrow streets and holler sweet obscenities at my cousins and me while we pretended to ignore them?

He turns and heads back to his table. There's a woman I hadn't noticed before sitting there waiting for him. She's around my age, a little thick around the middle and in need of serious exfoliation. And her eyes are shooting daggers at me.

Yeeee! Ranya? Ranya Hayek, is that you?"
        I look up. Two women, one in a salmon pink headscarf

covering her hairline and cascading in a silky curtain down to her shoulders, the other with poker-straight honey-colored hair and matching skin, are making their way to my table.

Leave it to the Universe to kick you in the shins just when you've never been more down. I needed the social equivalent of a Nepalese ashram buried in some mountainous wasteland, and instead I was about to be thrown into a lion's den while "It's a Small World After All" ran in a loop inside my head.

"It's such a small world, isn't it?" Soheir says, swooping down for the obligatory air kisses, her hair swooshing across my face.

I could cry.

If you had been around in the days when oil had made the desert bloom with the spoils of sudden wealth, chances are you would have met a Sabah or a Soheir. I happened to have gone to school with this particular pair in Riyadh, where my father, an industrial engineer from the small city of Sidon in Lebanon, was stationed. The Gulf area had come into a lot of money—fast—so they were happy enough to handsomely compensate anyone who could help transition them out of the Iron Age to something resembling the twentieth century. My father, educated at the American University of Beirut, was one such person. And that's how I, the daughter of a modest workingman from a regular working family, came to rub elbows with petrodollar heiresses like Sabah and Soheir el-Bustani.

"*Ma'sha'allah,* you look great!" Soheir coos. "Still, after all these years. How long has it been, Sabah?"

"Too many to count," says the less ditzy of the sisters.

"Can we sit?" asks Soheir.

"Of course . . . shame on you for asking!" I try to swallow back the hard knot of foreboding gathering at the back of my throat. There has to be a way out of this. Naturally, my cell phone, which had been ringing off the hook ever since I set foot off the plane at Heathrow, now slumbers mutely in my purse.

"That's not your husband over there, is it?" Sabah's gaze flits to somewhere just above and behind my head.

It's a lucky thing I didn't actually have anything in my mouth at the moment she uttered those words, because I immediately proceeded to choke on my own saliva.

Should I add "access to a teleporter" to the list of things-I-should-have-known-about-Dodi-before-I-married-him-but-didn't?

"*Sa'ha,*" Soheir mumbles the Arabic expression for "bless you," pummeling my back with her heavily bejeweled fist in the process. "Are you all right?"

"I'm fine," I manage, laboriously sucking in short gasps of air.

I whip around to find only the American, Georges, at the table behind me. He catches my stare and smiles. I turn right back, hoping he'd missed my cheeks exploding in bouquets of bright pink fireworks.

"That's just . . . someone I met here," I mumble.

Sabah betrays just a hint of disapproval. "Sorry, I just assumed . . . you know, since you were clearly getting along—"

"Oh, shush!" Soheir jumps in. "Ever since you took the *hijaab* you think everyone should be as stuffy as you. Let the poor girl talk to whomever she wants." She rolls her eyes before setting her gaze back on me. "Congratulations, by the way." She leans in and lays a dainty hand over mine. "We heard. You must be over the moon! Where is he?"

"Who?" I blink numbly.

"Your *husband*." She blinks back, her pasted smile freezing in place.

I inadvertently let out a snort. Some things never change. Or is it the people who don't change?

Sabah, Soheir, and I used to be part of a bigger *shillah*—a clique—back in our Riyadh school days. Loosely assembled though it was, a pastiche of girls who talked a little louder, held their noses a little higher, and flitted around in social circles a little brighter than the rest, I could imagine some ties in the old gang had resisted the pull of time and place. And with all the possible topics of conversation and debate this world holds for us, all they ever seemed to talk about was the weather and who had bought what from Europe or America to wear to which wedding. I'd spent the better part of my life convinced I had nothing in common with these girls. That if I socialized with them, it was for lack of more stimulating company. Sure I shopped a lot, but I'd also read Dickens and Zola and Flaubert not because anyone made me but to prove to myself I wasn't above intellectual improvement. I volunteered at the Red Crescent blood drive . . . once. I could tell a Monet from a Manet, and it was certainly *not* because I thought it was a talent my future husband might appreciate. And yet, sitting across from Sabah and Soheir today, I can't help but wonder if the biggest mistake of my life hadn't been my abysmal choice of a husband but in ever thinking I was any different from the pair of empty, vacant child-women in front of me.

"I don't know where my husband is, and you know what? I don't really care," I finally say.

They both gape at me quizzically as if trying to figure out the joke (another thing they were never very good at).

Calmly I stand up, grab my handbag, and leave the room.

Zahra

She is as proud and aloof as ever, and, as I should have predicted, has no idea who I am.

And why would she? Those who flit through life on the wings of entitlement seldom stop to take notice of the plebeians who fill in the gray nooks of their otherwise sunny lives.

When Ranya finally noticed me sitting at the table with Georges, her tall, dark, and handsome hero of the hour, it was only because I happened to occupy that peripheral space that included him, much like the wastebasket tucked discreetly at the foot of the bar behind us. Only even the wastebasket is cleverly embellished with a gold and cream floral motif that elevates it from a mere object of basic utility to a piece of art.

I'd bet that even on my best hair day, that elegant garbage can is more likely to garner an admiring glance than I am.

This is not false modesty. Given the laws of genes and environmental conditioning, I could have not been any other way. Allow me to explain.

Every family comes with a similar set of clichés—the smart sister, the pretty sister, the prodigal son, the dependable one. Mine is no different, even if it happens to be stuck in a god-forsaken, decrepit town of dust and desperation—Bethlehem—deep inside the Palestinian Territories, subsisting on religious tourism and olive oil pressing.

We're a smallish family by West Bank Palestinian standards. Five kids, nothing to brag about. The funny thing about us though (not ha-ha funny, sad funny) is our makeup: five girls. Four pretty ones, and me, the smart one. I suppose I should count myself lucky that in an ironic twist of fate, my sisters, much more likely to make a decent match than graduate from university, would find themselves trapped by their looks while I would be shipped off overseas to slightly better-off relations who could foot the bill for my education in a last-ditch effort so that in the absence of a son, my brains might be relied upon instead to hold the family's head over the tides of poverty. And now here I am. In London on a business trip with my boss, as far away from the tiny whitewashed stone house I grew up in as can be.

"So, Zahra, where were we?"

Georges sinks back into his seat, trying—and not succeeding—to take his eyes off Ranya while she's forgotten all about him already, chattering away with a pair of equally vapid-looking and well-off acquaintances.

"*Suéltate*. It has to go," I say.

He rubs his forehead with a hand the size of a squash racket's face.

"I can't, Zahra, and not just because of Joe, either." He shakes his head apologetically. But the resentment in his eyes belies the decisiveness of his tone.

"I know it's not Joe. Come on, don't you think I know you by now?" I can feel myself blush at my overfamiliarity. I'm not his mother, his girlfriend, or even his close friend. Not since college at any rate, and even then, we weren't the kind of friends who hung out together if not compelled by some academic motivation. Not usually, anyway. I am an employee. He's my employer. That's all there is, all there ever will be, between us.

He looks up from the patch of napkin he'd been studying intently.

"You almost sounded human for a second there, Zee. Careful, you're slipping." He winks.

He needs to stop doing that.

Making girls feel pretty and special. With some men it's a numbers game. The flattery-will-get-you-anywhere technique. Except with Georges, it's genuine niceness. I was painfully slow to realize that. Everyone's best friend and, ironically, a doormat to every girl who'd cozied up to him only to have her teeny-tiny thong charmed off at first chance by his younger brother Joe. I've seen so many of these insipid girls come and go I feel like I know them as well as I do my own sisters. Girls just like Ranya. Sun-kissed by life. Spoiled. Smug. Certain that they can have anything they set their big brown eyes on. Except they'd meet their match with Joe.

I'd love to meet the one lucky enough to be in the right place at the right time when Joe finally decides to cross the threshold to adulthood and settle—because let's face it, every man settles down eventually, if only to feel the thrill of two-timing his beautiful, expensive wife. I want to meet this phantom woman, and then watch her fall from her throne of smug superiority, down to where I sit every day. Unloved and barely noticed.

God help me.

I reach in the tiny exposed space between my neck and chest, courtesy of the one undone button of my white shirt, and tug at the cross hanging on the thin gold chain.

They call this kind of crucifix baroque. Meaning it depicts an acutely suffering Christ. Just the way I like him. The deity of the hopeless, the miserable, the bleak. People like Ranya didn't need Baroque Christ. Come to think of it, I think she's Muslim—I seem to remember that from our elementary school days in Riyadh when I was a poor, pity-case charge of reluctant relatives and she was a playground princess. In light of this, I suppose she wouldn't need any kind of Christ at all, even if she didn't have all that money, the mile-high legs, and the cute little un-Arabic nose as added insult.

I shake out my hair, straighten my back, and try to get my mind back to the matter at hand.

"The magazine has to go. We're headed for a recession soon what with the housing bust, and luxury goods are vulnerable. Consolidation is the word of the day. Focusing on your competitive advantage, which is selling luxury products, not advertising. Plus it's not making any money—how many times do we have to go through this?"

"I thought synergy was the word of the day. . . ." He feigns confusion.

I frown and cross my arms.

"First of all," he underlines his point by raising a thumb, "the resilience of the American consumer is unparalleled. The more things go belly-up, the more we absolutely have to have the latest Tom Ford sunglasses that Nicole Richie was seen wearing, even if we're maxed out on three credit cards already and the new shape makes you look bug-eyed."

I open my mouth to cut in, but he doesn't give me the chance.

"Second of all," he glares, "wealth doesn't just dissipate into thin air—it passes hands. Gets reshuffled. And the more ob-sessed people are with celebrities, the bigger their appetite for something that might get them closer to Mischa or Lindsay, or Scarlett . . . like perfume, an expensive scarf, a twenty-five-dollar lipstick when the six-dollar drugstore brand that comes from the same factory vat would do just as well."

"I don't see what this has to do with the maga—"

"*Thirdly,* I don't think it's *Suéltate* you have a problem with. I think you just don't like Rio."

"*Like* her? What's to like? She's the only person I know who talks like Jennifer Lopez and thinks she's Rosa Parks. If I have to hear her throw her 'back in ghetto' attitude in my face one more time, I'm going to punch something."

"Really?" He throws his head back and has a good laugh at my expense. "You need to loosen up, Zahra. Seriously. Rio's cool. She's had a lot to prove in her life, that's all. Not everyone gets the benefit of a top-school scholarship."

She's had a lot to prove in her life.

To say that the words slap me across the face is to put it so mildly that we could be talking about a Caribbean winter. But how is he to know when he's never seen me as anything beyond the quiet girl in his college study group? When everyone else would call it a day and declare their intent to hit the local bars I'd feign fatigue, illness, a visiting relative, or even must-see TV to get out of it. Eventually they gave up, or maybe they'd concluded I was a freak and any relationship to me was best left academic. Not that they all came from well-to-do families, many were on scholarship too, even Georges, but I was willing to bet a full year's tuition that I was the only one bankrolling a family of seven. I didn't think it was anyone's business then, or when I left Morrison & Fitch Capital Management five years ago and joined Mallouk Enterprises.

"The magazine stays for now, if for no other reason than to keep Joe out of my hair until his next bright idea."

I want to tell Georges that his brother had long since found something more lucrative and befitting of his lifestyle choices than the daily grind of running a magazine, even if his name still appeared in bold print on the masthead, next to "Managing Director." But it's not my place to get involved in family affairs. I let my boss go on, uninterrupted.

"So here's the game plan for this meeting: we need to get La Prairie on board by offering to pull the plug on the Crème de la Mer campaign. Also, and this should make you happy, since the magazine's circulation is showing promise, I think we can get an advertising discount. . . ."

Here his voice trails as his gaze follows the cloud of Estée Lauder pleasures perfume and the seductively swinging hips that go along with it past our table and out the door.

Of course I would have no clue which perfume Ranya is wearing, out of the hundreds of specimens Mallouk Enterprises carries in its stores, if pleasures weren't our number-one bestseller three retail cycles running. I've been around long enough to have figured out that it's always much better, if a little less exciting, to focus on stats and figures than the tight knot of disappointment squeezing your gut. Because if there's one thing I've never run short of in my life, it's disappointment.

Ranya

"Mama, stop crying."

I stare at the sheets of rain falling outside my window in streaming swathes of depressing gray, my eyes glazing over. Snuggled in a giant four-poster bed befitted with ridiculously soft cream sheets and a cart laden with all the carbs my fat cells have ever longed for and been denied, my sleepy, jet-lagged eyes wander over to the gorgeous breakfast nook in the corner, the fluffy twin bathrobes hanging in the half-open closet, the two little gold-wrapped chocolates the cleaning ladies had left on my pillows. Instead of easing my pain, all the earthly comforts of this suite just remind

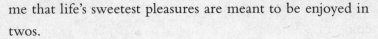

me that life's sweetest pleasures are meant to be enjoyed in twos.

"Why did you do this? To us? To your family? How could you justify your behavior to yourself?"

"I didn't do anything wrong, Mama." I sigh, my pulse quickening. This was going worse than I'd hoped. "I told you, he's *gay,* Mom. . . . What did you expect me to do?"

Silence.

I know she's just as uncomfortable hearing that word as I am saying it.

"How can you be sure?" she says, barely above a whisper.

"I'm sure."

"How?"

"Mom, please."

"I'm just saying, *habibti,* maybe you left a little too . . . hastily. Your mother-in-law won't stop calling—she's in hysterics, every time—begging, pleading that you come back and sort this out with Muhammad. . . . I can't accuse her son of . . . of being . . . of *that* if you don't tell me everything. Ranya, I beg you, be reasonable."

Be reasonable. There was nothing even remotely reasonable about this situation. I hadn't asked for any of this, and yet, because I had been the one to walk away, the burden of proof would fall on me. I would be asked to build a case, one piece of evidence at a time, and provide a solid explanation as to why I hadn't noticed something was awry.

Hadn't we been engaged two whole years? What were we doing all this time?

I'll tell you what—absolutely nothing. Fantasizing out loud about second homes we'd buy together, posh spots we'd vacation at, and what we'd name our three children. All that before we'd even shared a proper kiss.

"Tell Ikraam to stay out of this." No more "Auntie Ikraam" for that viper of a woman who'd managed to make me suffer through a marriage that would give Britney Spears a run for her money in the brevity department. We'd hardly gotten back from our honeymoon when Ikraam had made it known she wouldn't be one of those modern, stay-out-of-my-offspring's-affairs kind of mother-in-law. If it wasn't tireless hints about grandchildren, it was tips on how to properly dust a room, lessons in coupon cutting, jabs at any outfit color coordinations deemed too out-there for a newly married woman.

"What happened, darling?" my mother begins again, more softly this time. "Tell me."

"I . . . I . . ."

The truth is I was spending a weekday late morning in Holt Renfrew, the closest thing Montreal has to a Saks Fifth Avenue, as I was increasingly apt to do those days. The fights with Dodi were getting more frequent and had started taking on a mean edge. Since I don't drink, smoke, get high, or do yoga, the best I could do was worship at the altar of consumerism. For the past seven days and six nights my thoughts had been consumed by a gorgeous little Hermès passport holder in fuchsia croc leather, and one of Dodi's longest silent treatment punishments yet—one week, or 25 percent of our married life to date.

I had to have the passport holder.

It beckoned to me.

It howled my name in the middle of the night like an errant wind, begging to be heard.

I had to feed the beast. Even though the adorable little indulgence would be destined to spend the first few weeks in its new home hidden away from Dodi's fury in the back of the fancy underwear drawer, which, let's face it, no one was going into anyway.

At ten thirty that morning, an hour when only women with access to too much time and other people's credit cards haunted the halls of the department store, I sauntered into the Hermès in-store boutique, glassed in by three walls lined with all manner of exquisiteness.

He never saw me.

He stood idly by while a man, young, on-purpose five o'clock shadow carelessly slathered across his defined cheekbones, inspected the very same passport holder I was coming for. The one he was holding was flaming red. Minor detail.

And there was Dodi, standing right next to him, his hand ever so delicately skimming the small of that glossy-as-a-magazine-ad man's back, right in that unassuming yet utterly erotic spot where it met with the man's taut rear end, straining in its toned fullness against the filmy fabric of his off-white pants.

You always know who the other woman is, even when the other woman is a man. The air somehow electrifies, your senses heighten, you develop X-ray vision, or the blood-thirsty, radar-honing instincts of a vampire bat. You know. It's evolutionary. I can't explain it, but that's just the way it is.

What's even more is that I knew perfectly well who that ass belonged to—I'd spent a few afternoons basking in its presence myself, when its owner was dictating decorating suggestions to Dodi and me right after we'd moved in.

Paolo Barros. Interior designer and home wrecker extraordinaire to those who demand only the best.

"I just knew, Mom. I saw him." I roll over to my side, clutching the receiver between my ear and my shoulder.

"You saw him what?" she insists.

"With . . . the guy."

"Where, dear, where?"

"At . . ." And then it occurs to me. *What if she doesn't believe me?*

"Well, I didn't see him per se. . . ."

"Per what? Ranya, what are you saying?"

"I . . ." I falter. "I mean, I didn't *see him,* see him, but . . . I saw something on his computer." I'd seen something like this on *Guiding Light . . .* or was it *Days of Our Lives*? It doesn't matter. All that matters is that I never lay eyes on Dodi again.

"What? Please, Ranya, for the love of God!"

"A picture . . . of . . . a man!"

I surprise myself at the ease with which this flamboyant

lie just rolls off my tongue, like I'd been doing this since I was old enough to speak.

"What kind of picture, honey?"

"A really obscene one. . . . The man was . . . *naked*!"

What I would give to have seen her face when I said that.

"There was even a message . . . to his *lover,* Mom," I continue. "He was making plans to meet at a club the same night he told me he had a business meeting set up. . . . It was too much, Mama—I had to leave."

The other end of the line is so silent I'm afraid my mother might have fainted back at "lover."

"Mama? . . . You understand, right? You see how I had no choice?"

A long, heavy sigh. "Why couldn't you have come home? Don't you know you'll always have a place here with us, no matter what happens?"

Of course I know. I fidget guiltily, wrapping the telephone cord in complicated swirls around my arm. I didn't know it at the time, but even throughout that tortured month of marriage, my misery had been tempered by my first gasps of real freedom. Dodi wanted little to do with me. When we fought—something my mother told me was perfectly normal when two people were just getting used to each other—he'd sulk into silence and storm off, thinking he was punishing me. Meanwhile, I indulged in this new world of independence. I turned upside down the cabinet organization system my mother had used since times unknown and made up my own method. I decorated and re-decorated the flat, losing myself in the freedom of having no one's opinion to consider but my own. I bought myself Lily Pulitzer overalls covered in pink and lavender rosebuds and taught myself how to paint. The living room accent wall went from red to green to blue in the four weeks I lived in that apartment building. The neighbors must have thought I was crazy. Dodi was probably just happy I'd found some-thing to channel my energy into that didn't involve him.

"I was . . . I was embarrassed. I didn't feel like I could face anyone. I still don't, to be honest."

"Don't worry, sweetheart. Your father and I will take care of everything. I'm going to see your mother-in-law, and give her a good piece of my mind. Did you save that message?"

Uh-oh. My mind races. . . . What do I say? What do I say?

"Uh . . . y-y-eah . . . actually I don't remember any-more. . . . I was so panicked at the time. . . ."

"What do you mean you don't remember?" The sympa-thy that had laced my mother's voice for the duration of the conversation suddenly vaporizes. "Ranya, are you sure you're being completely honest with me?"

It's a lucky thing this conversation isn't taking place face-to-face. My skin is positively pulsing with heat.

"Mom, please don't stress me out right now. I'm suffer-ing enough without your input, thank you very much."

"I'm sorry, *habibti*." She sighs. "I really am. You just take it easy and rest, your father and I will call a lawyer. You don't worry about a thing. Everything will be settled by the time you come back."

Under normal circumstances I would've gotten a good earful for that bout of uncalled-for insolence, but it seems that a dash of personal tragedy interfering with my mother's dreams of domestic bliss for her only daughter is counteracting her unflagging penchant for making me feel like a five-year-old.

"When do you want us to book your ticket for?" she coos soothingly.

"What ticket?"

"Your ticket home, naturally. Or did you think you were going to run around Europe by yourself indefinitely?"

I jolt up in bed, sending the headboard smacking hard against the cream painted wall.

"Mother, I'm not even close to being ready to go anywhere near Dodi yet. He could rot in Hell for all I care!"

The line cackles ominously, making my mother's prolonged silence all the more unsettling.

"He's still your *husband*," she hisses icily.

"Why does everyone keep using that word? I *HATE* that word. I never, ever want to hear that f—" I catch myself just in time. "That stupid word again."

"Everyone? Who's everyone? Has anyone seen you in London?"

Smart as a whip, my mother. And no less stinging when she wants to be.

"Do you remember Sabah and Soheir el-Bustani?"

"God help us. . . ." Her voice trails.

"It's not so bad, Mama—"

"Not so bad? *Not so bad?* You had to run into the two biggest gossips west of Beirut! They'll run to their mother and soon enough everyone from here to the moon will know what you've done!"

"Is that all you care about? What people will say?"

"Are you telling me you don't care about your reputation?"

"That . . . that . . . that good-for-nothing piece of *shit* broke my heart, Mom, and you want me to worry about my *reputation?*" The words tumble out of my mouth faster than I can rein them in.

It's true. I might not have loved Dodi the way people do in epic romances. We weren't really friends, and certainly not soul mates. But we'd made a pact to embark on a journey together, a partnership where we would always be there for each other. I'd believed in it.

"I'm not asking you to stay married to the man, Ranya. Your father and I will be happy to let you ride out this mess at your grandmother's flat in Cyprus if you're not ready to come back to Montreal, but if you persist in acting out like a child and bringing shame to this family in the process, then I'm—"

"You're what? Not going to talk to me for a week, like the time I took the *hijaab* back in high school?"

Looking back, I'll admit that brief moment in my youth

wasn't my proudest. After all, who takes a sacred oath to modesty and God and turns it into an act of teenage rebellion?

She draws a sharp, horrified breath.

"Ranya," she struggles to maintain some sanity in her voice, "if you're not on the next plane home or to your grandmother's, then you're not seeing another dime from us."

No way. I don't believe it. She would never. This is my mother we're talking about. The woman who thinks nothing of fixing me a stuffed-vine-leaves casserole in the middle of the night if that's what I'm craving. The one who still pleads leniency on my behalf when my father gets the monthly Visa statement. She can't be abandoning me *now,* in my darkest hour . . . *can she?*

"You're not being serious." I chuckle lightly.

"Watch me," she huffs.

Silence.

"Well?" she says.

How much is my freedom worth to me? I'd do a quick mental calculation, but I've never been very good at math.

"No." I take a deep breath.

"No what?"

"I love you and Dad with all my heart. I would never do anything to hurt you on purpose. But I can't come home. And I don't want to go to Nana's, either. I'm not a child. I can take care of myself."

"Ranya, why are you being so difficult? What's gotten into you? Ah!" she gasps sharply. "I know what's going on. . . ."

"What?"

"Have you met someone? Are you making all this up?"

This time I nearly drop the receiver as my blood turns to ice in my veins and my whole body starts shaking.

"*How could you?*" I wheeze. "*To your own daughter* . . . Mother, my husband likes to fuck men. What's so difficult to understand about that?"

"That's enough! Since when do you say such obscenities?"

"Since my life turned into one big fat obscenity, Mom." I slam down the phone.

Zahra

Georges has decided he wants to see a little bit of the city while he's here and is dragging me along with him. It's not that I don't care about the parliament buildings, or the London Eye or the National Gallery, but we're looking more and more like a honeymooning couple, a very chaste honeymooning couple, and frankly, I don't know how much more of Georges's platonic affection I can take.

"Good old Renaissance humor," he says, balancing on the tips of his worn-out Adidas sneakers. I don't know very many multimillionaires who wear worn-out anything around London's finer museums.

"Did you know that was meant as a wedding present? Look—the size is just right to fit over the headboard of a bed."

"Or a fireplace," I offer.

"Or that," he replies cautiously, "but I don't know how much the commissioner's Florentine neighbors would have liked a nearly life-sized picture of Venus and Mars post-coitus hanging in the living room."

I tilt my head to one side and examine Venus's placid face while she in turn gazes at a snoozing Mars on the other side of the painting.

"Hey—are you blushing?"

I'd missed it. They've just had sex. I'd seen nothing in the canvas beyond the obvious, a random mythological scene, a near-naked man, a woman in a white transparent dress propped up against throw cushions, a few horned half-man, half-goat things against a country scene. Who cares?

"Look, it's a pretty picture—they all are—but I'm not really into this kind of thing; can we go?"

"But we just got here. . . ." He reaches for my hand and tucks it gently underneath his folded arm. "Behind every one of these paintings is a story. It would take years to go through every single one here and understand all the work that went into it, why the artist chose this type of brush-stroke over the other, what he was thinking when he painted it, what he was trying to cover up, or who he was trying to suck up to . . . all fascinating stuff, but we'll start small. And if you're good, then maybe I'll take you out for fish-and-chips and a fascinating debate about where the commodities market is headed. What do you say?"

"Well . . . if there's fish-and-chips involved . . ."

We study the rest of the Botticellis, meander over to the Bellinis, and decide to attack van Gogh next when who do I see turn the corner, looking like a fabulously well-heeled deer in the headlights, but her.

Ranya.

Georges's arm falters under my own, and just before she sees us, he lets my hand drop.

I never did mind before, who his flavor of the month happened to be, so it really shouldn't be bothering me now.

Except it does.

Kind of like the idea of horrible dictators passing away peacefully in their sleep bothers me.

I know I'm supposed to believe she'll pay for it, someday, somehow, but sometimes I just don't know.

"Look who's there," Georges says, a feather's touch above a whisper.

I shrug and try to keep along our artistic appreciation path.

"Let's go say hi." He doesn't wait for an answer. Just strides across the polished wood floor, his sneakers hastening him along noiselessly until he's hovering about a foot behind her. She senses his presence, turns, and looks scared out of her wits for a moment before recovering and planting a quick kiss on his right, then left cheek.

Just like old friends.

I'm a fidgeter. Whether I'm sprawled on my living room couch, wolfing down a pepperoni pizza and watching *Grey's Anatomy* on TiVo in the comfort of my sheep pajamas and grandma slippers, or trying not to doze off during sales presentations at work, I fidget and fret. I play with the hem of my skirt if I happen to be wearing one, I get up and sit and get up again if at all possible, or I bite the edges of my lips until they're raw. This is why I never seem to be wearing any lipstick—I leave my condo every day at the crack of dawn with the best of intentions and a fairly well-put-together face. But after forty-five minutes in Miami rush hour traffic, a quick breakfast of rainbow-sprinkled doughnuts or a bagel with garlic-herb cream cheese, a morning meeting or two, I know I look like I'd never even bothered in the first place. Sometimes I wonder why I do.

Today I'm wearing roomy pleated pants I hope are hiding a newly sprouted belly pooch courtesy of last night's room service, pointy-toed office shoes I bought my first year out of college (the tip is not so much pointy anymore as it is turned in on itself, fairy-tale-genie style), and a navy sweater under a trench coat. It's not a terrible outfit—not in the seventh grade homeroom teacher way at least—not really sloppy, either, not if you didn't look down at the shoes. It just doesn't call attention to itself, which is usually what I look for in an outfit. Except watching Ranya effortlessly soaking up every bit of Georges's attention, I wonder why I can never get myself to try harder.

I resume old fidgeting habits, staring at my feet instead,

tap, tap, tapping them gently against the blond wood of the floor. With hundreds of beautiful paintings to gaze at, the best I could do is stare at my ugly shoes.

"Zahra!"

I look up. Georges is motioning me to join Ranya and him next to a portrait of a stoic-looking old man who might be a pope. Or a bishop or a mayor or a cardinal.

I don't want to, but what choice do I have?

"You remember Ranya, Zahra?" He looks over from me to her to me again, nudging me with his eyes to say something nice. I don't take the bait.

"I don't think we were formally introduced," she says, and holds out a pretty olive-skinned hand with inky-black nails for me to shake. I wonder what she's doing in London, in this museum, in front of me. "Although to be honest, I have the funniest feeling we've met before," she continues.

This is it. My chance. I could humiliate her. Or, at the very least, embarrass her a little bit. Show Georges the kind of girl she is before he falls head over heels. Because people don't change that much over the course of twenty years. Their personality traits are wrought from their parents' genes, before their first breath out of the womb. Unpleasant babies turn into finicky adults; happy children are more apt to grow into those outgoing people who'd befriend walls rather than stay dull and silent.

I wait too long to speak. The moment passes me by.

"Listen, I was thinking," Georges looks at me, "it's just about lunchtime and we still have a while before our meeting with the Jo Malone people," and then back at Ranya, "so why don't we grab something down at the cafeteria. I've eaten here before; it's pretty good as far as English food goes."

I raise a suspicious eye at Ranya and find she's staring at me with just as much mistrust. I'm not going to be the first to decline and look like the bad guy. Or girl. Ranya is welcome to do all the dirty work herself.

She's as silent as a tomb for a couple of seconds, but instead of the "no" I was sure would escape her lips, she says this: "Are you sure?"

At which Georges leaps, of course, and leads her by the small of her back toward the exit of the Sainsbury Wing, leaving me behind to take leave of the Van Eycks, the Bermejos, and the Dürers I never wanted to see in the first place.

Ranya

I should have never come to London.

Arabs love London.

Maybe it's because we can identify with the guarded stuffiness, the deference to decorum, or because it's the sort of place where *Al-Sharq Al-Awsat* newspapers are sold alongside *Hello* and "Mind the Gap" T-shirts. Perhaps it's because this is the last remaining bastion of the Western Hemisphere where it was possible for a hairy-chested Muslim playboy, heir to England's brightest beacon of consumerism, to share a bed with the loveliest, most adored English Rose of them all.

Or maybe we just like to change things up with cucumber sandwiches and milk with our tea instead of fig cookies and mint sprigs.

In any case, when I had first set foot onto English soil, my second thought, after wondering exactly how I was ever supposed to slip back into polite society again, was how fast I could get to Harrods. But after the little tête-à-tête with my mother last night, I'm thinking a brief spell away from the shops is probably a better idea.

With that in mind, I slipped on my high-heeled Patrick Cox boots at the first hint of sunlight, the satin trench I'd torn off the coatrack just before I shut the door on my old life, and set out for a walk to clear my thoughts (if not so much my lungs), try to take in some culture, and maybe find myself a not-too-dodgy-looking pawnshop along the way.

I let my feet drag me down Oxford, past street venders hocking the latest in designer knockoffs and scarf-and-glove sets, slowing down and tearing up a little when I get to Selfridges but bravely sticking to my path. I cross women in pastel-colored peacoats and matching wide-brimmed hats stepping in and out of chauffeured cars along the streets of Mayfair, and grab a latte somewhere in Soho, lamenting the loss of the three pounds I should have held on to.

But somewhere between Russell & Bromley and Nicole Farhi on Bond Street, I just couldn't go on.

The solid sheet of panic I had been trying to keep at bay since I left Montreal had been slowly gaining on me, like a buzzing wave of locusts at the horizon, getting closer and louder, until I felt as though I would keel over and suffocate under the weight of dread and despair.

I needed to talk to someone. If my mother was anything to go by, I could guess at the kind of reaction my predicament and subsequent transatlantic escape would elicit from my friends. As with like-minded members of an elite political party, we all got along wonderfully as long as we stuck to acceptable party lines. Should you ever err into the territory of taboo, however, you were on your own.

And so it hits me, standing in the swankiest neighborhood in one of the poshest cities in the entire world, that in all these years of flitting from one party to the next, one social call to another, of making friends on two different continents, I didn't have a single one I could trust. If I broke down and confessed, I risked having my secret broadcast all over the Montreal gossip networks, bouncing off some satellite circling the Earth's atmosphere and beaming down to the Middle East, infiltrating genteel Persian-rug-carpeted living rooms where dowagers tsk-tsked away amongst themselves, taking care not to infect their daughters' ears with my tale of sordid scandal, shaking their heads and wondering if I'd get another shot at happiness when even the first had come to me so late.

I decided I would call Ali before I gave in to panic and went home, tail between my legs, back to my life just as it was before.

Until I one-upped her with my superior skills at setting

my poor parents' faces ablaze with shame, Aline was the black sheep of the clan. I'll take this opportunity to note that in our family, dating, in the normal sense of the word, was all the salacious behavior it took to lay claim to this title. That Ali's boyfriend of three years was an *ajnabi*—a "foreigner" (i.e., non-Arab)—was enough to have her inducted into the Hall of Shame.

I punch the numbers into my cell phone and wait for her to pick up.

"Hello?"

"Hi there!" I trill, trying to mimic the fluffiness of a fine soufflé.

"Ranya? Oh my God!"

"How's everything?"

"How's everything? Ranya, how the fuck are *you*?"

I'd always found my young cousin's generous use of profanity very endearing.

"Did my mother tell you?" I hold my breath.

"She didn't say very much. Just that you're fine, and that you've left Dodi, and we're not supposed to tell anyone yet because you're confused right now and need to think things through."

Confused? *Me?* I'm fuming so much I'm afraid I might burst into flames.

I proceed to give Ali an abbreviated version of the story I told my mother, hating myself for lying to my credulous, loving cousin who'd done nothing but look up at me with her big gold-speckled brown eyes her whole childhood. I've never been a liar. I've never had any reason to be. Everything about my life had been cultivated and studied and thought through, so that there wasn't room even for a whiff of scandal. I know it might sound—well, a little *boring* when you look at it that way, but I prefer to think of it as safe.

Liar or not, and though I trust Ali with my life, I can't risk having the truth floating somewhere out there just yet. I am wide open, with nothing else to protect me.

"I'm really sorry, Ranya. Of all the people in the world, you're the last person I would have expected something like this to happen to."

Maybe if someone as good as Ali loved me and even looked up to me once upon a time, maybe I was still redeemable.

"Ali . . ." I let my forehead drop against the Nicole Farhi window, causing the saleslady to rap sharply against it from the inner side of the glass, her eyebrows knitted and her lips pursed with bitchiness.

It seems my degradation is starting to manifest itself outwardly. I'm sure if this had been yesterday, on a similarly fashionable street, I might have been treated like the potential customer I would have been instead of the street urchin I am turning into.

"What is it?"

"I'm scared."

"Of what?"

"I've never done anything like this before . . . ," I say. "What will people say?"

"You think Maya and all those other girls at your wedding wouldn't find ways to criticize you even if this whole mess hadn't happened? Come *on,* gossip is our national sport. Besides, by the time they're finished with Dodi everyone will have forgotten all about you."

The thought of Dodi squirming under the spotlights of social scrutiny makes me feel a tiny bit better.

"What am I supposed to do now, Ali?" It nearly comes out as a sob.

"What have you always wanted to do?"

Hmm. Good question. Except that I'm not sure I want to know the answer. Because if I searched my soul deep enough, I might find that I was never really passionate about anything. I passed time. I was very good at it. So good that you might have been easily misled into thinking I had it all figured out. All I had accomplished was mastering the art of waiting for the right boy to come along, and filling my life with nonsense to fend off boredom in the meantime.

"That's just it," I say. "I don't know anymore."

"Well, there's your answer. Go figure it out."

I wish I had even a tiny speckle of her confidence.

"You know I can't. Mama and Baba will never be able to show their faces in public again."

"And how do you think Dodi's parents are feeling right now?"

Something tugs at me, as if there were something slightly selfish about not feeling a whiff of concern for the man who had promised, at least in public, to love and honor and protect me for the rest of our lives. An unsettling question worms its way through my heart—is it possible that he might be in even more agony right now than I am? I stamp the unwelcome thought right out by reminding myself of how he'd condemned me to suffer along with him, me, a perfectly innocent bystander. And why should I ever forgive him for that?

"Ranya," Ali says, "stop worrying. Just go with the flow, for once in your life. Your parents will understand, and so will everyone else."

Oh, really?

"So if I stay, you'll come visit me?" I smile through my discomfort and try to shift the subject off my parents and the likelihood they'll understand.

"Only if you promise to have the time of your life and fuck the first hot Englishman that lays eyes on you."

My mind automatically deflects to that handsome do-gooder from the hotel, and I blush instantly. What am I thinking? My mother is perfectly right about one thing—I am, in fact, for better or for worse, still married. Dodi can do whatever he wants, but I'm not about to take that as license to do the same. I scold Ali for good measure. She calls me a "repressed nut" and promises me I'll have some sense knocked into me soon. Preferably against a headboard of a king-size bed. I scold her some more and hang up after a prolonged and tearful good-bye.

What I don't tell Ali is that if I don't figure out a way to survive, she's going to be seeing me a lot sooner than she thought.

I'm not entirely sure why I stopped at Trafalgar Square. The imposing marble lions guarding the fountains? The throngs of happy, carefree vacationers snapping away with their tiny cameras? Or a vague, sepia-tinged memory my mind managed to dig up that van Gogh's *Sunflowers* lay beyond the doors of the National Gallery building at the head of the square?

I'd considered majoring in art history once. The thought had threaded itself into my consciousness during my first ever trip to Paris with my parents. It was probably conceived the first time I set a rubber t-strapped shoe onto the cobblestone streets of Montmartre, was nurtured by the sights of beret-wearing artists sketching likenesses of passersby with warp speed, and blossomed with every statue, painting, and sculpted fountain we came across.

I carried that dream with me until I realized that an art history major would impress no one, but at least it might lend me a semblance of substance when making small talk. Since then I let it burn quietly, like a pilot light I nurtured, by taking a few classes, reading up on the subject, and even fund-raising for Montreal galleries from time to time.

The last people I expected I would be having lunch with at the museum cafeteria were Georges Mallouk and his sour-faced friend.

"I'll have the goat cheese and artichoke salad please." I hand my leather-bound menu to the waitress.

"To drink, madam?"

"Just a Diet Coke, thanks."

Georges raises an eyebrow at me.

"Are you sure you wouldn't like a glass of wine with your salad? Isn't that what vacations were made for?"

"I don't drink."

"Oh" is all he says.

Zahra snorts and looks down at her menu.

"We never had a chance to talk back in the lounge," Georges says. "What brings you to London? The fashion, the culture, the theater maybe? Business . . . ?" he ventures as an afterthought, afraid to offend me by suggesting I don't have anything to do with my time except waste it.

I was hoping to hide out from the little hiccup that's popped up in my faux marriage until everything blew over and my parents took care of the whole ugly mess while I shopped until every credit card I had in my possession cried out for mercy.

"I'm visiting a friend."

"Where does she live?"

"She has a flat in Kensington. Close to the park." I'm impressed at how easily the fabricated stories are rolling off my tongue these days.

"And she didn't offer to put you up at her place?"

"I didn't want to impose."

"Nice friend." His eyes twinkle. Does he believe me? Am I that transparent? Could I seriously be worrying about what this perfect stranger thinks about me?

"Are you enjoying the city? We're getting some pretty good weather for this time of the year."

"Sure. I've been . . . shopping a lot."

I hang my head, waiting for the flicker of interest in his gaze to die out, and for him to steer the conversation somewhere marginally interesting. Like back to the weather.

"Have you been to Alexander McQueen yet?" he says instead. "His collection is great this season. Much better than McCartney's. Maybe I'm being cynical, but I wonder if Stella got to be the UK's fashion darling on account of her dad rather than her own talent."

He's got to be kidding me.

"Don't look so shocked, please." He laughs. "I'm in the industry—sort of. You shouldn't miss Pringle while you're here. Their pink-on-black argyle is set to become the next Burberry beige plaid."

I close my mouth, which I realize I'd left gaping.

"What do you do?" I edge a little closer across the table, feeling Zahra recoil on her side as I lean in. She's barely looked my way since we sat down, and hasn't uttered a single word. *What is this girl's problem?* I wonder. But even as I articulate the vague unease into an actual thought, I see it, as plainly as the salt and pepper shakers in the middle of the table.

She likes him. Georges. So that automatically makes me the enemy.

I can't suppress a surreptitious smile.

No worries, Zahra. I'll be out of your hair soon enough.

"It's a little complicated. . . ." Georges winces.

"He's chairman and CEO of Mallouk Enterprises," Zahra says, with a pinched look on her face that makes me want to toss my Diet Coke at it.

"Sorry." I shrug. "I'm afraid I haven't heard of it."

The insult registers nicely. Her nostrils flare ever so subtly, and she raises her blue goblet of water to her lips.

"We're a family-run business in the States. Dabblers—that's what I like to call us." He smiles into his pinot noir and takes a sip. "A little bit of this, a little bit of that . . ."

"What's 'a little bit of this and a little bit of that'?"

"I guess you could say we're into luxury. Think of anything related to luxury and we probably have a stake in it: jets, hotels, casinos, wine; we even have a magazine—but those are just peripheral investments. Our main business is duty-free. In airports, at Caribbean cruise ship destinations, that kind of stuff."

I don't remember much about the first time I ever walked into a classroom, or felt the warm tickle of the ocean on my toes. But the first time I pressed my nose against the glass panes of a duty-free cosmetics counter at an airport terminal still lingers in my memory in scents of pressed powders, flashes of Chanel's signature black compacts, or the pastel green, pink, and cream packaging of Clinique. Despite the endless varieties on the market today, it's the originals that still hold my heart in their overbranded palms—the ones my mother would carefully lay in the Bedouin-style handwoven basket on top of her dresser, the one with little brass coins dangling off the sides. Sephora could promise me mineral makeup that did my skin good or cream blush that was activated by my body's natural heat, but I would always find peace and nostalgic comfort in those same designers I remembered from my childhood.

"Sounds like a really interesting line of work. I thought you were a stockbroker or a lawyer or something along those lines," I say.

"It's funny you should say that." He chuckles lightly. "The law was on my short list of things-I-might-like-to-do-when-I-grow-up. But my father thought it might be more useful for the family if I went to business school." He shakes his head, his gaze focused on the filet mignon just landed in front of him.

Both Zahra and I shift a little in the not-too-comfortable chairs. Our eyes meet for a second, and we quickly look away.

"Let's see. . . . Astronaut, ballet dancer, cowboy, princess . . . *lawyer*?" I count off my fingers.

"You forgot dragon slayer." He laughs. "Touché. But those courtroom drama movies did make an impression. Maybe I was thinking more along the lines of cowboy-in-a-suit kind of lawyer than actual blood-sucking lawyer."

This time we're both laughing, and for a fraction of a second I manage to forget that I am a penniless social refugee, forsaken by her family and probably soon to be discovered by her gay husband and left to rot in the posh streets of London, a reminder to all plastic-wielding, jet-setting fashionistas just how precarious their cushioned existences really are.

I need a plan.

"Tell me about the magazine. Maybe I've read it," I say breezily.

"I doubt it," he begins. "It started off as a totally different animal, but these days it's called *Suéltate*—loosely translated as 'Cut Loose.' It's aimed at the Miami and Caribbean Latin market."

"Why would your company be into that? Seems like a bit of a departure from your other ventures."

Georges throws Zahra an affectionate sideways glance.

"You're right—some would say that. Honestly, getting into it was a bit of an accident. A last-minute turnaround since what we were doing before wasn't working. But the Latin market is just exploding right now. Both in the States and south of the border. So we're keeping it."

Zahra glares at him.

"For now."

We all munch away for a few minutes. I wonder how long Dodi will wait before trying me again.

My cell phone had been ringing nonstop in the first couple of hours after I'd landed in London. So much so that I had to turn it off. Not to sound like a clichéd relic from the fifties or anything, but mine really was the kind of husband who expected his made-from-scratch dinner piping hot and on the table when he arrived home from work, whenever that happened to be. And, at first at least, I was happy to oblige. Until after one too many arguments about where I had been if dinner happened not to be on the table at precisely the right hour and what I might have been doing had erupted, and our prolonged silent-treatment spells had turned routine. That's about the time I added to my expanding list of spousal disappointments the entry: thankless bastard.

This morning though, riled up from the "chat" with my mother the night before, I switched the phone back on.

I had twenty-seven messages.

Twenty-five were from Dodi. One was from my mother, and one from the butcher, kindly letting me know my special order of halal beef was ready for pickup.

The messages had ranged from irate (first three), to positively enraged (next four), to brink-of-nuclear-meltdown intensity, and then strangely turned to pleading and cajoling around message number seventeen. By the last one it almost sounded like my coming back home was optional.

"What about you?" Zahra finally breaks her silence.

Where *have* I seen this girl before? "What do you mean?"

"I mean, what do you do when you're not making cross-continental social calls?" she says smugly.

Once again, I'd left myself wide-open and unprepared. But I hadn't counted on sitting in a London museum café, having lunch with an American business mogul and his dour handmaiden, either.

"I, um, I work . . ." What's a good old innocuous occupation I know something about? ". . . in art."

"That sounds interesting." Zahra takes a swig of her wine. "What exactly is it that you *do,* if you don't mind my asking?"

That's it.

I calmly lay my fork down, mid goat-cheese-and-arugula bite, and meet her belligerent glare.

Who does this Zahra woman think she is and why is she looking at me like she's daring me to call her imaginary bluff as if we were actors in an Old Western showdown?

I search her face for something, a sign, a clue to what's behind the animosity.

And then I see it.

Like one of those 3-D paintings that made you squint and hold your head this way and then that before you eventually figured out what it was you were looking at. And once you saw that boat breaking against curlicue waves or the rocket ship soaring into swirly clouds, you were shocked at how you could have missed it the first time.

The pointy little elfin ears poking out of the oily, puddle brown hair should have given her away. It hasn't changed very much since we were kids. Neither had her waistless, watermelon-like shape: not quite fat, but definitely not slim, either. Even back in grammar school she reminded me of that song about the short, stout kettle. And now to look at her, she still does.

Then I remember the first time we exchanged words. And I feel myself go red from the nape of my neck up through my cheeks and all the way to my hairline.

It was in kindergarten, the only grade I can remember where girls and boys could attend class together in Saudi.

I have only one faint memory of that entire year involving Zahra, a collage, and a boy—all brewed together into one bittersweet flashback stew.

I couldn't tell you the boy's name. All I remember about him was his height—the tallest boy in class—and even at that age I had a notion of who was cute and who was not. He definitely was. Maybe it's the baseball cap I still see him wearing in the shadows of my mind, or the confidence he carried himself with, fully aware of the superior place his looks garnered him in the pecking order of the schoolyard. Or maybe I liked him because I suspected he liked me right back.

Well, the day came when he had his chance to prove his deference to me. He pulled through with flying colors.

Our teacher had asked us to put together a collage using paper cutouts of all kinds of innocuous, sweet scenes: I think I remember . . . a dog, a giraffe. Maybe the theme was "zoo," or maybe it was "afternoon tea." My logic is a little shaky here, since kindergarten kids are just as apt to put a giraffe in a Victorian drawing room as they are to put a sofa in the jungle.

Zahra—another little girl whose name I couldn't have told you if the grown version of her weren't seated across from me right now—was also in my class. Her bumbling little fingers produced the most god-awful cutout of a stick girl I had ever seen. It didn't belong in the same collage as the masterpiece of a baby carriage I'd fashioned out of hot pink construction paper and blunt-tip scissors.

Stick girl had to go.

So I tore her up in tiny little pieces. Lots and lots of them, so Zahra couldn't put her back together again.

I'm not saying it was my finest hour—only that I seem to have been born with an instinct for quality, which has morphed over the years into an appreciation for the finer things in life, like goose-feather throw pillows and premium denim.

I don't remember if there were any tears, only that the general mood of the class toward me that day wasn't especially friendly. They all took Zahra's side, of course. All of them, except for one. A tall boy in a baseball cap and a tongue dyed grape juice purple.

It warmed my haughty little heart so much that I had been right, he *did* like me, that it took away the sting of being relegated to the corner of the classroom for the rest of the day.

And now here she is, the same hapless little girl who couldn't muster enough courage to stand up to me, with a glamorous job that flies her to such swanky locales as London and a handsome boss with kind liquid brown eyes and a disarming smile.

And look at me. Jobless, husbandless, hopeless, and yes, hapless, too.

You'd think she'd be a tad more appreciative of the happy ending fate had reserved just for her instead of wasting all her energy glaring at me, as if all that stood between me and sailing into the Mediterranean sunset with Georges by my side was a flattering Pucci two-piece.

"Thanks so much for lunch, Georges, but I should get going. Zahra—I hope you have a nice trip back to the States." She looks at me a little perplexed, like she's wondering what I'm up to.

"What? I thought we were having a great time . . . ," Georges says, looking confused.

"Georges, you're a really nice person—"

"'Nice person'? Uh-oh—I think I just got the kiss of death. . . . I'm not trying to scare you off, I'm really not—"

"Well then, just let her go!"

Georges and I both turn to Zahra and freeze, stunned.

"Excuse me." She tosses her napkin on the table and darts across the crowded dining area to the ladies' room, her face twisted and indignant.

"Zahra! Shit, Ranya, I'm sorry." He runs a hand through his hair. "What did I say?"

"I don't think it was you," I say gently, throwing a quick look at my watch. I've already been here too long. I need to figure out what I'm going to do about money. About Dodi. God, what if he calls?

"Can you please go talk to her? Look—" He lets out a long, heavy sigh. "I'm really sorry, this isn't your problem, but I'd appreciate it. . . ." His eyebrows knot into the cutest mask of vulnerable concern I've ever seen on a man that big.

"I don't think she'll appreciate me butting into her business. . . ."

"Please? I can't go in there, and honestly, I'm not very good at watching women cry. I turn to mush."

"I . . . um . . . okay," I surrender.

"Thank you." He grazes my shoulder with the tips of his fingers, a gesture somewhere between heartfelt gratitude and an awkward inability to deal with high-wattage emotional situations. Still, some of that warmth seeps through his fingers and sneaks up my arm. I pull back before the heat can reach my face, or any other nefarious parts of my body, parts that I prefer to stay nice and cold, just the way I like them, thank you very much.

"I'd better go see her."

As soon as I turn back, I hear the unmistakable opening chords of a familiar tango tune I fear more than an afterlife in the seventh circle of Hell.

My phone.

I stare at the razor-thin handset, which I have an increasing urge to dub Satan's Handmaid of Ill Tidings, and toss a quick glance over my shoulder. Georges is nervously scratching away at the nape of his neck, looking this way and that, and shifting in his seat. I duck surreptitiously into the corner by the ladies' room and wonder if freaky Zahra can wait a few more minutes.

Conversations such as these, ones that hold entire sets of

Royal Doulton tableware and the reputations of two up-standing, heretofore unscathed families in the balance, should *not* be had at the intersection point of a busy kitchen and a bathroom. And yet . . . a masochistic impulse is seducing me into answering. Is Dodi worried sick about me? Is he going to beg me to come back? Does he love me? Or will this be another attempt by my mother to bring me to my senses? There's only one way to find out.

I flip the phone open.

My home number flashes on the screen. *My* home. My apartment. The one I shared with my husband. The faithless bastard.

"Hello?" Cool, confident, in control. I'm not the one with Hermès-wielding interior decorators hiding in my closet.

"Please don't hang up—"

"I won't. I want an explanation."

"For *what,* you craz—"

Pause. Deep breath.

I really should hang up, but at the same time I just can't bear the suspense. How is he planning on getting out of this?

"I'm sorry," he starts over. "I mean, I don't understand, honey. What happened? Why did you leave like that, without telling anybody?"

"Dodi . . ." I pause for effect. "I know."

"You know? Know what? What the hell is there to know?"

His voice slowly rises in a crescendo, the same way it always does when we're about to get into a fight. But this time, I am prepared. I have ammunition.

"You picked well. Paolo's a great guy. Hot, too! Maybe I would've had a go at him. If he were straight, I mean."

I can just imagine Dodi in his ratty old pajamas—a present from his dearly beloved mother—squirming like the vermin he is in the leather swivel chair of our home office. "Still there, darling?"

". . . how . . . ?" he nearly chokes over the word.

"Holt Renfrew. Did he enjoy that red croc passport holder? Were you hoping you'd get a deal if you picked up the pink one for your wife while you were at it? Oh, wait—I forgot. It would never occur to you to buy me anything because you hate me. At least now I know why no matter what I did for you or your stupid mother, it was never good enough. God, I was such an idiot."

I'm not going to cry. I'm going to keep it together. None of this is my fault. I have nothing to feel bad about. I'm so angry I could kill him.

"Ranya . . . sweetheart—"

"How could you do this to me?"

I'm shaking so hard I can barely see straight.

"*Hayati,* Ranya—my heart, my soul, my life . . . whatever you want, I'll give it to you. You don't understand—it's not at all like you think, I *promise* you. Ranya, *habibti,* my darling, you're my wife. . . . I can change, we can work this out."

I thought I could do this, but I can't. I really, really

can't. I lean against the wall, my face sinking into the supple lapels of my beautiful coat, a remnant of the life I'd left . . . how many hours ago? I don't know. . . . Days have been bleeding into nights, moments of lucidity melting into self-doubt and regret.

"It won't be like it was before, I swear to you. I swear on my life, I'll make sure my mother stays out of our marriage, we'll do anything you want, go anywhere. . . . Ranya, I swear to God things won't be the same."

"I don't know. . . ." I consider asking him to wire me a few thousand as a measure of goodwill. But that would be blackmail. Not to mention it would make me lower than scum.

As swiftly as his tone had turned kind and almost human on me, it flips back to the tone I'm better acquainted with.

"You're my *wife,* damn it, you'll come home when I tell you to."

"*You* don't get to call me your wife anymore, do you understand me?"

"Where are you going to go, anyway? Back to your parents? Stay over there by yourself like some sort of tramp? Who's ever going to want you after this? You're almost thirty-two years old, for God's sake! Where's your self-respect?"

I think about the choices he laid before me. Stay here, in London, and accept my fate as a woman fallen, or go home, shrouded in the cloak of respectability, cared for, provided for, valued, for the rest of my life.

"Respectability is overrated, darling. You'll be hearing from my lawyer."

I click the phone shut and stare at it. What now?

I adjust my coat over my shoulders, lift my head, and right there in front of me, her arms folded across her chest, is Zahra.

Zahra

So you're married? No rings—is that a new fashion statement I haven't read about in *Vogue*?"

Ranya stares down at her fingers where once I imagine
there must have been something huge and fabulous and
befitting of a spoiled little shallow diva.

Arrogant cow.

"I know you know who I am," she says, looking up.

I don't say anything. Why should I? I don't owe her a
thing.

"I don't think it's fair to hold a grudge for . . . what?
How long has it been? Twenty-five years?" She continues

undaunted. "But I'll say it: I'm sorry. For whatever hardship I might have caused you back then, I'm really, truly sorry."

She shifts her weight on her ridiculously high-heeled boots and then looks at them, in what I can only guess is shame, or perhaps a pointless attempt at manipulation, and then lifts her glassy, doe-eyed gaze back at me.

"I don't know what kind of relationship you have with Georges, but, and I promise you this, I'm not here to upset it. I'm just passing through town from . . . from . . . on my way to . . ."

And then she breaks down. Face in hands, silent sobbing interrupted by big, loud, mucousy gasps for air.

Oh, no.

"Ranya, get ahold of yourself. We're in public."

I'd spent a full minute, my face perched over the bathroom sink, rallying all my courage to face off with a great and formidable foe, one that now stands before me with . . . a runny nose and swollen red eyes? This can't be right.

I pat her shoulder and smile awkwardly at a gangly kid who's staring at us funny.

"What's the point? I'm pathetic!" she wails. "It doesn't get any worse than this!"

Any second now Georges is going to come looking for us. And if he sees her in tears, pitiable as she is right now, it's all over.

"Uh . . . why don't you step in here for a second . . . ?" I try to drag her toward the bathroom, struggling to hold the heavy swinging door open with the tips of three toes while I hold on to her at the same time. Nothing doing, the girl won't budge.

"He's right, Zahra, why would anyone ever want me?" she wails. "I'm too old to be a rebel, I have no dreams, no aspirations . . . and . . . and . . ."

"You have mascara running all the way down your cheeks. I think it's about to dribble all over your coat."

That does the trick. She darts out of my reach and into the bathroom so fast I nearly lose my balance.

"Zahra—hey, what's going on? Are you okay?"

Georges is standing in front of me, looking so cute and concerned it pierces my heart with a hundred little pins, like a seamstress's needle cushion.

"I'm fine. It was nothing."

"What have you guys been talking about all this time?"

"Nothing . . . just . . . girl talk."

"Girl talk? Really?"

"Yes." I try to break away to the bathroom before Little Miss Sparkly Pants reemerges and charms Georges's own khakis off.

And speaking of the devil in black jeans and fuck-me boots, Ranya materializes behind me, immaculate, pristinely groomed, in complete control of herself, without a whiff of helplessness about her.

"Sorry, guys, I was just speaking to my . . . friend." She throws a cautious glance in my direction. I keep my face cool and placid.

"She wants to meet up at Harvey Nics for a quick round."

"Here, please take this." Georges presses a business card in a bewildered Ranya's hand. "I don't mean to offend you, it's just we didn't have a chance to talk or anything. . . ." The poor boy seems genuinely flustered. Understandable, since it's been a long time since he's had to do the chasing. "If you're ever in Miami . . ."

"Yes, of course, thank you. . . . And thanks for lunch," she tosses over her shoulder, swiftly scurrying out of the restaurant.

I gratefully finger the edges of Baroque Christ, a little bump under my shirt, and utter a prayer of thanks under my breath. It's true. She doesn't seem to want anything to do with Georges and me.

We are leaving before the end of the week. In less than seventy-two hours I will be nestled comfortably in the leather swivel chair behind the oak desk with chrome accents of my office, a mug full of tasteless coffee in one hand, the weekly regional sales reports in the other. Georges will be battling off the affections of yet another raven-haired Miami Latina with an ass out to there and aspirations of being inducted into the social climbing hall of fame. Joe will manage to lure her into his bed instead, and promptly discard her like last week's gossip news. Rio will be getting on my nerves with her pleas to beef up the magazine staff, and my mother will still be sending me letters detailing the minutiae of which neighbor had to build another room to accommodate their

son's new bride, which girl managed to snag an overseas husband, and how my father's arthritis is getting worse and if it
keeps up, he might not manage to make his olive wood
sculptures anymore, not that there are any tourists to buy
them these days anyway.

Ranya will be a distant memory. And everything will
be just as it was before.

Ranya

Still shaking from my confrontation with Dodi, I take the long way back to the hotel, opting to rub shoulders with camera-carrying tourists and hurried locals threading through the handbag knockoff carts, pawnshops, and currency exchange stalls on Oxford rather than take one of the anonymous, more dignified streets leading to Park Lane. I pass more than one dilapidated shop promising to exchange my jewelry for $$$ (their words—not mine) with the ubiquitous tobacco-chewing, mustached man standing under the awning, his thick, curly arm hair disappearing under a football jersey.

I almost feel like I could make a life for myself here. But that would take a job. Or money. My father's or Dodi's, since all I have to my name are eleven gold liras—Lebanese pounds.

In a deeply traditional community that likes to maintain a nostalgic relationship to the past, it should come as no surprise that my personal net worth consists only of a lifetime's worth of gifts in jewelry, and eleven little solid gold coins I was given by various relatives as a baby.

It was meant as symbolic safety net. No one actually expects you to cash in your baby gifts. You're supposed to bequeath those to your own children one day.

Unless your life had fallen into the realm of true tragedy, of course.

I feel the velvet-wrapped, Ziploc-bag-stashed golden liras, platinum watch, 2.5-karat pink diamond solitaire, eternity band, and an assortment of gold chains, pendants, rings, and bracelets I've gotten at various momentous points in my life since I was born weighing down my handbag.

This is it. This is where my old life ends and the new one starts.

"Hey, pretty lady, come on inside, take a look," one of the burly men with forearms as thick as my thighs, a toothpick jutting out of the corner of his mouth, calls out to me.

Old Ranya would have let her jaw drop in mock disgust and spun on her heels, nose high in the air, and made her annoyance known.

New Ranya swallows her pride like a spoonful of Buckley's

and musters up a half smile, the best she can do under the circumstance, and says, "Good afternoon, I wonder if I could interest you in some antique gold coins?"

My lone duffel bag and various add-ons like the makeup case, the pretty hatbox that looks like it might have leaped off a screen broadcasting a black-and-white movie, are all packed and sitting by the door of my room, waiting to be called into action.

I'm going home.

I couldn't do it.

As soon as the hateful pawnshop man established I was not a potential buyer but a sad, down-on-her luck seller, he turned on me.

He led me to a dank, dark little room behind the counter where a bunch of other dodgy figures were sitting around a card table, partaking in a very loud, very lively conversation I couldn't understand a word of.

"What have you got?" he asked, taking a seat behind an old steel desk that looked like a relic from a 1970s classroom.

I timidly emptied the contents of my velvet pouch before him.

He picked up the solitaire first. "Hmpf."

Then the eternity band, followed by another grunt.

"You know how many solitaires ve hef here?" he said.

"No."

"Too many."

"Oh." I didn't know what else to say. "But this one's from Tiffany's!" I tried to act the part of a hardened sales professional.

"Hmphf." He shrugged. "Diamonds are like cars. You'll never get vat you paid for."

"Oh." Again, that seemed to sum up my feelings.

"Now these . . . ," he said, picking up the gold liras. "These we ken do something with."

I ended up tearfully parting company with a few gold chains and the eternity band for a pittance. But I couldn't leave my poor innocent coins in that horrible place, next to the guns and the tacky 14-karat gold medallions. They'd done nothing wrong. As for my engagement ring . . . it was too soon.

I was going to have to find a job.

Or go home.

I chose the latter because, seriously, who in their right mind would hire me? What am I qualified to do? I don't know how to put together a résumé. I have no skills. No goals. No address. I am, effectively, a stylish bag lady.

I call Reception and ask for a porter to bring my things downstairs. I cast one last glance at my place of residence for the last few days, shut the door behind me, and head down to the lobby.

"Checkout please," I chirp pleasantly to the attendant.

I tell him my name, he punches a few buttons at an invisible keyboard, consults an invisible screen, and then pauses. His face, just seconds ago a mask of impervious professional boredom, is suddenly and most unexpectedly plucked to life.

"Excuse me, madam." He turns his back to me.

I might have asked if there was a problem, but what would be the good in that? If I were listed as a fugitive would he really tell me? Actually, now that I think about it, maybe I should turn around . . . but then that *would* make me a fugitive, wouldn't it, skipping out on a bill, a doubtlessly huge one no less? What to do . . . what to do . . .

The suspense lasts quite some time, and I am treated to a symphony of loud sighs and exaggerated whimpers, weight shifting, and watch gazing from the growing line behind me. I turn back and smile, shrugging my shoulders and wiggling my eyebrows in the best waitstaff-can-be-so-sufferable-can't-they stance I can muster.

Then he appears, with a security guard, the frown from a few minutes ago a little deeper and meaner-looking this time.

"Madam, can you please come with us?"

Whatever it is, it's a mistake.

"What is it?"

"It would be better if you came with us."

"I'm not budging, not one inch, until you tell me what's wrong."

I may be a soon-to-be-divorcée, but that doesn't make me gullible. I don't need a man to take care of me. Or my parents. I know not to go into back rooms with strangers, even if they're British and say "brilliant" in reference to things and "gorgeous" about food. They might as well be bucktoothed mass murderers from a backwater Kentucky town for all I care. I'm not going anywhere.

The checkout clerk is clearly not amused. He eyes me for a second, almost like he's toying with me.

"Madam," he finally says, "it seems your credit card was reported stolen yesterday."

Miami

Rio

"*Ay, papi!*"

"You love that, don't you?" Joe laughs and slaps my elliptical-machine-hardened *culo,* then cups the flesh into a lusty pinch.

"Ow! Not so hard, *chavo,*" I squeal, but of course I didn't really mean it. Joe can pinch me as hard as he wants to. He can give me bruises up and down my legs and I'd still come begging for more. Not that I'm a sucker for the rough stuff, but I'm a sucker for Joe and that makes all the difference. When Osvaldo, my last boyfriend, pushed me a little too hard against the wall one night, I kneed him, right there in his smooth, shaven *huevos*. The boy had practically gone cross-eyed. But Osvaldo, cute, soulful, and *apasionado* though he was, was most often unemployed and a bit of a drunk. And he didn't choose to get himself shitfaced at the Delano or Mansion or anywhere the cool drunks hung out, either. Oh, no. Osvaldo stuck to the seediest places on Calle Ocho, far from the Beach, where you could still find old men slapping dominoes on peeling Formica tables and planning their grand return to Cuba once that *hijo de puta* Castro was good and dead. (Apparently just plain retired isn't good enough.)

Joe is different. Joe is the complete opposite of any man I've ever been with, the opposite of all the men in my family, my *papá,* my *tíos,* even my baby bro, Rafael. There isn't the smallest whiff of small-town about Joe. Joe is sophistication incarnate. Joe is machismo, self-assured sexiness, bad boy, playboy, mama's boy, and altar boy all rolled into one. And Joe is money. The kind of money that gambles in Monaco, not Reno, and owns the kind of yachts that line the docks of Biscayne Bay. Sort of like a cross between a hot, young, blond Desi Arnaz and a Ralph Lauren model, resplendent in Hugo Boss linen pants and bright polo shirt fabulousness. And straight, which, for Miami Beach, is a triumph of hope over likelihood.

"How bad do you want me, babe? I wanna hear it." Joe digs his fingers into the folds of my thighs and pushes hard.

"So bad it hurts, baby . . . don't stop. . . ." I shift a little to the right . . . twist my back . . . just a little more. . . .

"In Spanish."

Joe's rhythmic thrusting slows down to a pulse just when I'm about to go over the edge. Damn that *cabrón*.

"¡*Dale, papi* . . . *dale duro* . . . *sí, así!*" Just a little faster . . . faster . . . I thrash around on the Indian-print orange and fuchsia sheets, just the way I know he likes it. I'm getting closer. . . . Closer. . . . Maybe if I squeeze my eyes shut and focus . . . if I squish those Kegel muscles I've written about only *Dios* knows how many times . . . and then, just like that, there it is. . . . I see shadows of blue and black and green and kaleidoscopey swishes and swirls playing across the inner screens of my tightly clasped eyelids. My body jerks and twists uncontrollably, feeling nothing but wave after wave of hot, sticky pleasure until my arms turn into jelly and I sink face-first into the mattress. Seconds later, before I have a chance to catch my breath, I feel his weight collapse on me.

That's another thing the guy has going for him—flawless timing.

We lie there, speechless, motionless, the Eastern music floating to the bed from the iPod in the corner of the room enfolding us in a cocoon of Zen-like oneness with the universe. For exactly ten seconds.

"You horny little skank." Joe stands up, scratches his balls, and reaches for the pack of cigarettes in the Diesel jeans he'd left in a heap on the floor.

"No smoking in the apartment." I grab a pillow and fling it at him, missing the bulging muscle of his calf by a whole foot. "And don't call me a skank, *pendejo*."

"Right. You're a regular nun, babe."

I would have rather called him an asshole, but insulting your boss's brother in a language he could understand isn't something I was likely to advise my loyal readers in the Tía Elvira feature. There was no real-life Tía Elvira, of course— she was nothing more than a buxom cartoon with thick hips and a graying bob—but who would take relationship advice from a single thirty-one-year-old *hondureña* whose entire love life over the last year and a half amounted to little more than a string of ill-advised booty calls? With an *árabe* no less?

Ay, papi indeed. *Papi* would have my head hung over the living room mantel of the little house he built on Avenida San Isidro with his own two hands (and *tíos* Santiago and Francisco's, too) if he knew. *And over there, right next to the hunting rifle and the pictures of Rafael at six months, and again at a year, and then at his graduation, we have the daughter who betrayed me. . . .*

Right.

But *papi* was back in Honduras and I, Rosario Maria Piñera Vargas, am living the kind of life I could only dream about growing up in La Ceiba. Minus the cheating, no-good, sonofabitch boyfriend, of course. But that's not really fair, is it? It's not cheating when the man tells you up front he has no intention of ever marrying you, that if it weren't for the fact you worked for the family business you wouldn't even know what his goddamned mother looked like, that when the time came—*if* it came—he was going to settle down with one of his kind because that's just what *árabes* did. Keeping the culture alive and all that *mierda*.

What culture? Bigamy? Misogyny? A language that made it sound like you were cultivating a nice, juicy phlegm ball in the back of your throat?

But there's something to be said for an *árabe* who can find your G-spot on the first try.

Until I met Joe, a G-spot was just something I read (and occasionally wrote) about in magazines. When I did pontificate on the subject, it was mostly to assuage women's fears—"there, there, *m'hija,* it's okay if you're on boyfriend number twelve and still don't know your G-spot from a hole in your Club Monaco sweater; not all women have one, *sabes . . . ,*" which, of course, turned out to be a load of crap. Most men just don't try hard enough. Or maybe they think investing some time charting the ins and outs of a woman's body (pun intended, ha-ha. This is just the kind of humorless drivel that makes for excellent magazine copy) is just too gay. I could probably hand in 750 words on the irony of that alone.

Whatever, *chica.* Don't ask me why I put up with this shit. I have no freaking clue.

I reach for the Kate Spade notebook I keep on my nightstand and pencil in *Elvira—careers—BS.* That's "BS" for brainstorm, *mala*—I like my cuss words as much as the next liberated, post-feminist Latina, but I'm not needlessly vulgar.

He chuckles and plops down on the comforter while

every nerve covering every square inch of my bronzed (Chanel self-tanner—I was doing a feature) body recoils at the infamy of his ass germs mating with the gorgeous fabric I picked up in India and had custom sewn into a duvet by a near-blind Cuban woman on Washington and Fifteenth.

"Got anything to eat?" he says after a prolonged and needlessly noisy yawn.

"You know I don't cook." That's a lie. I do cook, and fairly well, too (thanks to the "Latina Diet" section), but I'm no man's doormat. Sex is one thing. A person could learn to dissociate the physical stuff from the rest of it, like Joe Mallouk and his ilk have mastered, but once you start cooking for them it's only a matter of time before you're expecting them to sleep over every once in a while, call you just to say hello, meet your friends, and generally setting yourself up for a royal fall. Not that I'm that much of a cynic, seriously—there had been good boyfriends down the road—but this is Joe. There's only so much you can expect from him.

"Have you spoken to your brother?" I prop myself up in bed and pull the covers around me, wiggling around until I'm happy with the precise angle of my back against the headboard and my butt in the mattress. I reach over for the stack of magazines on the nightstand and flip open the first one: *Vanidades*. A girl's got to keep up with competition, you know.

"No, why should I?"

"Because him and Zahra are meeting with all the heads

of UK suppliers to Mallouk Duty-Free? Because the out-
come of those meetings determines our magazine's budget
for the next fiscal year? Good enough reason for you?"

Joe turns to me and traces the slope of my nose down to
the tip with his index finger. "*My* magazine, Rio."

My head swivels abruptly toward Maria Menounos's
face on the plasma screen before he can see the rage reflecting in mine.

The *hijo de puta* has the *cojones* to call *Suéltate* his magazine.
His magazine. Like he'd had *anything* to do with it. If it weren't
for me, the thing would still be an eighteen-by-twelve
monstrosity called *Rave,* appealing mainly to that strung-
out-on-PCP heroin-chic niche market that finances its precarious lifestyle by mooching, high-stakes hooking, or
appealing to Daddy's pity. In Joe's case it would be Mommy,
since Daddy passed on ten years ago and, from what I can
gather, never really liked Joe more than he had to anyway.

The problem with that crowd is that they're notoriously
fickle, and, apologies for stating the obvious here, they don't
exactly like to waste time reading, even something that was
90 percent pictures, when they could be getting high.

Rave went for three issues, bleeding red from every over-
hyped, overrated, and underselling orifice until Georges
accepted my proposal to turn it around.

Funny thing is, I was never even about the fashion thing.
I like it, sure, sort of like someone can come to appreciate
fine wine with a few classes, even come close to loving it

after a trip to Napa or Burgundy or whatever, but it never got into my blood like most of the girls who traipsed through the gloomy, dank offices of Mallouk Enterprises looking for their big break in the industry. And every time one of those cutesy, made-up-to-perfection, wide-eyed Anna Wintour–worshipping fashionistas paraded their particular interpretation of style in front of me since I became editor in chief of *Suéltate,* it was all I could do to keep from bursting out in throaty, gut-tickling laughter.

Suéltate and "the industry" hadn't existed in the same stratosphere until I came along and molded the heap of unreadable trash, more apt to be lining kitty litter boxes than impressionable young women's handbags, into the kind of magazine that could stand up to *Vanidades, People en Español,* and *Cristina.*

Sure, my job description is still to hock overpriced creams and clothes and sunglasses (only the brands carried by the Mallouk network of luxury duty-free stores) to Latinos all over the Caribbean (and yes, Miami is the quintessential Caribbean city), but I get to choose the means. As long as circulation keeps up and I can show Georgie a positive correlation between products featured and sales, I have complete editorial control. He doesn't care about magazines. As far as I can tell, he only cares about money and his mother. And making sure Joe is kept at a safe distance from both.

The only caveat that comes with complete creative control is complete ass-kissing deference to Georgie in financial matters, and when Georgie decreed that the magazine didn't have the budget to hire another features writer, that meant I was not only editor in chief but also beauty and fitness editor, fashion editor, features editor, not to mention special correspondent, entertainment director, horoscope girl, and Tía Elvira. And when I set about revamping *Rave* into the up-to-the-Miami-minute Latina woman's magazine it is today, I needed a respectable alter ego to dole out the tidbits of wisdom I imagined a Hispanic Dr. Ruth would give.

Hey, muchacha, óyeme—*you think your man's wandering eye might be a full-on, packed-up-and-on-its-way-to-Timbuktu eye? Forget hunkering down in the kitchen and emerging fifteen hours later with a twenty-seven-course traditional Mexican* (or Cuban, or Nicaraguan, or Argentine, or whatever) *meal complete with homemade tortillas and get your curvy behind to Macy's intimates department instead. And while you're at it, the gym. And if the bastard still declares his God-and-Mama-given right to as much booty as crawls into his sorry lap, then get yourself a backbone,* mamita, *and drop him like last season's hemlines. You don't need this bullshit.*

Pity I have a hard time taking my own advice.

Under the covers, I feel fingers dancing on my thigh, creeping up from one side and slithering down toward the still moist spot farther in.

I can't believe it. The man is a phenomenon. I look over and sure enough, there it is, the outline of a bulge, right under the duvet.

"Are you serious?" I pick up his hand and flick it away.

"Aw, come on, babe, don't hold out on me for telling it like it is. . . ."

"Why don't you get back to Maria and let me work?"

He's not dissuaded in the least.

Joe shakes his head and pulls back the covers. "Suit yourself."

He gets up, fumbles around for the French Connection skintight biker shorts, the jeans, and the Euro-cut striped shirt. "I'm late for something anyway."

I want to say it's eleven at night, what could he possibly be late for? But I don't. That's the thing with being in love with an asshole—it can work, but only if you know your boundaries.

Zahra

Rodrigo lies on his back, one arm behind his neck, one leg propped over the other, completely naked and blowing smoke circles that look less like circles and more like a warped shape out of a Munch painting into the stale, air-conditioned room.

I wrap the coarse sheets around me, disgusted at the thought of how many times they'd been soiled with various body fluids—different body fluids of different people glued together in lustful, desperate embraces—but deciding I'd rather cocoon myself with this filth than watch my bloated, dirty reflection in the ceiling mirror.

"Why you gotta wrap yourself up like that with those sheets, baby? I love your body."

He reaches for me, but I turn away from him. I don't need to be patronized.

This is not my house. I would never bring someone like Rodrigo to the same place where I read the paper in the morning, snuggled into a fuzzy peach bathrobe and munching on day-old doughnuts. The same place Georges might drop by once in a while to strategize before whisking me away to an important supplier meeting (not a nice, quiet dinner in an unassuming restaurant, of course). I like to confine my self-whoring to cheap motels in those sections of Collins Avenue overrun by dollar stores and greasy Argentine *parilla* joints, far, far away from the classy, jazzy nouveau-Cuban bistros and pastel pink Art Deco buildings of the Beach. This is the Beach, too, technically, except it looks more like Miami Beach's skanky illegitimate half sister who sells herself after dark to fund her crack habit than the elegant stretch from the Biscayne Bay yacht marinas along Collins, down through trendy Lincoln Road Mall, and out to celebrity-ridden Ocean Drive.

"I wanna move to Canada." Rodrigo looks even nuttier and more doped out than usual.

"What? Why?" I pull the sheets tighter around me, my skin crawling up and down with every scratchy crinkle of fabric.

"Did you know it's legal to grow weed there? Can you

imagine that kind of freethinking? Doesn't it just, like, blow your mind?"

"It's not legal, it's decriminalized—that means you won't go to jail for possession, not that it's okay. And it's only in Quebec—can you speak French, genius?"

Rodrigo lays the lit stub into the plastic ashtray by the bed. He turns over on his side and spoons me, his chin stubble scratching my cheek. "I'm just messing with you, baby. You know I'd never leave you."

I don't understand men like this. Miami is full of them. Like it's somehow more commendable to lie to a woman through your miserably misaligned and yellowing teeth rather than tell her the truth—that the only reason you happen to find yourself in bed with her is because by some stroke of luck, she was standing next to you at the bar where you'd pissed away the last of your paycheck, and looked decent enough through the Dos Equis and tequila–induced haze. Maybe Latinas like to be lied to. Rio must enjoy it if she's managed to convince herself Joe might one day, through divine intervention maybe, discover a deep and profound love for her where once he'd seen nothing but a big round ass and thick receptive lips.

I don't know why I do this to myself. Boston was different. Everything about it oozed quiet sophistication, entitlement that came from a mix of money and education. Boston wasn't about flash and cheap glamour like Miami, or vain self-consciousness like New York. Boston was a me I didn't even know existed back in the Middle East. Unassuming.

Demure. More concerned about rising inflation than dipping hemlines. And the men—the men are everything Miami men, with the exception of Georges, are not. Boston men grow scruffy beards, cherish baseball games and Fenway Park hotdogs and pints of beer at the pubs with their buddies, clad in oversized Bruins jerseys, parkas, and earmuffs. Boston men are not, as their South Floridian brothers are, likely to stare at you blankly if you go on a riff about the disturbing direction of U.S. foreign policy, global warming, or the worrisome state of the dollar. In Cambridge I belonged to three different grassroots NGO campus arms, one concerned with human rights for Palestinians, another with raising money for local credit unions that lent money to village women so they could start businesses and support themselves. The third was a sort of bridge group that sought to open dialogue between on-campus Jewish organizations and Arab ones.

In Boston, I was happy.

I didn't have to go shopping on Newbury Street or stay abreast of the latest celebrity gossip to fit in.

The first time I had sex was after a protest. It was a good one—loud, well organized, and the turnout was phenomenal. He was a sophomore, a year younger, and reeked of marijuana and privilege. His shirt might have had holes at the seams and his jeans could have been frayed, but they were of that cut and quality that even I could tell didn't come cheap. And when we slipped into his car for some privacy after knocking kneecaps for twelve hours at the all-night vigil, it wasn't in a beat-up old Beetle but a sleek silver Audi. Instead of the musky odors of our tryst mingling with those of cigarettes and sweat, I became intoxicated on the fumes of Cool Water cologne and new-car smell.

I could justify my hippielike behavior at the time with the feeling that I was doing good for my people, fighting the good fight in America while they clung to their miserable scrap of an existence back home. But who was I kidding? I slept in a comfortable dorm, a solid roof over my head, a clean mattress under me, my door bolted, free of the fear that faceless soldiers would whisk me away into the night, never to return. The crowding never bothered me—if anything it reminded me of home. I crossed from Cambridge to Boston as often as I liked, with nothing more by way of "papers" than my student ID, never once worrying I might be detained at a checkpoint and denied reentry back into campus on account of a protest gone bad on the other side of town. But nestled in a virtual war zone though it is, Bethlehem was safe enough. My sisters were all fine. Some had even gotten married and my parents, cataract and arthritis ridden though they were, were still alive and kicking. I knew not who to thank for that except for Baroque Christ, who'd still been clinging to that thin wisp of a chain around my neck since the day I was born. So I thanked him every day. Every day that I sat in Advanced Macroeconomics, in International Relations, in Principles of Financial Analysis, I thanked him while I imagined my sister Abeer crouched down on the tiles of our old kitchen, tiles that seemed to me older than Jesus himself, her long embroidered tunic tucked tightly between her legs, grinding green *mulukheeyya* leaves into powder for the evening meal. In study hall late into the night I thanked him still, thinking about my mother heaving her heavy body around, sinking into the unsteady patio chair of our neighbor and letting out a tired breath, her palms over her knees, waiting for her cup of scalding tar black coffee.

Rodrigo nestles his prickly chin deeper into my neck.

I don't want to be here. I don't want this bubble of smuggled drug money and liposuctioned behinds and the bottomless pit of sunshine that is Miami. I don't want Rodrigo or any of the scruffy pseudorebels I've inflicted on myself since moving here for lack of the real thing. I want to be in Boston. But the banking world is a small one, and big, expensive mistakes can cost you your career. Like one mistake had cost me mine. One. Mistake. One nine-and-a-half-million-dollar mistake.

Which is why, for the last five years, I've had something else to thank Baroque Christ for every living, breathing moment of my existence: having met Georges Mallouk.

"What's the matter, baby?" Rodrigo pulls back a strand of my hair that had gotten caught in my earring.

"Nothing. I'm going to take a shower."

"What's with this obsession with personal hygiene? Do you have to take a shower every time we fuck? At least wait till I'm gone. Jesus, man."

I ignore him and pull the covers off the bed, entwining them around my body, Greek goddess–like, so I don't have to look at the disgusting rolls of my tummy, the cellulite spotting my upper thighs, or my deflated breasts flat against my chest, until I'm about to step into the tub. But I hear my BlackBerry vibrate in my purse before I can make it to the bathroom. I cannot ignore it. What if it's Georges? My family? It can't be anyone else, with the possible exception of Rio.

Rodrigo sighs loudly and flips onto his stomach in a show of disgust when he sees me reaching for the little black vibrating device. He's made his disapproval with my having sold out to "the man" apparent enough in the past. And I've made my utter and complete indifference to his sentiments equally explicit.

The screen flashes Georges's number.

I duck into the bathroom quickly and lock the door behind me. The walls are paperlike in their thinness, and I can only pray Rodrigo is too stoned to care what I'm doing in here.

"Georges?"

"Zahra—hey! Glad I caught you."

Oh, no. George never starts a conversation so . . . so . . . sunshiny. He's an efficient sort of man, stating the problem, and hence purpose, of his call in the first ten seconds of conversation. It's one of the things I love most about him.

"What's going on?" I mumble uncertainly.

Silence. Further proof something's gone terribly wrong.

"Georges? Are you there?"

"Yeah, I'm here. Look, I've got a favor to ask you. Can we meet up somewhere for a drink?"

I look at the closed door, imagining Rodrigo stretched out in the bed on the other side. My skin feels swarmed with a million little invisible bugs, crawling up and down, through orifices and in between creases of flesh. What am I doing here?

"Okay, I'm just . . . not at home right now. I need a little time to get ready. Can you at least tell me what this is about?"

He sighs. "Ranya. She needs a place to stay."

And just like that, the entire bathroom, seventies geometric motif shower curtain, rusty bathtub, and pukey pink tiles, goes into a freefall spin around me.

To: MunirwaMaryam _ Hayek@yahoo.com
From: R _ Hayek@yahoo.com
Subject: Don't Worry

Dear Mama and Baba,

It's very hard to put in words how sorry I am to have made you worry about me, as I'm sure you must have when you realized I wasn't on the flight you'd booked for me.

I'm sorry.

Very, very, very sorry.

But I wasn't ready to come home just yet. I hope you know how much I love and respect you, and how important your guidance is to me. I am nothing in this world if I cause you to lose your pride and faith in me, for even one second. That being said, know that I didn't take the decision to stay on abroad a little while longer lightly. I know this is something you think only crazy *ajaaneb* say, and that you think being around family is the best remedy, but I think for this time I need to do some thinking on my own. Just for a little while, I promise.

I also promise I won't be bothering you for money, or anything else, so long as I am away. And that I'll let you know if I'm in trouble. Not that I'm planning on getting in any trouble, of course. I'm just saying.

Lots of love, and I'll see you soon, *in sha'allah.*

Ranya

Ranya

The officers were really very nice, especially after I started crying. They brought me tea and a muffin, and managed to make me feel like I was making a social call in a cute little Notting Hill walk-up instead of being held in a dingy, depressing police station on suspicion of credit card fraud.

Of course this was after my father had faxed over a copy of the marriage certificate after my bumbling, nonsensical confession, extracted in between bouts of sobbing, had apparently not been convincing enough. They were really, really sorry (*really* sorry, miss—er, missus) for the whole mess and even offered to drive me to the airport and everything.

The bastard had reported the credit cards—our *joint* credit cards—stolen.

And barely an hour after I'd been arrested I was dropped off at Heathrow, an online ticket reservation code scrawled on the back of a Harrods receipt for a one-way ticket to Montreal courtesy of my parents and dictated over the police station landline with explicit instructions that I am to return home *immediately,* that they weren't having any more of my shenanigans, and what kind of way was this for a still-married woman to behave, homo-unmentionable husband or not?

So there was clearly only one thing in the whole world I could do.

Buy a ticket to Miami.

Mama and Baba, intoxicated and judgmentally impaired with the rush of ensuring absolutely nothing hindered my journey home as they were, made sure to purchase every kind of travel insurance known to man. Which included cancellation insurance of the most generous variety.

I'll admit, my behavior might appear, to a casual observer, to be a little sneaky. "Ratlike" might even spring to mind. That's what I'd think if this was happening to someone else. But the key point here is that I *really, truly, honestly* had no choice.

It's not that I don't think that somewhere behind the yelling, the head-beating over the mess I'd gotten myself neck-deep into, and numerous appeals for God to inject some sense into me, that my parents don't mean well. They do. They always have. It's just that I'm no longer convinced, as I once was, of their firm understanding of the Truth of the Universe.

Where once I might have understood the Truth to be that I needed to get back to Montreal because that was what my father had decreed was best, a flutter of uncertainty entered my soul as I stood in front of the Air Canada check-in counter, passport and Harrods receipt in hand, waiting for a sign.

And it came.

In the form of an Alexander McQueen digital advertisement just above the conveyor belt set to whisk my luggage away, radiating with a soft, almost heavenly artificial yellow glow.

There must be something else to life beyond waiting for Mr. Lebanese-Muslim-Parent-Approved-Right to walk into your life.

I wanted to find out what that something was. So here I am, one hastily composed e-mail to my parents later—in Miami, Florida, as opposed to Montreal, Canada.

I'm sure they'll forgive me. They always do.

So, tell me about yourself."
       All it takes is four little words to bring a cold sweat over me. Georges must have noticed, because he leans over the table and lays his hand gently on my arm—which is shaking through the pleasant heat and my long-sleeved sweater—and tells me to take it easy.

"All I was trying to find out is what you like to do, what you studied, maybe, you know, just the basics."

"Another virgin daiquiri, miss?" The tan waiter smiles down at me, all young, muscled arms and dark, smoldering goodness. I'm not sure if all of Miami is this body conscious, happy, and relaxed or if it's just the waitstaff and patrons of the Delano. Everywhere I look, leggy women in gold and turquoise sandals, bejeweled bikinis, and huge sunglasses are lounging in elegant white chairs or stretching out on white daybeds, very little of their lithe bodies left to the imagination. And almost invariably, equally attractive males in gold-rimmed Ray-Bans and tight shorts hover close by, alcohol-laden tumblers in hand, buzzing over the near-naked Venuses of southern Florida.

"I don't know anyone over the age of fifteen who still orders virgin daiquiris. Are you sure you don't want to give the real thing a try? This is Miami Beach after all." Georges smirks.

I cast an evil eye in his direction. "Do I have to be depraved to be in Miami?"

He raises his glass of red wine. "Does this make me depraved, then?"

"N-no . . . that's not what I meant. It's just not right for me."

"Oh, okay, I get it. Alcohol's fine for us Christian riffraff because we're going to hell anyway, right? We might as well have a good time of it while we're here."

"No! I didn't mean that, either!" My ears are burning. In

the space of an hour I've managed to offend the one man standing between me and my last hope of a not-too-dark future. How else am I going to find gainful employment when the most challenging thing I've done since university is roll vine leaves and minced meat into hors d'oeuvres?

I peer into his eyes beseechingly by way of an apology, but there's no sign of contempt, maybe just a bit of bemusement at this silly, not-so-little girl sipping virgin cocktails and wearing a sweater in the smoldering Miami heat in front of him.

"My mother taught me never to talk politics or religion with a lady. I'm sorry." He smiles benevolently. "You were going to give me some insight to who Ranya Hayek is and what she wants out of life."

I wonder if everyone else in the world would be as stumped by this question as I am. Is it really normal to not know who you are in your thirties? Or where you're going? Where do you start with a question like this when you're smack-dab in the middle of an existential crisis?

"I was born in Lebanon but didn't see much of it because of the war. My dad worked for a Saudi Arabian oil company—this was back when Dubai was just a patch of date palms and a well—until he retired. That's when we moved to Montreal, Beirut not really being an option. That's it, really."

That I spent the better part of my conscious life waiting for the same fairy tale that eventually befell my friends, my mother, and my aunts to happen to me and that my handsome sheik in gleaming white robes was probably enjoying a romp with our equally handsome interior decorator at this very moment isn't really anyone's business right now.

Georges leans a little closer across the table, treating me to a heavenly cloud of musky cologne and a brush of bare forearms against my fingertips.

I pull back instantly. His touch, the feel of little black curls creeping out from underneath rolled-up shirtsleeves, is more than I can bear. There was a time when small exchanges like these promised a future of something discussed only in hushed tones and innuendo when my mother thought me out of earshot, something I finally learned about from poring over issue after issue of *Cosmopolitan* and later, when my friends were marrying off, one by one, slipping slowly out of my life like fluffy clouds dragged across the sky by invisible hands. It was something I realized I wanted on the decaying docks stretching out into the Rea Sea, old and eaten away by salt and humidity, the only place my friends and I were set free to enjoy ourselves, away from watchful eyes. And the only place where boys worked up the nerve to talk to us.

Some girls pushed the envelope, the loose, *faltaneen* girls my mother warned against, but not me. These girls didn't content themselves with innocent flirting. They would disappear behind the sand dunes only to emerge a half an hour later, their makeup smudged, their faces flushed with a mixture of guilt and smug pride. Even if a part of me was jealous, I knew that if I waited, real happiness, not the shameful, elusive kind some indulged in, would be mine.

But somehow that something had eluded me too, and I was never going to wait for it again. Nor was I going to turn into those girls who'd lose themselves in one bed after the next, hoping to forget that their chances at security and a decent life kept slipping out of their grasp with every encounter, like a bar of wet soap.

It's time for Plan B. The fluttering in my stomach brought on by Georges's touch, so similar to those forbidden longings I once felt for Dodi, is not going to help me.

I'm going to go out and get myself a life. And this time I'm keeping men out of it.

"I was really surprised when you called to say you were in town," he says, an eyebrow tantalizingly askew. "Pleasantly, of course, but surprised all the same."

"I have a confession to make," I tease.

"Really, what?"

"I lied about why I was in London."

"Oh." Georges stiffens, leaning into the cushioned back of the chair.

"I was having some trouble with . . . my parents. I just didn't feel like I could be myself around them," I stammer. "They never made me feel like I was fit for very much, so I thought I'd go away for a while. Try to figure it all out on my own." This is as close as I could get to the truth without saying too much.

Georges seems to relax. "I know all about difficult parents, don't worry. And I think it was very brave of you to do that."

I scratch the back of my neck, shake out my hair, and cross my arms across my chest, all the while taking in the great white columns encapsulating us within their intimate, secluded space, the white curtains dancing lazily in the breeze, the white daybeds stationed around the empty pool in front of us, just begging for us to strip away our clothes and let the gentle late-afternoon sun kiss our bodies.

I suddenly realize my temples and inner thighs are damp with sweat. What kind of interview is this anyway?

"I majored in political science," I blurt out before he can notice I'm practically melting under his gaze. "Minor in French literature."

"Oh, yeah?"

"Yes. Why are you looking at me like that?"

"No, nothing." He shrugs. "It's just a very accomplished, genteel sort of thing to study. You must be a fantastic small talker. Not to mention you'd get along great with my mother."

"How come?"

"She studied in France, her family still has a place there, actually. She made sure we learned French when we were kids. It was brutal." He makes a pinched face as if someone had just asked him if he fancied sautéed rat for dinner. "Those messed-up irregular verbs . . ."

I start to laugh. He's so easy, so cozy and fun to be around. He talks to you as if he's known you forever.

"So what were you planning to do with this poli-sci degree besides make great cocktail party conversation?"

I'll admit I studied political science mostly because that's what my best friend at the time, Suzie, was going into and I didn't want to be exiled all the way across campus in the applied sciences wing when everybody knew the best wraps and lattes were served in the College of Liberal Arts cafeteria.

I was a good student, and could have gone into bio-chemistry just as easily as English lit or business, or even astrophysics. My problem, as it turned out, was simply that I lacked a driving passion, but (and please be honest here) so does pretty much everyone at nineteen.

I ended up enjoying political science at the end, and even envisioned myself a diplomat, a UN interpreter perhaps, a human rights commissioner, a member of the UNESCO World Heritage committee, maybe, but seriously, who did I think I was? Angelina Jolie? Or maybe I was subconsciously hoping I'd marry an ambassador one day.

I am tempted to launch into my whole wife-of-a-diplomat bit but think better of it.

"What about you, Mr. Mallouk?" I adopt my best mock-serious face. "How did you end up head of a giant private company that 'dabbles in this and that,' as you say?"

"My great-grandfather started out as a peddler. . . ."

Visions flood my mind of a homeless man in long dirt-covered rags and a fez, scraping the bottom of the American West barrel of capitalism on a horse-drawn buggy, scouring for miserable people to sell useless junk to. Was this smooth-talking art and fashion connoisseur sitting in front of me descended from an illustrious line of snake-oil salesmen?

"He came to America the same way everyone else did back then, on a ship that sailed into Ellis Island. He didn't speak a word of English, the only thing of any value he brought with him from back home was a letter from a cousin who'd made the same trip before him and said that anyone who worked hard enough could eventually afford to send his children to the best schools, and that they stood as much chance as anyone else of becoming doctors or lawyers or engineers, and have enough money left over to build the biggest, most lavish house back in the Old Country. Or so he claimed."

I take another sip of my virgin daiquiri and mull over how things really hadn't changed that much since Georges's great-grandfather's time.

"Anyway, the story goes that the cousin's letter was— excuse me—bull, because Americans liked Easterners even less back then than they do now. They called my great-grandfather a Turk even though that was the last thing he was. He was the 'Mess'ican' of his time: Anyone from the Middle East had to be a Turk, just like Spanish speakers in the U.S. are all Mexicans. Or Cubans if you happen to live in Florida."

"Sorry, but where exactly is 'back home'?"

"Today we'd say northern Lebanon, but back then the whole area was just a big blob with no defined borders. All my great-grandfather ever knew of his country was his village, and maybe a couple of neighboring ones. I think what finally motivated him to pull up the stakes and take the show else- where wasn't so much money as the need to get away from the run-ins with the Turks and the occasional religious massacre or two. Every time there was a drought or nasty olive or silk or orange season, the neighboring Muslims would take it as a good excuse to come into town . . . and not to pay a friendly visit, either."

I blush.

He notices.

"Don't worry—it's been four generations. The grudge has lifted. At least against Lebanese Muslims . . . new ones seem to be born every day." He sighs. I don't need to ask him why. The civil war, pitting Lebanese against Lebanese, Lebanese against Palestinians, and Palestinians against the world.

An uncomfortable silence plagues our little corner of tropical heaven and I want to kick myself. All I want right now is a job that will keep me in unorthopedic hand-me- down shoes from the Miami branch of the Salvation Army and maybe even a roof over my head until I can think things through and come up with a new life plan. So far all I've done is sabotage my one chance.

"I would have made a *great* political scientist, for your information," I say brightly, "if only I'd ever figured out what political scientists actually *did*."

He cracks a hint of a smile. It's a start.

"If I had a chance to do it over again," a euphemism for

if-I-didn't-subscribe-to-the-Arabian-prince-and-his-Westmount-mansion-theory, "I think I would have gone into art history. Or journalism. Or maybe both. I was just trying to be realistic. . . . What kind of job do you get with art history, right?" Right. That's exactly why I stayed away from the arts. Less than glowing career prospects.

But for some odd reason, Georges's eyes light up.

"Journalism, huh? And have you done any magazine writing?"

I consider telling a blatant lie. I want whatever he's thinking of offering with every cell in my old spinster body.

"N-no . . . not magazine writing per se, but I did take a creative writing class once. And I've helped my mother put together the newsletter for her Syrian Ladies League of Quebec meetings before. Not that the ladies are all Syrian, but it's an old organization and the name stuck . . . you know. . . ." Nothing but incomprehensible babble seems to be escaping my lips. Lips that are now burning as I gaze at Georges's. If there's one thing I will never forgive Dodi for taking away from me, it's my maidenly innocence. Once upon a time I had the discipline of an infantry unit when it came to my feelings toward the opposite sex. Attractive men were over there, I was over here, and that was that. If the wrong kind of guy sent my hormones firing just a little too much out of control, I simply extracted myself from the situation.

Georges leans forward a little and I feel my heart start to pulse in my ears. Normally, this would be prime compromising-situation-self-extracting time. But I need this job. With no CV, no past, and consequently no future, what else am I supposed to do?

"You know about our main business—the duty-free industry."

"Y-yes. . . ." Please *please please please please* don't make him offer me the position of perfume spray girl, which, let's face it, is all I'm qualified to do.

"Well, we also publish this magazine. . . . Honestly, most businesses like ours just farm out these sorts of peripheral activities to a specialty firm, but, I don't know, *Suéltate* seems to be hitting a chord with our customers in southern Florida, so we've kept it under our control. My father was never one for farming out family business to strangers anyway, and you're not exactly a stranger anymore."

His dark broody eyes look up at me from under a rim of thick, straight lashes.

"Our editor in chief is a very competent woman, a little rough around the edges." He chuckles lightly to himself, and my fake smile freezes on my face, loud alarm sirens firing off in my brain. This can only mean trouble. Still, I don't want to go back to Montreal. I don't care what I have to do. "But she's very good. She's been after me to find her another staff writer, and honestly, I was going to get her an intern, but I think you'll do a better job at representing the magazine's image. You're the kind of woman I think our readership aspires to be—worldly, sophisticated, well traveled, and, well . . . attractive."

The rosy glow of health and general contentedness about him deepens into a red flush to rival the wine he reaches for. We sip our drinks quietly, each surveying the space above the other person's head.

I think about what he's just said. A staff writer . . . it sounds so glamorous, so . . . Marlo Thomas meets Sarah Jessica. But in Miami. I would be so busy covering galas and sipping Pellegrinos that I'd have no time at all to think about Dodi or the fact that unless I abandon all the values I once held dear—something that turns my stomach just to think about—I will die alone and unloved. And disowned by the poor parents I deserted.

"When can I start?"

Georges bursts out laughing. "Wow—I was expecting you to play a little hardball and tell me that anything less than features editor is below you, but hey, this is cool, too. I'd order some champagne to celebrate, but I'm guessing that's still out of the question?"

I nod.

"Okay. Another virgin daiquiri it is. I'll take one, too, this time, see what I'm missing." With a twinkle of mischief in his eyes, he winks, but then his eyebrows furrow as if he'd forgotten something.

"I meant to ask you earlier—do you have a place to stay?"

I stare at my fingernails and notice the dark purply black is beginning to chip in the most unbecoming way. They probably stuck to metallics, pinks, and nudes in Miami anyway, so I should head over to a nail salon and remedy the situation as soon as possible. If I had a red cent to my name, that is.

Braided somewhere into this thought process is the question of exactly how I tell Georges, this person who for some unfathomable reason is going above and beyond in his efforts to make me comfortable, just how much of a mess I'm in. I have nothing to my name but what eleven little golden coins and some assorted jewelry would fetch.

"Actually . . . I was just going to stay here for a while. Until I get settled and all that."

"At the Delano? Are you serious? You sure you're not some oil princess down here playing pauper with us poor folk?" He gulps down the gooey pink slush that's been placed in front of him and grimaces.

Recovered, he says, "I'd offer you my house, but I'm pretty sure a nice girl like you would look at me like I'd completely lost it, even though I *am* a nice Lebanese boy who lives with his mother and three brothers. My sister was with us, too, until she got married and moved out five years ago."

My mouth flaps open. "There's five of you?"

He throws his head back in loud, throaty laughter. My knees shake just watching him. "The first question I usually get when I say that is how do I ever get any privacy, but yeah, we're a big, tight-knit group. It seems my great-granddad started the whole family closeness thing and my folks kept it going. It's pretty nice, I might do the same if I ever get the chance."

I want to ask how is it possible he hasn't had the chance

yet, unless there was something wrong with him, but then the thought of Dodi and our decimated fairy-tale life springs to mind.

"Zahra has a great condo—huge, overlooking Biscayne Bay. Perfect place to start fresh."

I look around me, squinting into the fierce early afternoon sun. Is this it? Do I take the plunge?

"I'm not sure Zahra likes me very much."

"Zahra comes off like she doesn't like anybody sometimes. I think it's just Miami she's not crazy about. Don't worry, I'll take care of it."

I wait for him to ask me what I want to do today, offer to show me the city. Ask me if I wanted to meet that big boisterous family of his, maybe. But he just turns his wrist over, tosses a glance at his watch, and shuffles to his feet. With a quick but warm kiss to my cheek, he tells me to get some rest, enjoy my evening, and that he'll call me as soon as he's settled things with Zahra. Tomorrow he'll take me to the office to meet my boss, Rio.

Oh my God. This is really happening.

Rio

Fuck you, Georges.

Or better yet, let that leggy, long-haired flesh-and-blood incarnation of Princess Jasmine in Cavalli boots and a tweed suit (in the Miami humidity, mind you) sitting in my waiting room, have *her* fuck you. She looks all prim and proper, but those girls are the worst. Just look at Zahra. What, *papi*? You think I don't know? She slept with a cousin of a friend of Rafael's once, and I wouldn't touch that guy with a ten-foot pole.

"I can have her help Behnaz with copyediting. Does she have experience with that at least?" That's what I say instead. Because seriously, what's the point? Should I risk my job, my standing in the company, for this *chava*? As if.

"An intern could do copyediting—why don't you let her have a crack at filler pieces, see what she does with that. She obviously looks the part and I have a good feeling about her—like she's just waiting for the right opportunity to prove herself."

Uh-huh. *Like she's proved herself under the table at your last fancy dinner?* I want to ask.

Stop it, Rosario Maria Piñera Vargas. *Stop it.* You don't know that for a *fact,* do you?

"Okay, no problem." I beam my most professional this-is-beyond-bullshit-but-what-am-I-going-to-do-about-it smile, my hands clasped together in front of me, my Fornarina-clad elbows jutting out all businesslike on either side.

I can employ her, but who's to say she won't quit after she figures out that *Suéltate* is no ragtag publication-cum-gravy-train her boyfriend might keep her busy with because she batted her eyelashes just so?

"Rio . . . you did say you needed help, didn't you?"

"That's true, but I did have someone more experienced in mind . . . someone I can train for a features editor position one day, maybe? Are you sure Ranya wouldn't be happier in sales under Daria?"

"Yes."

"Okay. You're the boss."

"Shall I let her in?"

"Sure thing." More smiling. Of the largely fake variety.

He returns the fake smile, insofar as a quintessentially nice guy like Georges can, and gets up. He heads for the door and motions her in. Ranya Hayek. My new staff writer. My new staff writer who'd somehow managed to bypass at least a dozen girls five times more qualified—and younger, to boot.

She's even prettier up close. A slightly less South Asian version of Aishwarya Rai, if you get what I mean, which lends her that exotically impossible-to-place air, like she could be an Italian with coffee bean–colored hair, a pale Pakistani, a Greek girl with wide, gold-speckled irises, even a dark, freckleless Irish chick.

Not like me.

No matter what I do, I am and will always be a Latina. Capital *L*. With the pouty lips, slight stature, and generous derriere cartoon versions of Latinas are saddled with. I can cut my wavy jet-black hair into an edgy bob, swear off lip liner forever, and punish my sorry ass on the elliptical five times a week, but I will always look the part of that quintessential Latina. Thank a generous dose of Mayan blood for that.

Georges does the introductions and scuttles away, claiming some urgent meeting at head office—is there any other kind?—squeezing Ranya's elbow on his way out. And if that weren't enough, she stares longingly after him, her gaze lingering at the door even after he's disappeared. *Ay, chica,* but could she have possibly been more obvious?

"Georges says you don't have a résumé. Is this your first job?" And I don't say that in a don't-worry-we're-all-friends-here tone, either. She throws me a look that reminds me of Bambi's mother . . . right before she got shot.

"I'll take that as a yes," I reply to her silence. I want to give it to her, straight, about how I've pitched young, bright, upstanding Miami Latina after deserving Latina to Georges, begging for a permanent staffer, and all she had to do was wiggle her compact little ass in front of him to get the job instead of, oh I don't know, getting a journalism degree from Yale like the adorable Guatemalan-American twenty-three-year-old I had to say no to three months ago, or some practical experience like the Peruvian-American with the master's in corporate communications, but I don't. I bite my tongue because Georges is my boss and whether I like it or not, Mallouk Enterprises is a family business, and I should be thanking my lucky stars the only Mallouk kid remotely interested in running a magazine happens to be too vapid or wasted most of the time to care. What I should most definitely *not* be doing is rocking the boat.

I sigh audibly. "You'll notice there aren't too many of us working here. Georges's name is on the masthead as CEO, but he's too busy running the rest of the empire to bother much with a little outfit like ours—we account for less than one percent of total Mallouk Enterprises revenue. Bear in mind, though, it's hard to get a handle on exactly how much of the in-store traffic is driven by advertising and editorial in *Suéltate*." Of course it's hard when a dumpy little accountant with a royal stick up her *culo* considers any numbers that marketing shows her to be worthless drivel.

"Have you met Joe yet?"

She shakes her head, probably still reeling from the shock of possibly having to do actual work. What the hell was that Georges thinking?

"Don't worry, you'll meet him, but there's no telling when. His job has more of a . . . 'hobnobbing' nature to it, so you're more likely to find him at some of the PR events *Suéltate* is regularly invited to attend." Right. If only. It usually takes a blowjob or two to convince him to come, with promises of getting there late and leaving early, and I'm only ever successful if he's having a slow week.

"So really, the actual grunt work comes down to me—I do most of the editorial work—Marisol, who's director of circulation, and Daria, who's in charge of advertising sales. Behnaz's official title is copy editor, but as the most junior one in the bunch, she's pretty much the receptionist-slash-coffee-getter-slash-concierge around here. Well, *was.*"

I feign my best innocently evil smile and look up (yes—because the girl literally *towers* over my five-foot-two self, scarlet-soled platform Louboutin knockoffs and all).

Ranya appears suitably mortified, though that might just be leftover mortification at the whole work thing. Hard to say.

"If you're wondering how we manage to put together an entire magazine on such a skeletal staff," not that there's any chance she is, but I have my pride after all, "it's called freelancing. We make ample use of that around here—everything from artwork to layout to features to production. All we do are fillers and regulars: advice, must-haves, Latin numerology, on-the-job . . . you might want to pay special attention to *that* column . . . that kind of stuff."

At this point in the conversation, Ranya's mouth begins to twitch like she might be trying to muster up something to say. I shift my weight onto my left hip, cross my arms, and wait for the mute wonder to speak.

"Am I . . . am I going to have a . . . cubicle?"

Ay, chica, the girl actually says the word "cubicle" like it's another word for "five-star beach house in the Maldives." *Te lo juro.*

Ranya

I do, in fact, get my own cubicle. I'd heard so much about these things, watched everyone—from my cousin Ali to Ally McBeal—organize their lives around time spent in them, that the moment Behnaz leads me to my very own one, my home for thirty-seven and a half hours every week, my heart soars with achievement. The stained carpet, the dirty layer of mock "dark oak" peeling at the corners, the hardened globs of blue poster glue on the wall facing my swiveling chair—all of these touches feel like authentic effects in a sitcom where I'm playing the part of the plucky ingénue who wins over the office with her spunk, good humor, and quick thinking.

If only I had but one of those qualities.

No matter—what's that saying? Fake it till you make it?

"It's not so bad," Behnaz says.

I like her. Her father moved the family to New Jersey when Behnaz was seven. Apparently, all it took was one trip to Wildwood to convince her she had to blow that aerosol stand (her words, not mine), even if it was back to Tehran. At eighteen, she hopped a bus to New York and got a job selling an unknown designer's clothes out of a trunk on commission. Poverty soon made her wonder if there wasn't another way of earning a living doing something that didn't make her want to puke at the thought of getting up in the morning and that kept her if not in designer duds, then at least in some decent knockoffs. Cue a degree in journalism, a couple of years as a blogger for a local newspaper, a bit of freelancing, and now this, receptionist/coffee girl/whatever-Rio-decrees gofer.

"Rio can be a total bitch sometimes, but she's fair. Although I've noticed she's a hell of a lot bitchier after a visit from Zahra. She's from corporate," Behnaz says in a hush.

Zahra? As in my new temporary roommate Zahra? I try to keep my face impassive.

"Why'd you leave New York for this?" I ask.

"Another winter and I would've torched myself. Seriously, how is it fair that some people never ever have to wear pantyhose—ever—and others have to bundle them-

selves up in coats that wouldn't weather a fistful of snow-
flakes just to look good? I mean honestly, I'd like to know if
Ralph Lauren is thinking 'winter in Tahiti' when he comes
up with some of his stuff.

"It's not just that," she continues. "There are five general
looks in this country: New York sophisticate, Miami chic,
California cool, Dallas debutante, and sweatpants-and-
scrunchies-ville, USA. I was a Miami girl in a New Yorker's
body."

I want to point out that she's actually an Iranian girl
who grew up in Jersey, but I'm starting to think that Behnaz
sees actual physical matter as merely a state of mind.

"Anything I owned that was black or beige went straight
to the Salvation Army as soon as I moved out here. I will
tolerate navy just because it's making a comeback, but that's
as far as I go."

Ah. I struggle to hold back a smile. It's obvious this girl
is in her element. I wonder if I could ever feel this way. I
look around the office, lined with cubicles, a little more on
the dingy side than I would have expected for a women's
magazine, buzzing with purpose and activity, but with a
few touches here and there I would imagine are totally different from what most office dwellers experience: no sullen,
bored faces anywhere in sight.

I let Behnaz rattle off a few more fashion axioms before
I interrupt. "So . . . what exactly do you do all day?"

"Rio's a very busy woman." Behnaz stiffens, taking
obvious pride in the fabulousness of her boss and, by

association, her own role as gatekeeper to all that fabulous-ness. "I'm always fielding calls from publicists, nobodies who think they're Donatella Versace or something, invit-ing Rio to this party or that, asking her if she wants the exclusive on their latest perfume, or lipstick, or novel, or whatever. I set up meetings with the photographers, the stylists, the makeup people, caterers, you know, regular stuff."

I feel myself get faint. Is this what I left Montreal for? My mother, my father, afternoon coffee rendezvous with my few remaining friends, my . . . my . . . All of a sudden a rush of tears well up behind my eyes. I turn away and exam-ine a rack of brightly colored clothing lining a wall of one of the cubicles, hoping Behnaz is too entranced with spicing up her job description to notice. I can't help it. I'm sorry. I know I'm not supposed to care, that I'm better off without him, that it was never a real marriage so how could I possi-bly have it in me to mourn it, but I just can't help it.

I think of our apartment. *My* apartment. I would have never dreamed of leaving my parents' home, it was just never done, and why would I? It would have been madness . . . paying rent, even assuming that I had a job that would have paid me enough to move out in the first place, coming home to an empty house instead of the sound of my mother's voice calling out from the kitchen for me to set the table, help with dinner, tell her about my day.

And yet.

When I married Dodi it had seemed that if nothing else

was going right, at least, for the first time, I had something besides shoe collections, jewelry, and a closet bursting with the fruits of countless shopping sprees that was mine. Something real, something *adult*.

The apartment.

It was the one area of my life where I simply didn't take anyone else's opinion into account. I decorated it in the complete opposite manner of my family home, emphasizing minimalism and function over useless beauty and Turkish tassels. Gone were the Swarovski ballerinas, bear cubs, and ducklings—a nightmare to dust—and in with the huge statement pieces, a lone, rectangular glass vase, a single white calla lily inside, on a massive, simple dark wood table.

And now I'd left that all behind. For what?

"Ranya?"

I realize Behnaz is now looking at me with what I think might be concern.

"Remember, all the phone numbers you'll need are on that call sheet, you have to arrange an appointment with the cover stylist for the America Ferrera issue, take care of catering, no red meat or cabbage in anything, and no smelly foods, either, and make travel arrangements for the freelancer who's interviewing America. Got it?"

"Absolutely!" I don't even bat an eyelash. Since curling into a little ball under my desk isn't an option right now, what choice do I have but to suck it up and figure it out somehow?

"Okay, good." Behnaz's cautious smile is tinged with

relief. "I'm moving over to that desk over there, just call me if you need anything."

"I will. Thanks."

"No problem."

And off she goes, leaving me to acquaint myself with this new life I've stumbled into.

Zahra

I'm fidgeting. I know I am. I shouldn't. I am an intelligent, experienced, poised, qualified, and all-around capable candidate and this fidgeting isn't saying any of these things. It's saying I'm terrified. Scared, self-conscious, conspicuous, self-doubting, and terrified.

"This way please, Miss Badalati." Even this secretary has more confidence than I do. Why wouldn't she, with her adorable brown freckles and glossy dark hair, falling with perfect, unfrizzy straightness on the lapels of a perfectly tailored suit.

I tried. Of course I did. I even went to Bal Harbor,

walked right into Nordstrom's, and did my best to pick out an outfit that exuded power, hid my bulging midsection and wide, flat behind. Isn't that what you're supposed to do? Highlight your best features and downplay your worst ones? What the magazines don't tell you is what to do when you don't have any decent features to speak of. What I ended up with instead is some sort of balloonlike contraption the ebullient saleslady had referred to as a "tulip skirt" that seems to have expanded my hips to three times their actual size, and a matching cropped jacket, which is doing nothing to camouflage this miserable fact. What would Rio and her fashion mongrels have to say about that?

The secretary leads me down a long hallway I'm well acquainted with even though I've never been in this particular building, the clickety-clack of her high heels echoing off the taupe walls, the smells of wood polish commingling with those of reheated lunches seeping out from beneath closed doors.

My first job out of MIT's Sloan School of Management was with Morrison & Fitch, one of the scores of financial powerhouses that dotted downtown Boston.

"Mama, you're not going to believe it!" I had bellowed over the cackle of the strained long-distance connection. "I've got a job! And not just any job—it's at the biggest investment bank in the city!" I couldn't keep her guessing very long. We had a tradition of disaster in the area—from dry spells that brought olive grove farmers to their knees to army raids that did a nasty number on the tourism trickle—which made my mother wary of any sort of news since it seldom foretold anything good.

"*Nurshkur'allah habibti,* may God shower you with His blessings," she said, but only after the slightest of hesitations. And in one swift instant, all the puffed-up pride I dared to take in the fact that I, Zahra Badalati, a nobody, a plain girl from the garbage-lined and forgotten town of Bethlehem on whom not a single admiring glance had ever been bestowed, had single-handedly managed to pluck herself, and possibly her family along with her, away from the brink of poverty.

My mother has hesitated, her showers of praise and effervescent ululations reserved, because secretly in her heart she'd always harbored the hope that I might one day get married.

Although welcome, news of a job simply didn't measure up.

"Your sister Mirvat is pregnant," she continued, her voice controlled but betraying bubbles of simmering delight. "She didn't want to tell anyone before the third month, but I knew. A mother always knows these things."

From then on exchanges about my work revolved around how much money I could afford to send and when, not about the box-sized studio apartment I rented in a dingy Boston suburb so that I could support myself on an entry-level salary and still have money left to send back home. As much as American living had taught me about self-reliance and its twin, watching out for number one, I never managed to shake the guilt that plagued me, that I was here and they were there, or the sense of indebtedness I felt toward my family. Abeer, Reema, Nura, and Mirvat had done without university so I could go. They were mothers so I could be a career woman. Would they have traded places with me if they'd ever had the chance?

The secretary and I continue walking for what seems like a long time. They are trying to intimidate me, and it's working. I feel sick to my stomach, like I used to the night before important exams, nights when I would lie on my back in bed, staring at the ceiling, begging God to just let me fall asleep, if only for a few hours. Just a few, so I wouldn't look completely terrible in the morning, so terrible that no amount of concealer could hide my fatigue, so I wouldn't spend the waking part of the day ahead in a hell of stifled yawns and drooping eyelids.

I hadn't slept last night, either, not even a wink, and this was only going to be the most important interview of my life.

"We're here," she says brightly. She carefully pushes a heavy wooden door open, ushers me inside, and, with one swoosh of her shiny mahogany hair, disappears behind me.

It's completely illogical, but suddenly I feel very alone. I take a deep breath, and turn to face the inquisitors.

"Hi, I'm Zahra." I stride over to the desk where they are sitting, all three of them, two men who smile at me with a hint of humanity, and one woman in a red blazer. I can't see the rest of her, because none of them rise from their chairs to shake my hand.

"Hello, Zahra, please take a seat," the pudgy one with round glasses says. He has a ring of brown hair from one ear to the other, around the back of his head, just like my father, except his is dusted with more gray. I smooth the skirt beneath me and lower myself carefully, making sure to keep my legs closed, just like I remember from career counseling in college.

Pudgy thanks me for taking the time to fly up to Boston on a moment's notice. I smile and try not to think of how I felt about lying to Georges.

"We certainly appreciate someone with your experience applying for what's actually a pretty junior position. We're certainly nowhere near as big as some of your previous employers," he glances down at the papers in front of him, shuffling them, as he says this, "but you'll find we have excellent advancement opportunities."

"We're fairly new in the hedge fund game," his colleague shoots back. This one is young, good-looking, boisterous. He's the business school kid who, when asked what his future aspirations were, boldly spat, "CEO of my own venture firm," in the lecturer's face. "I'm Tony, by the way, this is June, and that firecracker over there is Richard."

Richard follows with a nervous cackle, not terribly firecracker-like.

"We're looking for strong people to build our thoroughness and customer service brand. We're a small team, but we're going to be very aggressive."

I nod enthusiastically and try very hard to focus and not

think about how much I need this, how close I am to the end of my rope. I can sell the condo. Make enough to give my parents a hefty share, enough for my father to retire comfortably, without having to drag his skeletal frame, arthritic rheumatism and all, to work every day. Maybe even enough for my mother to stop beginning every phone call with a sigh and a shopping list of her various ailments, and why God had been so unkind to her in her old age when she'd been His humble servant all her life.

I want to ask if they expect me to be aggressive, but I swallow back the thought. It's too early in the game, and I'm too desperate.

June leans over, hands clasped in front of her, and begins to speak. "You have a very impressive résumé—a scholarship to MIT, four years at Morrison, rising up the ranks, albeit slowly. . . ." Her eyes meet mine.

I try to blink away the sting of her comment.

I hadn't been hired by the bluest of the blue-chip Boston firms because of my talents at sparkling small talk, a Rolodex fat with impressive names, or for possessing the charm, discretion, and persuasion skills of a seasoned Washington madam. Or so I thought.

Always the same story, the story of my life. While I sat at my cubicle researching, referencing and cross-referencing files, waiting for faxes from our associates in London, and coming in evenings for conference calls with Hong Kong, the playboys of the office managed to do with wild bachelor parties and strip club outings what I did with blood, sweat, and hard work. I was the one who devised controls and lobbied IT for the scanners that ought to have replaced the archaic fax machines still used to transmit the most sensitive, costly information imaginable, where an overlooked sentence instructing our firm to sell out of a stock or buy another could cost millions. When I presented my boss with a cost-benefit analysis to justify ditching the fax machines in favor of something a little more twenty-first century, he said, "A cost-benefit analysis? Seriously, Zahra, who does this? This is a business, not college."

They couldn't—wouldn't—tell me that my awkwardness embarrassed them at client meetings, that an impeccable performance record didn't quite measure up to research assistants who did their jobs well enough and dressed to kill, whose mere presence and the cadence of their velvety voices were enough to sway a potential client into handing over millions of dollars' worth of contracts.

I hadn't known when I proudly fumbled my way over the smooth hardwood of the lobby my first day of work that this was a country club. And I was never very good with any kind of club. It was high school and college all over again, but this time without Georges. And no matter how many management training seminars I attended, how many "Lunch and Learn" sessions designed to up my likeability IQ, it was Amanda Briggs, tall, thin, strong jawed, and brassy, who got the promotion, and then Victor Martinez, smooth-talking ex–college baseball star, men who both talked and walked a good game and women who would jump at the chance to show the big boys they could cuss and bellow and kick back at strip clubs with the best of them.

I might have continued like this forever if fate hadn't come along and pulled my future right out from under me in one big sweep of cosmic irony.

"I was very good at what I did and was pigeonholed into administration," I say.

Stay positive. No matter what, even if you feel your face is lighting up with your lies and indecision, just pretend. Style over substance. That's one thing America had taught me.

They shift in their chairs, uncomfortable.

My impulses start firing off red alerts. I need this. *Please, God, I need this.*

"I brought some recommendation letters, thank-you memos, and performance evaluations from my time at Morrison." I reach down for my briefcase, nearly knocking down the glass of water in front of me. I pray they can't see my hands shaking. I look through the papers without seeing, numb except for the nauseating churning in my stomach.

"Here they are." I mimic the carefree smiles I see girls beam all the time, from the braces-wearing ones at the Wendy's take-out counter to the sleek, bubbly ones Rio hired to work at *Suéltate,* brimming with demure confidence with every sashay of their nonexistent hips.

I hand the thick stack of papers over to the woman, thank-you e-mails for a file well done, for pushing through sensitive wire transfers mere minutes before the Federal Reserve was set to close for the day, for handling the setting up of off-shore bank accounts and meeting impossible deadlines.

"This is very impressive," Richard says.

I smile, this time out of relief. The conversation takes a more pleasant turn, from interrogation-style intimidation techniques to get-to-know-you questions, about where I saw myself five, then ten years down the line, how I liked Miami, why I moved there, and why I wanted to head back up to Boston.

"My current position is not challenging enough," I say, fully aware of how textbook it sounds.

June clears her throat. "Can you tell us about your move from hedge fund management to the duty-free business? It's a bit of an unusual career path."

Of course it was unusual. It was downright comical. Career suicide, the smooth MIT guys in polo shirts and frameless glasses would have called it. *It's not suicide when you're already dead.*

"I had to move to Miami for personal reasons . . . reasons which aren't there anymore."

This is a risky strategy, not to mention that it's not strictly true. Allusions to a personal life are tough. On the one hand, they're evidence of a personality, of that well-roundedness firms like their bright-eyed recruits to embody when they are about to come in but must then check at the door on their first day at work. At my age a personal life might come off as less like affability and more like persistent sappiness. The kind of sappiness that makes you put a personal relationship above a job. Bad. On the flip side, any sentence with the word "personal" in it is usually a cue for the recruiter to switch gears. Good.

"Was he worth it?" June grins, this time with a girly giggle and a knowing twinkle in her eye. "I'm sure he was." She waves. "You don't have to say anything. I didn't mean to pry."

I don't know if he was worth it. But that's never the point, is it? Who knows why people fall in love with other people, people who might seem totally random in a crowd but you know are lighting up somebody's life. Each time one of my sisters fell in love she made it seem like the world must stop spinning out of reverence for this momentous event. They would float, not walk, from one room to the next, sprint through the daily chores so they could spend as much time as possible in a trancelike state, dreaming of weddings and babies and presents and moonlit walks. They would suddenly start spouting nonsense about the miracle of having met the one person in this world who completed them. My mother would then send them off to do the laundry, and suggest to my father if perhaps moving up the wedding might not be such a bad idea.

I didn't fall in love with Georges because he was the only person in the universe for me. My love was not cut from the cloth of miracles but the fabric of the ordinary. The everyday mundaneness of being. And sitting next to Georges in class day after day, staying up all night with our books open in front of us and our minds wandering, I started noticing things like the slope of his eyelashes, the curve of his neck as he bent over his notes, the concentrated look his eyes would take on when he hit his stride sometime around 2:00 A.M.

Suddenly, sitting next to him wasn't enough. I wanted him. More than anything I'd ever wanted before, anything I ever thought I deserved. I just wanted him.

But I didn't relocate to Miami for him, I did it *because* of him. Two entirely different things.

"This all looks great, uh . . ." Tony stares at June for a second while waiting for his thoughts to coagulate in his brain. ". . . Zahra. We'll let you know in about a week's time either way, but if I may say so, we'd be thrilled to have someone of your experience on board."

"Thank you. . . . I, er . . ." I could never manage to let the words "you won't be sorry" roll off my tongue as seamlessly as some of my colleagues did. I choose to just grin and stay quiet.

"So, Morrison, huh?" Richard says, not to anyone in particular. "Those guys are our toughest competitors. Never miss a beat."

Tony swivels around and crosses one leg across the other, nearly swiping June with his shiny lace-up. "They did a while back, didn't they? I had a buddy who interned there, told me someone, an associate, had missed a request to redeem out of Nortel, just before the stock tanked. Ended up getting sued over it."

"Jesus, I wouldn't have wanted to be the sucker who messed that up." Richard shakes his head.

"It must have been when you were still there, Zahra. How the hell did that go down?"

All eyes are now on me, precisely when I am battling the rise of bile in my throat. The nausea of this morning, jumbled nerves, anxiety at having lied to Georges, memories of walking along Newbury Street and catching a quick pint with him in between classes, of his mother's horrible reaction when he finally introduced me, at my own cowardice, and finally the mistake that had cost my employer millions, and me my entire reputation, my future, my life. And then another memory of Georges, this time giving me another chance at a decent life again. And here I was betraying him.

The urge to vomit turns into a sudden sense of disconnection, as though Tony, June, and Richard were speaking to me with mouths full of marbles from across a canyon. I'm dizzy. Dizzy, and humiliated, and nauseated at the same time.

"Zahra?"

"Uh . . ."

I stare intently at Tony's light pink socks, his elbows leaning on the armrests of his swivel chair, his fingers noiselessly drumming against each other.

And I snap.

"That was me. It was my fault."

This was going so bad it was almost funny. What did I

expect for sneaking off to Boston and stabbing Georges in the back? He needs me. Given the chance, these people would toss me out on my behind, just like the bigwigs at Morrison did. It didn't matter that it was the most innocuous oversight you could think of. It didn't matter that when you really thought about it, it was the company's fault for having inadequate controls. Or that it was my first mistake in five years of loyal service and consistently glowing performance ratings in technical proficiency. None of that mattered. They just needed a scapegoat, and I was it.

June has paled to the same colorlessness as the naked walls. Richard is flushed a deep red and has puffed up with wheezing, his starched shirt collar digging into the folds of his chubby neck. Tony looks straight ahead at nothing, smacking his lips together comically, apparently unable to come up with a better reaction.

Suddenly they don't look like inquisitors at all. More like circus clowns.

I gather my things quietly, thank them for their time, and show myself out, fighting to suppress a smile.

Ranya

I nearly wept the first time I saw the apartment, with what I don't know.

Zahra's place is a stunning, wondrous monument to fabulousness, in a tall, sleek building flanked by other tall, fabulous buildings, as far as the eye could see, overlooking a beautiful blue bay that sparkles with what looks like bits of fairy dust everywhere the sun hits it. And impeccably clean, except for the piles of books and newspapers on coffee tables, some half-empty glasses and scrunched-up bags of chips here and there. Frankly, I'm not sure what I was expecting from Zahra, but it certainly wasn't this.

But even with the apple green accent walls, the airy minimalist spaces, and the pools, indoor and outdoor, it just wasn't home.

Not that home had anything good going for it these days, at least as far as I was concerned, but it was still home.

Georges had driven me over, my lone suitcase in the trunk of his Lexus sedan, handed it over to the doorman, who said he'd take care of it "right away, sir," and leaned against the front door, watching as Zahra told me to make myself at home. He then pecked me curtly on the cheek and disappeared in usual Georges fashion, with muffled talk of work and meetings and deadlines, leaving Zahra and me seated at the farthest ends of her enormous three-piece cream sofa set, awkwardly staring everywhere except at each other.

"This place has two bedrooms and two bathrooms, obviously you get the guest bedroom. Boyfriends are *not* welcome."

I nearly spat out my sip of Fiji water at that.

We stared at each other wordlessly for a few seconds.

"You have a beautiful apartment," I said tentatively.

She shrugged. "I wanted a place with a view. I've always loved the water. Then Georges bought me the services of a decorator as a housewarming present."

I wasn't sure whether or not to crack a smile at the admission—was it self-deprecating humor or a shocking lack of self-awareness?

In any case, she didn't match my attempts at friendly small talk with an inquiry about the weather, or my shoes, so we languished in a few more seconds of deadly silence, tiptoeing around the great pink elephant in the room.

Finally I'd had enough.

"I really want to thank you for your help—"

"No reason to thank me. I fully expect you to pay half the mortgage and help out with utilities," she interrupted.

I gulped back the bitter pill of humility. I hadn't paid a day's worth of rent in my entire life, but even I knew that Zahra's place hadn't come cheap, and the paltry sum Georges had mentioned as my starting salary in the car ride over might not cover it. Visions of going home, humbled, facing the twin wraths of Dodi and my parents, throbbed in my head.

I would make this work. Whatever it took, I would come out the other end happier, wiser, and better able to face my future with my head held high.

"If you don't mind," I got up carefully, my head beginning to buzz with anxiety, "I think I'd like to put my stuff away, maybe lie down for a bit. It was a long flight over here."

She rose noiselessly, walked me past an elegant dining room of cherrywood and deep green upholstery that I thought I recognized from the layout of a magazine, down a corridor adorned with black-and-white prints with a few splashes of color, to a door at the end.

"This is your room. There's a cleaning lady who comes in every week, the take-out menu is in the top kitchen drawer, left of the oven, and there's a strip mall with a small grocery store and a pharmacy across the overpass down the street. The phone book is in the living room. Did I forget anything?"

"Er, no, thanks."

"Okay. Good."

And just like that, she spun on her carpet slippers and started down the hallway.

"Um, Zahra?"

"What?"

"I just wanted to say . . . look, I'm not after Georges," I blurted out awkwardly.

"I don't really care either way, Ranya. It's none of my business."

And she disappeared before I had a chance to beg her not to tell a living soul what she'd overheard outside the restaurant bathroom, the last time I had spoken to my husband.

It's hard to imagine that was just a few days ago. It seemed like years.

· Rio

"Where's her ass?"

The *pendejo* from the modeling agency stares at me blankly, blinking absurdly and shifting his weight from one side to the other to buy himself some time while his gringo brain processes my question.

"I, um, I'm not exactly sure I understand." He folds his arms across his skinny chest and tries to look like he's actually got it together.

I take a deep breath, trying to convey my exasperation to this joke of an *hombre* in a pink dress shirt and suspenders. They don't make them like that in Honduras. Thank *God*.

"Her ass, Klein, where is it? I specifically asked for *Latinas* only."

"Look, we've only got six Latinas on contract, and five of them are booked all of this week. She's South Asian, what's the big deal?"

"The big deal is that I'm doing an embrace-your-curves issue and I've got a girl whose butt is as flat as a tortilla. Are you getting me now?"

He raises his hands up in mock surrender. "Then I suggest you go with a plus-size agency."

Plus-size? Is this clown kidding me? "Okay, whatever. Thank you for your time."

He nods and disappears behind my office door.

Ay, niña.

All in all it's a pretty fabulous time to be Latina in this country, what with the media finally getting that Ms. Everywoman is not a white, blond, six-feet-tall, rich, skinny size-two bitch. But sometimes . . . *no es fácil.* It's not easy. It never is.

I press down the bright red button on my phone. Conference.

"Ranya, make a call to all the modeling agencies in the area, including the plus-size ones." I shudder in revulsion at the thought that in this day and age a girl with booty still falls under the plus-size category. "I want one size-four JLo, one flat Penelope, an Eva M., and an America except taller and bigger. I want them all booked for Thursday." I don't ask her if she got all that, just hang up. It's the Latina body type quartet—bootilicious, petite, busty, and plus-size. With enough skin shade nuances, from creamy white to golden caramel to burnt sienna with blond highlights, to represent our *mujeres.* If Ranya didn't get that by now, that's her problem.

Don't get me wrong, *m'hija,* I'm not doing it on purpose. It's not like I have a Cruella De Vil complex or anything, I swear, but the girl has to work for her money. We all do. It's bad enough that Georges has called every day this week to make sure she's okay and that I'm being nice to her. Not that it's going to make me change my attitude or anything, I mean, I've got a magazine to run here, but to the girl's credit she hasn't ratted me out yet.

Now where was I?

Right. Zahra. Has the nerve to slam *Suéltate* with one of her "financial assessments"—entirely her fabrication, mind you, and then skip town on some mysterious "personal matter." Since when has that girl had anything more personal going on than a yeast infection, I ask you? Maybe it's another one of her clandestine booty calls she thinks no one has any idea about.

Sigh.

Any second now Georges is going to call and demand another meeting. My only hope is that with Zahra out of town, he might shove the report to the side and obsess over something else, like say, how the new Smashbox cosmetics line is doing in the Bahamas store, or whether or not Mallouk Enterprises should invest in the new luxury mall they're building over in the Cayman Islands.

My attention goes from the mound of press releases that have yet to be flipped through, to the "financial assessment" from hell staring me in the face, to my laptop.

Plus I need to peruse the dozens of proposals from free-lancers sitting in my inbox, in the hopes of finding something that maybe, just maybe, fits in with the *Suéltate* brand and that the magazine can actually afford. That I've tended to go with the riveting, hard-hitting, and well-researched yet expensive stories written by decent reporters in the past is where Zahra and I don't quite see eye-to-eye.

She says our angle is shopping and that my "visions of grandeur" (see, I told you she's a kook) are taking away from the focus of the venture. Her words. I would never utter such stupidities. As if you could distill art, creativity, and enlightenment down to a mission statement and bal-ance sheet. Not to mention the dissemination of Latina—and occasionally Latino—pride. I'll admit that part was me. But it was timely, in tune with the market at a time when salsa was fast replacing ketchup as America's condi-ment of choice and illegal immigration was the hottest ticket on the ballot.

I have a headache.

I switch on my laptop and click over to my inbox.

An avalanche of article proposals pop onto the screen, one after the other, interspersed by inquiries as to open po-sitions or internships here and there, some spam, and a flurry of Facebook activity.

I should really open up the proposals, but one particular

Facebook alert freezes my blood right in my veins. And it takes *a lot* to do that to a Latina, let me tell you.

Adam.

Son of a bitch.

I start to get heart palpitations. Okay, *breathe, chica.* You're not sixteen anymore. You're a successful editor in chief of an up-and-coming Miami women's magazine, a University of Miami graduate—with honors, might I add—and occupant of an ultracool bachelorette pad, not to mention a neat, if a little old, jet black Volkswagen Cabrio. Publicists all over the state, and some from Texas and New York and California, too, kiss your ass every day for an editorial mention in *Suéltate* magazine. And you're fucking the boss.

You're not a dopey kid anymore, stupid and gullible.

The subject header reads: *Hey You!*

Eloquence was never Adam's strong point. Or maybe he'd never progressed past the maturity level of an eighteen-year-old.

My eyes scan over the calming blue and white background, the sound of the words in my brain competing with the echo of the pounding of my heart.

```
Hey—
Long time no speak! Looks like life's
treating you pretty good. Not surprised, you
were always the smart cookie. ☺
I'm doing okay, can't complain, got three
```

kids now, how 'bout you? Single, though—we separated a few years back. Hey, if you've got a couple of your own maybe we could take them on a playdate sometime. Could be fun. ☺

You won't believe this, but I'm in the ad biz now, nothing too fancy, just a small outfit in Tallahassee, and the boss is talking about breaking into the Hispanic market for some of our clients. Couldn't believe my eyes when your name came up in one of the meetings!

Anyway, call me, let's talk.

Thinking of u,

Adam

That's the e-mail. I swear to God. This from the man who fucked me over in the worst way possible and then left me to rot.

I'm having a brain freeze. No ice cream or snow cones in sight. I lower my head and hold it in my hands. Why are my insides churning? Why why why?

"Hey, Rio . . . ?"

I swirl around and bark at the figure of a human in the door, seeing nothing in my white-hot rage. "What the hell do you want from me?" Ouch. That may have come off as a bit too crazy-banshee-like, even for me. But what do you expect under the circumstances?

It's Ranya. All doe-eyed and pathetic. She looks like she's going to cry. Good, that makes two of us.

"I'm sorry, I didn't mean to bother you. I just wanted to ask—never mind, I'll come back later." She retreats back to the bowels of the office, glassy-eyed, leaving me to ponder exactly how to deal with this blast from a past I wanted dead and buried.

I sigh and drop my face in my hands, before I remember I have an art meeting in half an hour, which means I won't have time for a quick touch-up if I make a mess of my makeup.

Something is rising in my throat. No, not bile. An ache. A miserable, forgotten ache I thought I'd done away with for good.

Get a grip.

The something rising in my throat is actually a sob. I swallow it, blink back a few times, press a Kleenex under my eyes to blot off any wayward mascara, and rest my fingers over the snow-white keys of my iBook.

For all the women who'd ever been wronged in the world, women who fantasized about that precise fuck-you moment in their lives when they'd finally get their chance at the Great Comeback, that moment of sweet revenge where they're on top of the world and poised to kick the *sinvergüenza* son of a bitch who'd dealt them a good one all those years back, I had to strike back. This is my chance, on a silver—no, *chica,* a fucking diamond-studded platinum platter—to kick the *cara de culo* right where it hurts the most: his wallet. And his pride.

Adam,

Nice to hear from you after all these years. Glad to see you're a family man now. No can do on the playdate, but would be happy to talk shop. I'll have my director of sales get back to you so you can put together an ad campaign. She's the best in the biz.

Thanks so much for thinking of me,

Rio

A girl has to know when to be a professional. That's the difference between a child-woman and an adult.

Okay, now I'm going to throw up.

I stand up slowly, walk over to the office door, and shut it gently. I should have probably slammed it. Little girls—especially little Latina girls—are always taught to be nice and quiet. What they don't teach you is that the loud bird gets the worm.

But all the sarcasm in the world isn't going to cut through the sobs that wrack my body, making my shoulders heave up and down.

I can't believe that after all this time, it still hurts so much.

Twenty minutes later, I've busied myself thinking about how *María Mercedes* magazine, named after one of the most popular Mexican telenovelas ever, has one-upped *Suéltate* yet again on the newsstands, and what I'm going to do about it.

See? Back to normal.

I stare at the cover of the latest *María Mercedes* issue and America Ferrera's smiley, wholesome face stares right back at me.

One-upped again.

Everything I want to do, Veronica Almonte, the editor in chief over there, seems to come up with first. To hear that scheming little blue-eyed bimbo, I'm the one who's copying *her*.

I swear, the next time I run into that nouveau-*cubana* biatch, a rum princess whose family defected from the homeland once it looked like they wouldn't be able to run their factories on pocket change and crooked smiles anymore, and whose product (I won't say what, but let's just say it rhymes with "Havarti") came out Puerto Rican on the side, I think I'll ask her which brand of yuppie champagne she was drinking while I was skipping along the garbage-lined streets of La Ceiba, wondering if *papi* would allow me to go to college one day.

I'm scrutinizing the table of contents when my door is suddenly pushed open.

"Who the—"

"Relax, it's me."

Joe saunters over to my desk, his dirty blond hair a sexy, ravish-me-now mess, the D&G striped shirt with the crazy-ass print I swiped from a cover shoot back in June wrinkled and open down half his chest, revealing a sliver of hairless, delicious flesh.

Anywhere in America Joe's outfit would be the height of cheese. But here in Miami it works. Don't ask.

Just like that, I feel my nipples strain against the gauzy, barely there Calvin Klein black bra I'd selected this morning to go under the white shirt I'm wearing.

Ay, chica, see what I mean?

"Missed me?"

It's a rhetorical question. Of course I did. He's daring me to ask him where he'd disappeared to for five working days without even a whiff of an explanation. That way he gets to tell me: *Why are you asking? You think you're my girlfriend now?*

No thanks. I'm not biting.

"No, but you did miss a few changes around here."

Shit. As soon as the words escape my lips I wish I could swallow them back. I've read enough pop psych books (I refuse to call them self-help—that would imply I *need* help, wouldn't it?) to know that it isn't entirely out of the question that the reason I can't stand Ranya is because I feel, on some level at least, intimidated by her. Just look at her—an Amazon with an innocent face and infuriatingly gentle way about her. You could almost fall under her "niceness" spell if you weren't careful.

I know, I know—Joe doesn't *do* nice, not to mention the distinct possibility that Georges might be doing Ranya on the sly. Not that this would stop Joe, mind you, but still. A girl's got to watch her back.

To my utter delight, my unwitting instance of verbal

incontinence ricochets off the top of his coiffed head, the sight of my nipples getting whatever attention span he has into a tight headlock.

"I can see your bra."

"That's the point."

"Isn't there some sort of color-matching underwear-with-your-clothes thing women usually stick to?" he says, coming around the side of my desk to where I am sitting.

I push my chair back to give him some space. It's suddenly getting hot in the room. Hot and sticky.

"Not if you're cool." I wish I'd reapplied mascara after my little . . . *episode.*

I feel the heat of his breath blowing down my shirt.

I don't have time for this.

"Joe—I don't have time for this."

He doesn't listen, too busy working the complicated clasps of my shirt.

"What is this, a suit of armor? Are you trying to make this harder?"

"No, it's Gucci. Now get off me."

Then next thing I know I've been lifted out of my chair, spun around, and have landed with my back flat on the desk, my legs wide-open and flailing.

"Joe . . . the door! What if someone comes in?"

"You're the only one in this office who works through lunch. Relax—there wasn't anyone when I came in. Besides, I'm the boss, remember?"

With that comes the curt *zzzzzzip!* of jeans being undone,

and a hurried fumbling my body is responding to while my brain continues to run in complicated circles.

"You're wet. . . ."

Veronica's icy blue gaze fixes me from the spot on the ground where the magazine had fallen to. A bolded sentence jumps out at me: **Being gordita—*curvy*—is *fine*. . . .**

Right. For other women, maybe. Namely those fat, pathetic blobs this publication panders to, but certainly not *moi*. For all her talk about curves and how it's okay to have, Veronica is as *flaca*—skinny—as they come. Doesn't miss a day at the squash club, her minions tell me. The squash club—have you ever heard of anything so lame?

"Is that yesterday's Big Mac?" He pokes the soft flesh beneath my belly button that no amount of sit-ups and interval training had succeeded in defeating.

"Shut up."

I clasp my eyes shut as he pounds away. The tinglings are building up, unfolding like tentacles through different parts of my body. I lift my head up half an inch, trying to sneak a peek at the door, as if one look from me would magically send any potential intruders away.

There's got to be a way.

"Tell me you want it," he gasps.

"Not here," I manage to summon enough breath in me to say.

I really hope no one's listening.

"Rio, I'm going to . . ."

"Wait. . . ." It's coming to me. . . . The hard knot of an idea is taking shape in the back of my brain. . . . What if . . .

"Rio . . . ," he whispers between clenched teeth.

"Wait!"

"I can't!"

It's coming. . . . Wait. . . . What if—

"Rio!"

"Yes! Oh my God, *yes*!"

Joe grins at me slyly through the sweat trickling down his temples.

What if we came up with a special *Suéltate* sex feature? It seems so simple, yet all we've ever focused on was shopping, diet, and the serious Latina issues like female rebels in the jungles of Bolivia or the ravages of a macho culture on a woman's psyche. Important, weighty stuff to balance out the plugs for Mallouk products.

I stare back at the upside-down face of Miss Prim and Proper Beauty Queen. *Her* magazine is too good for a sexual heath feature. Or too anal-retentive. All the better for me.

My body lifts off the desk and collapses back against it in rapid-fire convulsions.

I did it, just like I always do.

Ranya

It's Friday afternoon, seven days into my total life makeover, and I haven't dared open my Yahoo! Mail account yet.

I'm afraid.

So very, very afraid.

The time's come, though, when I can't hide anymore. At least I shouldn't, if I had one fleck of decency left in my whole body. Seeing as my mother's the type who gets suspicious if you say you're stepping out to the pharmacy and come back with a box of maxi pads *and* coffee breath, I figure she must have driven herself mad with freakish scenarios spinning round and round in her mind like a possessed carousel out of a Stephen King novel.

A decent daughter would put her out of her misery.

A decent daughter would call.

Any chance decency is just as overrated as respectability?

Probably not.

With a heavy sigh and an anvil of dread weighing down my stomach, I pick up the phone and dial. First digit. Second.

I make it to the fifth and stop, holding the receiver suspended in aerial limbo for a few seconds.

What are the odds my mother will:

a. Cajole me into coming back home with promises of a nice trip abroad together, maybe to Europe for some shopping, maybe to Cyprus to spend a couple of merry weeks trying to forget Dodi was ever born by doing little besides lounging about my grandmother's beach house all day long.

b. Fly into a blind rage at the sound of my voice, inform me that my selfish actions and utter disregard of my honor and reputation had sent my father into a mental breakdown, causing him to redirect his entire investment portfolio to a Lada factory in eastern Lithuania and thereby condemning the family to financial ruin.

c. Ask me how I was getting along, if I needed anything, and assure me there was no need to rush home.

Deciding that option A was a marginal possibility and C out of this galaxy, I place the receiver back in its cradle and turn to my computer screen instead.

I type in the URL for my Yahoo! Mail address, my heart somewhere in the vicinity of my ankles. My blood pounding in my ears, I scan the different subject lines one by one until I've gone back six months in my inbox.

Nothing.

I look again, slowly this time. Still nothing.

I cast a sideways glance at the phone, sitting there at the corner of the desk. Quietly. Watching me.

Taunting me.

I still won't do it.

I turn back to the screen, draw in a sharp breath, and start pounding the keyboard fast, not leaving much room for thought. Or fear.

> Dear Mom,
>
> You'll never guess where I am. . . .
>
> Miami! As in Florida, USA.
>
> You wouldn't believe it, but I ran into an old friend from Riyadh [no need to split hairs here about the actual meaning of "old friend" as it is employed in common vernacular]. Zahra Bada- lati . . . do you remember her? [Obviously not, since even I barely acknowledged her existence back then.] Zahra is really great. She's letting

me stay at her place, so you don't have to worry about me being all alone. [As if that was her foremost concern right now.]

Anyway, I'm really sorry I haven't called since arriving in Miami, I've been busy [Do I say that when I'm not at work I'm a sobbing, bumbling mess whose only company is the cast of *Grey's Anatomy* and Zahra's tabby cat?] shopping, and catching up with Zahra and trying to get my mind off . . . things. I'm sure you understand.

Please give Dad a big hug and kiss for me and I'll e-mail again soon.

Love you,

Ranya

There. Done.

I shut off the computer and prepare to face my first weekend as a (quasi) single woman on her own in Miami.

What do you mean you don't drink? How are you supposed to get shitfaced then?"

I thought that out of all people, Behnaz would understand. Perched at the edge of a round leather bar stool, she glowers at me over the rim of her fourth Bellini in half that many hours.

"You know how it is. . . ."

"No, I don't. You're out here on your own for the first time in your life and you won't even take a sip of champagne? What did you bother leaving home for?"

Why does everyone react this way when I tell them I don't drink? It's really starting to get on my nerves.

"I really don't get what the big deal is." I try to get myself understood over the insanely loud music exploding out of the speakers. In honor of my first weekend in the city, Behnaz rounded up Daria and Marisol for a night out on the town, Miami-style. Which, as it turns out, means South Beach, *the* place to be according to my self-appointed city guide. We started the night off with dinner somewhere on the strip, a very retro place with psychedelic wall hangings and low cushioned booths in every conceivable shade of orange. Then halfway through dessert the lights dimmed and the music that was steadily getting louder all night suddenly turned deafening. That's when Behnaz suggested we hop over to Mansion, which was apparently much more happening, and besides, she'd gotten us on the guest list. And even though we managed to skip ahead of a hefty lineup to get in here, we still had to cough up twenty dollars each to get in.

"Think of alcohol as lubricant." Daria winks.

"Lubricant for what?"

All three of them convulse in peals of shrieking laughter.

"You're really something, aren't you?" Marisol says, wiping a tear from the corner of her eye. "For picking up, dummy."

Now why would I want to do that? As if coming out here was just a great big plot to get myself laid once and for all.

Oh my God.

Is that what my parents think I'm doing here?

My heart starts beating in a flurry of nervous activity, and my temples moisten. But my body calms down when I remember that no one really knows what happened between Dodi and me.

"I thought I read something about how the Koran doesn't even really say you can't have alcohol," offers Daria, taking a big slurp of her lime margarita to underline her point.

"Well . . . that's not *exactly* true. . . ."

"But sort of?" Marisol leans forward.

I turn to Behnaz, but she's no help. I'm not sure how she managed this, but she seems to have locked lips with a kid—he can't be much older than eighteen—with a nearly shaven head and chin stubble who'd been buzzing around us with his buddies for a while.

I suddenly feel old. Old and awkward, and completely out of my element.

"Look, I think I'm going to head home. I'm tired," I lie. I have nothing to look forward to tonight except slamming my pillow, tossing and turning in the hopes of beating the insomnia that's plagued me since I moved here.

"Hey—isn't that Joe over there? He's so fucking hot!" Behnaz interrupts her romantic interlude to squeal into my ear.

She's a nice girl, I swear, but I don't know how much more of this I can take. I think I might even prefer—God help me—Zahra's icy company over this.

"Come, let me introduce you!" she yelps.

"Wait!" I try to untangle my hand from her grasp. "Who is he?"

She stares at me dumbfounded for a second, and then bursts into ripples of giggly laughter. "He's our *boss*—d'uh! Didn't you see him coming out of Rio's office today?"

"N-no. . . ." I must have been too panicked over finding "that article about the top ten flans in Miami, but not the one by that asshole Julio, or the one with the recipe from Rosa's, the other one," for Rio.

"He's never in the office, so you should definitely introduce yourself." Behnaz lunges for my hand again, but I pull away quickly.

"What's the matter?"

I look down at my clothes and then back up at Joe. So that's Joe. My boss. Georges's brother. Georges's brother? Seriously? I would have never guessed. Where Georges is broad-shouldered bulk stuffed into suits, dark curly hair contained into close, severe cuts, and serious and concentrated, Joe is loose and fluid and effervescent all at once. He'd casually draped himself over a white armchair in a far corner of the club and was locked in a conversation that seemed to run the gamut back and forth from bubbly to intense with a blonde in a turquoise mini and gold platforms.

I stare down at my own outfit of salmon pink paillette mod dress, complete with towering silver heels and a fringed clutch. It doesn't exactly scream "serious, capable, hard worker" to the casual observer.

Behnaz rolls her eyes. "You look *hot,* now come on."

"No, sorry, I really should go."

She gapes at me incredulously, shaking her head.

Call me crazy, but I don't want my first meeting with my boss to take place against a backdrop of mind-thrashing music, gyrating bodies slick with sweat, and even the occasional pole dancer. For once in my life I want to be taken seriously, not to be seen in a dress cut up to there and shoes that scream I-want-to-land-a-husband-right-now. And I wasn't going to let the fact that Joe looks like sex in linen pants and leather flip-flops change my mind.

"Can I ask you something?" Behnaz tilts her wide green eyes up at me. "Have you ever kissed a guy?"

"Wha . . . ?" Who does she think she is, asking me something like that? Of course I've kissed a guy! There was the kiss at the wedding, awkward and stilted, but there were over six hundred guests at that wedding, so what do you expect? And of course he kissed me later that night, too, but I was so emotional and hollowed out from having cried my guts out at the sight of my parents driving away, leaving me with this man by my side as if I weren't their responsibility anymore. . . . What kind of prelude to romance is that, I ask you?

But Behnaz wouldn't know any of that. She doesn't even know I'm married.

I lay my hands on each hip, ready to let this little imp know exactly how I feel about her nosiness, when she giggles spastically like an Energizer bunny on crack, bringing a hand up to shield her mouth and sending what must be fifty gold bangles jiggling. She stumbles backward before managing to catch her footing, and narrowly escapes sloshing her drink all over an unsuspecting bystander's bald head.

"Uh-oh, I think I'm drunk!" precedes another fit of giggles.

"You think? Come on, let's get back to Daria and Marisol."

"They're gone!" I look up from trying to latch on to Behnaz's fidgeting elbow and I realize she's right—Daria and Marisol are not at the bar.

"Wait here. Don't move!" I instruct her.

She bobs her head up and down with such great big contortions of her neck that I feel fairly certain she didn't understand a damn word I said.

I lead her with me to the dance floor while she burps and hiccups a dinner that I figure must have included a hefty dose of garlic.

"Excuse me, can you watch her please? I'm going to take a quick look around the dance floor," I say to a big burly man with a gold earring and dark sunglasses standing right off the space in the middle of the room.

"Sorry, miss, but I can't let you through."

"What do you mean?"

"It's VIP only for the dance floor."

"What? Are you kidding me?"

Behnaz erupts in another fit of giggles. "I'm going to pee my pants!" she says, squeezing her legs together and jumping up and down as though she were a toddler.

"Sorry, lady. Those are the rules." He folds his leg-of-mutton-sized arms over his chest and glares down at me. At least I think he's glaring at me, what with the indoor sunglasses look.

"I just want to find my friends—"

Even as I say the word I realize they aren't my friends at all. They're just girls who took pity on me and dragged me along to a place I don't belong. I can't play at carefree party girl this late in the game, no matter what I tell myself.

"Ranya . . . I think I'm going to puke."

"It's okay," I sigh. "Let's get out of here. We'll stop by the ladies' room on the way."

"Thanks, dude, you're the best." Another hiccup, followed by a stumble.

Out of the corner of my eye I spot a solid mass of purple sparkles and black leather that might be Daria. She's on the far side of the bar, splayed up against the wall, lip-locked with a young Latino in baggy jeans and a tight T-shirt. It's hard to tell from this angle, but something about the tight curves of his muscles makes him look like he might be half her age. Good for her, but definitely not for me.

Just a few steps short of the bathroom, Behnaz barfs all over her hair and my shoes.

Zahra's apartment is deathly quiet. I crack open the front door as quietly as I can, but the dry hinges announce my arrival with a loud screech.

I check the console. If it weren't for her keys in the blue ceramic dish centered under the brass-framed mirror, I would never have any idea if she were home or not. Or even in the country. That's how much she speaks to me.

I slip off my sandals and tiptoe over to the huge stainless-steel fridge, famished all of a sudden. As I expected, it's packed with all kinds of junk—doughnuts, ice cream, leftover pizza, sodas and juice cocktails, a bottle of wine, and a good four or five different kinds of cheese.

No wonder the poor girl couldn't shake off that spare tire.

I scavenge around for whatever I can find that would do the least amount of damage and miraculously come up with an apple and a half-eaten tub of tabouleh parsley salad that Zahra must have gotten from the Arabic grocer all the way across town. She told me about him once, on a rare occasion when we managed to exchange more than two words unrelated to the weather and when I was expecting to come up with my first rent check.

The answer to that, by the way, was that I still didn't

know but was optimistically hoping I'd find out the next time I checked my Yahoo! Mail account.

I walk barefooted across the kitchen tiles and feel a furry tube on paws threading itself between my calves.

"Hey there, Waleed, I didn't know you were up. Did I wake you?"

I struggle to lift the big orange cat with one arm, hoping he doesn't wake up Zahra with his meows.

When I had laughed at his name Zahra had scowled and stormed off to her room, so I never did figure out where the poor fur ball had gotten his moniker from. So far he was the closest thing I'd ever had to male companionship, probably because of the extra bits of sandwich meat I slip him when Zahra's not looking.

We nestle together on the couch quietly, Waleed laying his cute little head on my lap for me to stroke. There's not much use in me heading off to bed right now, to toss and turn while my imagination catapults across great leaps of time and space, giving me a headache and sometimes, when panic grips me, those dreaded heart palpitations, too.

It's funny how much my world can spin from okay to wildly out of control in a matter of a thought or two. Little positive things seem possible when I'm sitting at the café on the first floor of the office building, sharing coffee and a Danish with Behnaz and trying to decipher Rio's mood or how we would make over Zahra. I even manage to giggle along when Behnaz starts recounting a sexual exploit or how she plans to catch the attention of the cute barista who works at the Collins Starbucks down at the Beach. But then Rio might ask me to help come up with filler copy for the Latina diet section or excavate the mail bag for some original, relevant dilemmas we haven't covered in the last dozen issues. That's when my chest feels like it's gripped in a vise, tight, and I'm flooded with fear and inertia. *What am I doing here?* my brain taunts, over and over again, and I'm left to concede: *I have no fucking clue.*

Fucking. There. I said it. I have no fucking, fucking clue.

What was I hoping to achieve with this little adventure?

What was I going to do when I inevitably had to go home?

Who would look at me? Who would want me? I'm nothing like Rio, or even Zahra, or the women *Suéltate* is trying to reach with centerfold spreads of day-to-night outfits, or tips on multitasking or even how to treat a persistent urinary tract infection. These were women who worked and partied and worried about landing not just any man but the *right* man, and then holding on to him with skimpy lingerie and discussions on neo-liberalism and how Clinton was doing in the polls. Women who had sex while their kids watched Saturday morning cartoons and who knew five different ways of making tuna casserole, for God's sake.

Women who weren't me and, what's worse, would never *be* me. Just like I would never be them. I wasn't going to radically alter everything I'd ever believed in just to fit in.

"I'm too old for that, Waleed," I sigh into the sleepy cat's face.

He meows back for me to leave him in peace and go back to stroking his neck, underlining his protest with a pronounced back arch.

No, I wasn't going to go out and get myself laid just because my husband would rather do the milkman than touch me.

I'm just going to grow up, plain and simple.

I gently lift Waleed off my legs and lay him on the carpeted floor.

More tiptoeing, this time to Zahra's study—the girl has a study; how grown-up is that? I can't even remember the last time I sat down and read something that wasn't a gossip magazine. That's another thing that's going to have to change. Since I don't think I'm going to have much of a social life to speak of, I'm going to remake myself from inside out. That means rekindling those interests other than shopping and hanging out with women whose sole ambition in life is to land a man. Any man who could keep them in pretty much the same lifestyle their parents had provided them. He didn't have to be good-looking, or young, or particularly smart. Pliable and easily manipulated usually did just fine.

I press a button and Zahra's laptop comes to life, noiselessly. She hadn't bothered to password lock it before going to bed, so I can easily navigate over to my Yahoo! page.

I gasp, my blood eking to a frozen halt in my veins.

There's an e-mail from my mother.

To: R _ Hayek@yahoo.com

From: MunirwaMaryam _ Hayek@yahoo.com

Subject: Re: Don't Worry

Ranya,

I would try to tell you how disappointed your father and I are in you, but I can't. I just don't have the words. Never in my entire life would I have expected you to be so callous and selfish with your own family, even as we indulged you all these years.

Muhammad is beside himself with worry over you; his mother is furious, threatening to tell people you ran away with another man. I'm not even sure I believe all those awful things you said about your husband anymore, seeing how cold you have been to us, your own mother and father. To think you couldn't even bother yourself to call.

You are my daughter and I would welcome you back with open arms anytime you find your senses again and come home—but right now, Ranya, I have never been more ashamed of you, or blamed myself more for having been so indulgent with you.

You can do whatever you like. I don't care anymore.

And that's how it ends.

I sit in Zahra's leather chair, in shock. My ears plug, as if I were on an airplane, and my body folds in on itself. I can hear nothing outside of my head, everything fades away into nonexistence.

They don't believe me.

Rio

When I step onto the dirty upholstered floor of the office this morning, I trill a loud, happy "good morning" at the cramped communal writing space in the middle of the windowless room where my entire staff, minus Joe of course, is busily typing away like good little minions. It was Joe's only concession to Georges, in exchange for big bro's bankrolling Joe's doomed *Rave* idea, that the offices should be set up as cheaply as possible. Joe was a little miffed at the time but eventually could be brought to see that a dilapidated look might somehow come off as underground, even edgy, with the right attitude and window dressing.

The girls all look up at me incredulously.

"What?" I bark. Honestly—is that what you get for trying to spread a little lightness around here?

Behnaz and Ranya instantly dip their heads, cowed down to their bones, while Daria and Marisol just raise their little button noses at me. They can do that—they're a tremendous asset to the magazine, the only assets besides me, you might say, and they know it. Not like a certain little hussy I could think of.

"Ranya, any messages for me?" I say more briskly than I strictly needed to.

"Er . . . yes, Georges says he's dropping by in about an hour. He wants to meet with you."

Good. He could sit in on the meeting—my grand coup.

"Is he bringing *her*?" I hiss.

"Er . . ."

"Zahra!"

"He didn't say." She cowers.

Honestly, it doesn't matter what you say to this girl, she always looks like a newborn kitten that wants to be folded up into a ball and hugged. It just makes me want to kick her harder so she could maybe, possibly, grow a backbone one day.

"Never mind." I sigh and retreat to the quiet serenity of my office. "Meeting in an hour, I want everyone there," I toss back behind me before shutting the door with a loud bang.

I barely have time to collect my thoughts when I hear a soft tap.

"Not now!" I need to prepare for this, especially if Georges is going to attend. I need to convince him that come rain or shine, or Miami humidity, I *will* get circulation up, that ad sales *will* skyrocket, and that this magazine will become a venture he can be proud of instead of some sort of patched-up version of Joe's ex–business pariah, something he's going to hold on to just long enough for Joe to find something else to keep him busy. And I might just have the ticket.

And I'll do it while sticking to my mission of elevating Latina pride in this country, showing my ladies we can do anything we want to do, be anything we want to be, and that we won't do it by flat-ironing our hair stick straight or dieting our *culos* into oblivion. We're going to get ahead *our* way.

"Rio?"

Shit—it's him.

I leap out of my chair and bound over to the door.

"Hi, Georges. I wasn't expecting you so early."

"Sorry." He narrows his eyes at me and seats himself in one of the cheap, mismatched chairs across from my desk. Maybe it's time to broach the sticky topic of an office face-lift.

"What's up?" I toss, casually.

He sighs and rubs his forehead, slightly disheveling the hairs his stylist had taught him to comb carefully forward. Not a good sign.

"What's wrong?"

"Nothing. I just—"

"Look, before you say anything, we have a meeting this morning I want you to attend since you're here anyway." I try to think fast. Whatever news he came here to tell me, I need to turn it around, like, *now.*

"What about?"

"I want to take *Suéltate* in a slightly different direction. Throw our readership a little curveball I think they're ready for, distance ourselves from the competition." I'm aware I'm talking fast. Too fast. I think I might be coming off as nervous, but I can't help it.

I see his head shake from side to side and his mouth start to form a protest. *Coño,* this is worse than I thought.

Beads of moisture are pricking the nape of my neck, just above the crisp starched cotton of my shirtdress.

"I'm not sure this is the right time for a redesign, Rio."

"It won't cost you a thing." I say this with the intonation and heartbeat of a desperate woman flinging herself at the feet of the one man who can pluck her from misery, but I manage to casually lean back against my desk, arms folded in a way I am praying conveys confidence and self-control.

"Good, I'm glad, but it's not just that, Rio." He sighs again. "Zahra's right, this isn't core business, and while you managed not to have the magazine bleed red, it's ballooning into a monster we don't really know much about and, frankly, never really wanted to know about in the first place. It's not you, Rio, it's us."

I wait for a voice-over to boom out into the ether: *We were just never that into you.*

I would rather have Joe pronounce he's getting married than hear this. My insides feel gouged, my throat dry, and my spirit utterly crushed.

No matter how big of a mess I'd made of my personal life, I could always hold the magazine up to my parents, the shopkeepers, the fruit peddlers and hunched-over old ladies of Avenida San Isidro. *Oye, mi gente,* Rosita made it. She might not have an alcoholic husband with a job at the PepsiCo factory down the street and five kids hanging off her hips, but she's somebody. *Was* somebody.

I take a deep, labored breath. "What about the people who work here, Georges?"

He shifts in his seat, having been caught off guard. I am Rio the Iron Lady of the office after all.

"Joe isn't the only one vested in this enterprise, you know," I say.

"Joe isn't vested in this and you know it. Please don't use people as bait, Rio. That's not how it is. They're all bright; they'll find something else. Easy."

Yes, but where else do *I* get to be editor in chief with enough maneuvering room to take me to the moon and back?

"What about Ranya?" I say carefully. This could completely backfire in my face. I would be total, utter, toast. "With this new direction we're taking, and so as not to cost you one extra cent in redesign, I was going to assign her more writing responsibility. Maybe even some features." I balance a pen between my fingers.

"Do you think she's ready for that?"

"Absolutely." I do not even blink when I look Georges in the eye for one long, tense moment.

He hesitates, glancing down at his black polished shoes.

I pounce. "Just come to the meeting, we'll talk again afterward."

"When is it?" He looks at his watch. "My day's pretty packed."

"Right now."

I reach over my desk, grabbing whatever notes and backup I can, stride confidently to the door, and bellow to the room, "Everyone in the boardroom."

Ranya looks up meekly. "But I thought—"

"Now!"

There isn't a second to lose.

Ranya

Every few minutes I nervously refresh my Yahoo! account, minimized at the bottom right corner of my screen, in the hopes my mother wrote back to me.

And confessed it's all a bad joke and my father would be sending me ten grand, as a goodwill gesture, and I would call her and we'd laugh the whole ordeal off together.

Where there is no hope, there are wildly spun fantasies. I can't help it.

I file into the cramped conference room behind the rest of the crew but ahead of Rio, who is hanging back, surveying us all from her diminutive though no less intimidating angle. Sometimes I want to tell her, if I weren't such a nice girl, I might just stomp her down to the ground one of these days.

Georges sidles up to me and squeezes my elbow gently.

My insides suddenly go aflutter.

He's been calling to check up on me every once in a while, but he always sounds a little tongue-tied, a little off his game, not the confident man I met in London what now seems like ages ago.

"How are you holding up?"

"Fine," I say. He sounds more big-brotherly than usual.

It always feels like he might be on the brink of asking me out on a date, but he never does. Not that I would know anything about being asked out on dates. I'd always been very careful about not inviting undue attention in public—when random boys would make eye contact with me on the street or the bus, or even at a busy nightspot, I would always turn away, not wanting to get myself in a situation I couldn't get out of. I was pretty extreme, I have to admit, but then again I was also pretty young. I thought I knew everything there was to know and if there was something I happened not to know, well, it was probably because I didn't need to.

For a girl who'd been so bright in the classroom, I had to admit I was pretty stupid, too.

"Whoa—what the!"

Georges topples forward as a ripple of girly shrieks rips through the room.

"Watch out!" yells Daria.

"Hey, Bro, you're such a stiff you can't take a tackle anymore?"

"What the hell is the matter with you?" Georges says, straightening his suit jacket.

Behind Georges is Joe, this time not standing across a dark, smoky, crowded room but right there in front of me. And he's even better-looking up close. Like sunshine if it had a tan, a dimple, and a smirk.

He stares at me for a few seconds, the corner of his mouth tilted in amused confusion.

"And who's this?" he asks no one in particular.

Rio stops shuffling her notes, thrusts her hips forward, and stares right at the both of us, with one hand draping her thigh.

She has that look about her she gets when I've taken down hastily recorded phone messages but couldn't make out the first few digits of the phone number, or when I've forgotten to run spellcheck on those few-and-far-in-between filler pieces she's thrown my way so far.

Exasperation personified.

"That's Ranya, our new staff writer. Haven't you guys met?" Behnaz says brightly.

Georges suddenly looks sullen.

I'm overcome by an urge to go to him, ask him what's wrong, but he's already flanked by Daria and Marisol, the both of them yawning into their morning lattes.

I have no choice but to sit between Joe and Rio.

"Okay, people, are we ready now?" With her hands clasped together on the table and her waxed eyebrow arched, the room sinks into quietness, amidst a final flurry of cleared throats, soda cans sizzling open, and a sneeze.

"First of all, I'd like to thank Georges for joining us today."

He nods.

"Before we get down to the purpose of this meeting, let's go around the table for our usual roundup. Daria?"

"Have you made a decision on January's cover yet?" She crosses her arms defiantly, leaving me in awe of that kind of confidence.

"I thought we settled this," Rio huffs.

"Actually, we didn't. Nelly Furtado's people have been calling. They want an answer."

"I already told you no, Daria, Nelly's not Latina, and what kind of Latina magazine would we be if we had a Portuguese artist—a *Canadian* Portuguese artist—on the cover, no less?" Rio huffed.

I notice Georges's attention perk up at this last bit.

Daria rips into Rio again, this time with a generous dose of sarcasm lacing her voice. "If we say no to the cover, they'll pull the ads, and they were planning a massive campaign for her latest album. We were even discussing a pull-out centerfold. Two pages, heavy paper, glossy. They're happy to pay premium for the coverage."

This time Rio falters. She glances over at Georges nervously, her lips parted in mid–thought formulation.

"Look, I just don't want to see my bonus affected if we didn't meet our sales quotas on account of whether or not a girl is Latina enough," Daria, part Peruvian herself, practically spits.

Daria and Rio stare each other down while the rest of us sink low into our chairs. Except for Georges, who's following the discourse intently, his brows furrowed in a rather sexy way, and Joe, who seems to be enjoying the scene very much.

"Okay," Rio finally concedes, "we'll talk about this after the meeting." She looks nervously at Georges for a brief moment, before reverting her attention back to us.

"Does anyone else have any pressing issues they want to discuss this morning?" The words coming out of her mouth are inviting, but her tone is as frosty as Chanel's latest shade of winter white eye shadow.

No one dares say anything.

"Marisol—how are the latest circulation numbers?"

"Newsstand was up with the Eva Longoria issue but dipped when we featured Julieta Venegas."

I can sense Rio deflating before my eyes.

Georges clears his throat. "Who's Julieta Venegas?"

"A fantastic up-and-coming Latina songstress."

"How up-and-coming?"

"She's won a Latin Grammy," Rio counters.

"Has she crossed over to the English market?"

"N-noo . . . ," Rio says carefully.

"So we can conclude that Latin artists with no crossover

appeal don't sell magazines? At least not *our* magazine." The words come out kindly enough, but Rio manages to take offense anyway.

"How many times a year do you expect me to put Jennifer Lopez on the cover?"

"Does the focus have to be strictly Latina? The Mallouk brand in general aims to be very cosmopolitan. Would it be so bad if that was reflected in our magazine as well? Look around, Rio, just this little meeting here happens to be pretty cosmopolitan, don't you think?"

"We're veering off course here." Rio stops and takes a sip of water from a bottle she'd brought in with her. I've never seen her so frazzled.

"I asked you all in here today not to change the course of this magazine—which is doing remarkably well given our constraints," and here she eyes both Georges and Joe contemptuously, "but 'remarkably' isn't good enough. We need to not just match the competition but surpass it. We're a magazine with an agenda and a social conscience. We don't just show where high fashion is going next season, we educate our readers as to how they can incorporate it into their own wardrobes, emphasizing value and functionality and, of course, fun. It's this last bit I wanted to address this morning." Here Rio finally pauses to catch her breath.

"In addition to having features urging Latinas to be more aware of issues affecting our country and the Americas at large, *Suéltate* must reflect its founding principles much more closely—that Latina women break loose of all that has constrained them so far, politically, socially, culturally, and . . . sexually."

The room, quiet before, now stills completely. We all surreptitiously lean forward, waiting for the explanation. What does she mean exactly?

"I think it might be time *Suéltate* feature a 'Sexy Modern Latina' section, much like some of our competitors like *Marie Claire* or *Glamour,* but not going as far as *Cosmopolitan.* What's truly innovative about this is that Latinas have traditionally suffered from the Madonna-slash-whore complex instead of viewing sexuality as an empowering, vital area of life."

Listening to Rio speak, I'm wondering if maybe Latin culture might be more similar to my own Arab one than I thought. I think back to the lazy days at the dock in Beirut, about girls who dressed for the beach as they might have for a soirée—high heels, dark lipstick, full-on mascara and blush, and lengths of gold chains wrapped in varying lengths around their necks. Innocent and stupid as I was, I wondered why they would fret over getting their hair wet—what was the point of coming out then?—and when the sons of prominent families that occupied the private cabins along the shores of our gated beach would show up, started acting differently, lying back against the sand in ridiculous poses, flipping their hair, cracking up over the silliest things. And how they'd pretty much ignore me after that, so when they finally disappeared behind the bend with the boy of the day, I wasn't too bothered to see them go. I never thought too hard about what they were doing while they were gone.

Maybe I never had much imagination, or maybe I was afraid that once I started thinking of it, a mysterious, insidious current might start pulling me along to where they were.

Those were the only two kinds of girls on the beach in those days: me and them. And the last thing I wanted was to be one of them.

"And I assume we'll be paying freelancers for these articles?" Georges interrupts.

"No, I was thinking Ranya could take over that section since everyone else's plates are pretty full. Ranya?" Rio glares pointedly in my direction.

"Wha . . . what?"

"What do you mean, 'what'? Is there a problem? I thought you would welcome more responsibility." Rio crosses her arms at this while her eyes dart between Georges and me. "Well?"

"I . . ." I turn to Georges pleadingly, and to his credit, he seems just as pained about the whole ridiculous idea as I am.

Joe, on the other hand, is looking at me in a way that makes me feel very naked all of a sudden, and this in spite of high-waisted trouser jeans and a cardigan.

"I'm not sure that's the kind of thing Ranya would enjoy doing," Georges says. "What about Behnaz?"

"Yeah! What about me?" Behnaz pipes up.

"I've liked Ranya's filler pieces lately. She's showing promise for someone with no experience to speak of. I think she might do wonders with this feature, and besides, Behnaz has a million other things to do."

Behnaz opens her mouth in protest but is instantly silenced by a nasty glare from Rio's direction.

If there was ever a time to stand up, apologize, and explain that this was all a mistake, a misunderstanding, and hightail it back home with the comfort that I at least gave it my best shot, this was it.

"Are you sure you want to do this?" Georges leans in toward me.

Rio, meanwhile, casts me a glare warning me to watch what I say next very, very carefully.

I tilt my head up toward Georges, look straight into his dark liquid eyes, and smile. "I can do this. Don't worry. It'll be fine."

Rio

We wait for everyone else to file out of the room, none of us saying a word.

The air is still pungent with something, but it's impossible to tell what now that the stink had mated with the four different perfumes, two brands of cologne (one I happen to know is Givenchy Blue for men), hair-care products, deodorants, coffee breath, and various other assorted personal odors. Maybe there's a dead rat in the ventilation tubes, who knows.

Ranya is the last to leave, shutting the door behind us and, with it, drowning out the sound of Behnaz's shrill

"you'll never guess what!" to an unseen listener, Daria asking Marisol if she's ready for another coffee run, while
phones bleep and fluorescent lights hum.

Now the only sound in the room is that of Joe tapping
his pen annoyingly against the cheap wood of the conference table.

"Will y—" *you stop it!* I swallow back with a cough, re-
membering Georges's watchful presence. I focus on a spot
on the carpet somewhere behind his head, waiting for him
to speak. It's a sort of indecipherable color—the carpet, not
his head—like white, with specks of black thrown in, sort of
like an explosion of the yucky gray of concrete and slush,
different shades of Ordinary you don't often see in sorbet-
colored Miami. I consider taking advantage of this wonderful visual aid to bring up the topic of office redesign—I
know, I know, *es una obsesión, chica*—but it's just too awful a
fate for such a fabulous magazine.

Because we could be fabulous. The market is ripe; the
minorities of the world are shaking their fists in the air
raging against the Stepfordization of our lives, from
skinny, no-ass white models gracing the covers of our
publications to old, fat, repressed white men telling us
why it's a good thing to be bombing a bunch of brown
people for reasons no one can quite understand, while
pushing back another set of brown people to the other
side of an arbitrary border, a border *other* old, fat, balding,
repressed white men drew with the blood of innocents
hundreds of years ago.

I shake—with what? Rage? Fear? The contained fury of impotence? I don't know. It's all too much. Sometimes I just want to bury my head in my hands and cry at the hopelessness of it all. Then, a second or three later, I'm over it. Moving on with my life. Doing the dishes because the sink is starting to stink. Picking my outfit for the next day even though I know the camisole was probably embroidered by a Filipino nine-year-old, the pants sewn by a woman in Bangladesh who makes less in a week than I spend on coffee in a day. Taking out the garbage because it's garbage day, not even bothering to separate the paper and glass from the real garbage of decomposing food and assorted disgustingness, just because I'm too tired, too lazy, too *whatever* to bother. And then I have the balls to be angry at Republicans. Where do I get off? No wonder it's so easy for them to poke holes in our armor. We have no armor. We're just a jumbled mess of miseries and powerless frustrations. Blame it on the White Man. On Greed. On Multinationals. On stupid, stupid brown people who won't stop killing each other long enough to focus on killing the white man. On slavery. On Disaster Capitalism. On Stalin and Mao and Lenin and Marx. No, not Marx, I like him. He meant to do good. . . . What happened? What am I doing here? Where do I fit into all of this?

"Are you okay?" Georges rubs the back of my shoulder gently. He can be really sweet sometimes—actually, most of the time—which makes it that much harder to be angry with him. Kind of like Marx. Means well but unable to sway this cruel and nonsensical world.

I'm not making any sense. I'm just angry. Angry and desperate.

"Don't shut us down, please." I hold his gaze, my heart breaking almost as much as when Adam left me, telling me I could do whatever I wanted but that he wouldn't be a part of it. This almost hurts more. There was light after Adam— *much, much, much* after him, but it came. What would come after this?

"I'm going to ask Zahra to monitor sales closely for the next couple of issues. If we see a correlation between your ad campaigns and a spike in brands we're promoting in our stores, I'll be happy to keep the magazine going. But Rio, I have to be honest with you, I just don't see us doing this for much longer. Zahra's right—it's not core business, and it takes too much energy and money to keep it running. Even if it *is* marginally profitable."

What about doing good? I want to scream. Isn't that worth *anything?*

"It's a good magazine. . . . I'm sure we can . . . sell . . . if we want to."

The word "sell" comes out of Georges's mouth as a whisper, or else maybe my senses are leaving me completely. Sell it. Sell my baby.

"I'd make a strong recommendation you stay on as editor in chief. And if . . . anything happens, Rio, you know you'll always have a place at Mallouk Enterprises. I can't promise doing what, but you'll always have a place with us."

I lift my head and stare at Joe. Looking at him always makes my blood boil. Usually with exasperation, but with the added occasional bonus of lust. Some might call it passion, I call it a perfect recipe for keeping genuine feelings out of your life.

Which is exactly what I need right now. It's better than dissolving into a puddle of pathetic weakness right here in the conference room, in front of the two men who hold my life between them as if it were a plaything. A forgettable trinket, to be traded in when a more attractive, younger (in Joe's case) or more convenient and better suited to the bottom line (Georges's) one comes along.

"Thanks, Georges, I appreciate your support. I promise you'll be wowed with our next issue. After that . . . it's all up to you."

I quickly look away and blink furiously. I need to get out of here. Two breakdowns in two days. What's happening to me?

"Is there anything else?"

Georges looks defeated. And all of this is going directly over Joe's head. Joe who insists on attending important meetings when he happens to be in, not because he cares but because he thinks that's what a managing director should be doing. The other things a managing director should also be doing, like supervising staff, brainstorming ideas, budgeting, and directing the vision of the publication, he couldn't be bothered with.

"No, that's all."

"Thanks."

And off I go to cry it out in the safety of my office, once more.

Ranya

A sex columnist. This is what I'd become. If this was God's doing, then He's one hell of a prankster. There was a time when I would have been horrified with this level of blasphemy, but I'm now completely and utterly beyond redemption.

A sex columnist.

What would my mother say?

She wouldn't have a chance to say anything—she would have keeled over and died of humiliation before she had the chance. Not a heart attack—Humiliation. Capital *H*.

With my status now raised to "staff writer" from the

lowly post of "whatever" girl, I was at least now freer with my time. After the meeting I'd quizzed Rio on what exactly she wanted out of this section, and she said she wasn't quite sure herself yet and why don't I just riffle through the mail and see if anything doesn't inspire me.

That, or she suggested I go down to the beach and see what people were up to, maybe interview a couple on their mating habits.

And since I hadn't had much time to check out South Beach since I'd gotten here, I pounced on the opportunity.

Just as I was grabbing my purse, I felt a presence hovering above my desk.

Joe.

"I didn't get a chance to introduce myself properly back there."

If I was susceptible to such things, the way his stare bored right into me might have made my panties melt off. But I am not.

"I'm Joe Mallouk, the managing director." He offers his hand.

"I know," I say, taking it.

"You know, when I first saw you I thought maybe you were one of the models called into the office for a story or some pictures or something."

Even though the line is as cheesy as they come, I can't help but blush and try to hide my face behind a curtain of hair, nervously pulling at the ends.

It was the delivery, I think. Smooth and flawless, like it could only be either entirely sincere or else practiced to perfection.

"I have to go." I don't know what else to say. "Rio wants me to start researching right away. . . ."

"Does that mean you're just going to go down there and pluck the first guy on the street and 'research' the afternoon away? If that's the issue, I'm happy to help."

I blush the bright red of the Andy Warhol print hanging behind Joe's head even as he starts laughing at me.

"Don't be so embarrassed, that was just my roundabout way of asking if you needed any company."

"I'm not sure. . . ." I fumble with the clasp on my handbag.

"Are you new to the city?"

"How did you guess?"

"The accent, for one thing, plus you're the only person I've seen today without a tan. Is Rio working you that hard?"

"It's not Rio. . . . I just don't really know where to go here."

"In Miami? Are you kidding? We're going to have to take care of that right now."

"No!" It comes out more forceful than intended. "I mean, I need to get some stuff done first; it's going to be boring for you. . . ." I am so dull and unimaginative, I'm even boring myself.

"Okay then." He smirks. "Plans tonight?"

"What?"

"Plans? More specifically dinner plans?"

I can see Behnaz's mouth drop open from a far corner in my field of vision.

I want so much to say no—for starters, what would Georges say? Not to mention the teeny-tiny detail that I am *married,* but now hardly seems like the time to mention it. Or that I'm contemplating fleeing right back to where I came from, seeing that I am broke, friendless, utterly unqualified for my job, and completely out of my league.

And as far as Georges is concerned, I'm really not sure how the thought of him figures into the equation. Do I want to *go out* with Georges? Please! If he wanted to ask me out he would have done that by now, and I am still light-years away from a relationship, seeing as I have yet to extricate myself from my current one. And hadn't I sworn off relationships anyway? I am thirty-two and (virtually) never been kissed, just like the title of that movie years ago. I am intrinsically flawed, and there's no need to add more drama to my life.

There's just one problem.

I hadn't counted on the small detail that at this point in my life, turning away from the promise of intimacy is a hell of a lot harder than it was when I was sixteen.

"I'll pick you up at nine. Dress up like you're going to run into Madonna."

"Am I?" I panic.

"Possibly." He winks.

For all their inner dinginess and patchwork of mismatched furniture, the offices of *Suéltate* are located in what is, apparently, the hottest place to be in this city—South Beach.

Rarely have I seen such a spectacle of on-display body consciousness, from the ubiquitous tight white capris paired with loud halter tops and platforms to teeny-tiny shorts, even tinier bikinis, and taut bronzed bodies as far down Ocean Drive as the eye can see.

Even the name, Ocean Drive, rolls so tantalizingly on my tongue that I almost want to strip down to that level of sizzling beach glamour.

Or maybe it has something to do with the fact that I can't stop thinking of Joe, a man who seems to be the personification of this easy, sexy, beachy cool.

It's hot.

Scandalously hot.

Or maybe it's all the layers of clothes I'm wearing. And that they're all black, my color of choice in Montreal. It's not just the clothes, either. It's the hair, a uniform shade of chocolate brown, the skin tone, a pallid, positively unglowing olive, and the fact that I haven't waxed anything in forever.

I couldn't wear a bikini if I wanted to.

I meander down Ocean and turn up to Lincoln when the taunts of the tall, busty women manning the spill of restaurants along the beach, practically begging walkers by to come in, get to be too much. I keep walking until the smattering of stores becomes more concentrated, and names I remember from a time when I had the money and carefreeness to shop with athletic dedication come into view, plus a few others I've never heard of. The street turns into an enormous, Euro-Riviera-ish pedestrian mall, with an eclectic mix of peddlers selling everything from paintings to hippie jewelry to freshly squeezed juice lining the middle of the boardwalk.

I am a shopping addict, in a shopper's paradise, and I can't shop.

Oh, the irony.

It's almost as ironic as a virgin being assigned to write the "Sexy Modern Latina" section of *Suéltate* magazine.

This is not ironic, it is utterly ridiculous.

I thread in and out of shops way too expensive for my current budget, stopping to peruse menus of charming little sidewalk cafés I can't afford, when I spot one very different sort of store: a bookstore.

An adorable little one at that, not chainlike in any way, where the ever-present red banners have been replaced by lots of old, unpolished wood, and where books are stacked in offbeat mixes, as opposed to the usual barrage of bestsellers by the door. And it had its very own café.

It's been ages—years—since I'd picked up a book.

I weave through Fiction, Biographies, Gardening, Business, and stop when I get to Art. I'm met with stacks and stacks of lovely books. Gorgeous coffee table books, books about artists, design, Miami style, Cuban style, Pop Art,

something called MiMo, and volumes of Art Deco literature.

I want them all.

I can't have them all.

I pick up a volume about Venetian architecture and flip
it over to see the price.

Oh my God.

I'm going to need a budget. Of course I know what a
budget is, I could have been heard talking about a mysterious
"budget" in my pre-sky-falling-over-my-head days, but it
was strictly in the abstract, as in, "I'm not sure this Moschino
fringed leather jacket is in the budget." What that really
meant was I thought I'd burned one too many line items on
my father's credit card statement and that it was perhaps better if I waited until next month.

I walk out of the store with a pocket notebook, a kitschy
souvenir pen, and a colorful *Wallpaper* City Guide* of Miami,
which I'd decided on because of its cool architectural angle.

Plus it was the cheapest one.

After about twenty minutes of strolling through Lincoln
Road Mall and wrestling with long divisions and shadows of
multiplication tables I learned a lifetime ago, I figure that between what was left of my modest cashed-in jewelry stash, the
pocket change in my personal bank account, and the pittance
Suéltate paid me, I would have to renegotiate rent with Zahra
or else I was bound to wander the streets of Miami, a Bigfoot
of unwaxed body hair, wrapped in New York–style black.

And how was I ever going to get my "Sexy Modern Latina" mojo on looking like that?

But first things first. I walk up and down the stylish boardwalk looking for someplace halfway affordable to begin my transformation, find myself winding around tucked-away back alleys and tiny streets lined with everything from designer denim stores to kosher meat delis and drag-queen-manned sex shops.

And then I spot it—a crowded window advertising everything from henna to threading to waxing and Eastern massage, tucked away at the top of an inconspicuous flight of stairs, shrouded almost entirely by neon. "Madame Vilma's Beauty Spa," reads the bloodred paint.

Welcome to Madame Vilma's," says a pretty girl behind the counter. "Have you been here before?"

I shake my head no and she says not to worry, she'll be with me in a second, and sure enough, seconds later I am led down a narrow hallway lit with red incense candles and draped with sarilike gauzy fabric in shades of fiery orange, fuchsia, purple, gold, and, of course, red.

"What are we doing today?" she asks brightly once we're in a softly lit room, the door shut behind us.

"Er . . . I'm not sure—maybe just the legs and some bikini?" I'm furiously doing the math in my head, wondering what I can afford.

"Sure. Just hop over here." She points to the table in the

middle of the room and hands me a towel to drape myself with.

I lie back as per instructions and try to get as comfortable as possible, under the circumstances.

The girl eyes me up and down. She has gorgeous skin, the color of almonds if they got a golden Miami tan, dusted with shimmer in all the right places, and eyebrows shaped to heights of perfection I'd only seen in the most exclusive of spas. Good eyebrows are key—I liked her already.

"Can I say something?" she says, eyeing the area around my bikini line cautiously.

Oh, no.

"What is it?" Was I so far along the Bigfoot spectrum as to be beyond help?

"You just got here, right?"

"Yes. . . ."

"Are you planning on going to the beach soon?"

"Of course."

"How do you feel about Brazilians?" She flicks the switch on the wax heating contraption and starts lining up white strips of cloth on the table beside me.

My entire body breaks out into a sweat.

"Er, no, I don't think that's going to be necessary. . . ." I am beyond mortified.

"Oh, come on." She swats my arm. "A gorgeous girl like you is bound to have a man waiting at home. You've never had this done before, have you? He's going to flip!"

She picks up the first piece of cloth and slathers it with the thick, pasty wax.

"I don't have a man waiting at home, or anywhere for that matter." I'm not entirely sure this is a lie.

"What?" She squints, incredulously.

"Promise."

"You must be Indian then—has anyone ever told you you look like Aishwarya Rai?"

"No to the first, yes to the second." I giggle nervously.

"Re-e-eally?" she trills. "You're not Latina, that's for sure. I've seen so many of them here, I can tell. Let me guess. . . . Middle Eastern?"

"You're the first person here to guess right!"

"Ha! That's because I'm good." She winks. "And modest."

"I'm Lebanese, actually."

"Huh." She raises one of those perfect eyebrows as she starts to slather hot wax on my exposed thigh. "Lots of Lebanese here, though you wouldn't know it sometimes. They're more American than the Americans."

I think of Georges and Joe—how different the Lebanese are in Montreal, more raw, more connected to their roots— and I have to concur.

"There's a big old Maronite church in Coral Gables—that would be where all the rich ones live. Maybe you should head there after this, remedy this man situation you've got on your hands."

"What, me? Oow!"

"I'm sorry, sweetie, beauty hurts."

And off goes another wax-laden linen strip, and half my nerve endings along with it.

"I'm not . . . aahhh! . . . interested in . . . oh my God . . . men." I wipe my damp forehead with the back of my arm.

"Lift your leg for me please. . . . No, higher . . . higher . . . good girl. Got to get those pesky little hairs all the way in the back, so a man's not afraid to go back there! And what do you mean you're not interested in men? Don't tell me—"

"Oh, no, no no no. . . ." Every time I tell myself I've come across the worst day of my life, the Universe, ever eager to please, promptly delivers another gem.

I was splattered on a waxing table, underwearless, and discussing my nonexistent sex life and possible lesbianhood with a perfect stranger. A stranger who was now better acquainted with my intimate bits than I ever was myself.

"There!" she says after an excruciating ten minutes. "All done. You might not want to wear your pretty lacy things tonight, you're bleeding pretty bad, but don't worry! It'll be all gone in the morning. Next time it won't hurt as much, I promise. Now let's do those arms. . . ."

Having bonded over intense pain and extreme emotions running the gamut from mere whimpering to flat-out crying out for mercy, I feel emboldened to ask my petite, delicate-featured yet shockingly savage waxer if she was the Madame Vilma advertised on the window.

"That would be my mother-in-law." She rolls her eyes.

"She's in Pakistan now, visiting relatives, so I'm free to do things like roll my eyes and call her a bitch. I'm Priya."

I gasp. "You called your mother-in-law a bitch?" I'd certainly had the thought—more than once—over the course of my engagement to Dodi, and then our very brief marriage during which her bitchiness had reached epic proportions, but I'd never dared say it out loud, not even to a perfect stranger who would never meet her, not in a million years.

Priya laughs. "She's not here, is she? Besides, she *is* a bitch and someone should tell her. Just not me, because then I would be dead as a dog in the streets of Beijing."

"Priya!"

She erupts in wicked laughter. I've never met anyone so unguarded.

"You're shocking." I shake my head, sitting up and wriggling my bruised and battered body back into my clothes.

"Not as shocking as you. What's this thing about not being interested in men? Are you saving yourself for the second coming of Christ or something?" She starts tidying up her work space, pressing knobs and replacing the crinkled and blood-speckled sheet of hospital paper.

I have to think about this. What do I say? Is my story even plausible? Isn't it wrong to be talking so scandalously about my husband to this girl I've just met? Will this come back to bite me in the behind somehow?

"I'm Muslim, first of all, and not terribly concerned with the second coming of Christ."

"No way—me, too! I was sure you were one of those Maronites, all spiffy and shiny and, well . . . rich-looking. Was that wrong of me to say?"

"No, of course not. I appreciate your honesty."

"Though I have to tell you, sweetie, wool blends and Miami don't mix."

"I know, I had no choice. . . . I'd packed for London. . . ."

"London?"

"I . . . I . . ." I can't hold it in anymore. Between a roommate who won't talk to me, a boss who wants me to drop dead, parents who've disowned me, a husband who'd probably sicced a bounty hunter after me by now, and a pair of mysterious men I suspect would be a challenge to figure out even if I weren't completely useless in that department, I didn't have one friendly soul to pour my heart out to in the entire world.

In a jumbled mess, it all comes tumbling out, from the trauma of having caught my husband and my trusted decorator in a too-close-for-comfort pose, at my favorite department store, no less, to running into a successful Zahra after all these years and meeting Georges, and my flight from reality. I tell Priya about Rio, the magazine, the new section I'm supposed to be responsible for, about my parents, my fears, and even my date tonight.

"D-do you have someone to see after me?" I sniff. "Don't worry, I'll pay for your time. I'm sorry. . . ." I feel myself about to crumple again when she grabs me by the shoulders and shakes me.

"What are you going to wear tonight?"

"What?"

"On your date with Joe, tonight. What are you wearing?"

"Did you hear anything I said?"

"Of course I did, sweetie, but what are you going to do about it? You can only play the hand you're dealt, but play it to the best of your abilities."

I couldn't help but marvel at her confidence, for such a young-looking girl.

"It's not your fault Dodi's gay. It's not!" she repeats when she sees my sheepish, downturned face. "Honestly, it can't be easy to be him, so try not to get too angry, either."

"So what am I supposed to do then?" I moan.

She hesitates, but only for a second. "Be the best damn sex columnist you can be!"

"What about Joe? How is he going to react when I tell him about . . . you know . . . that—"

"That you're a virgin? Simple. Don't. Not until you feel comfortable with him. Anyway, are you even sure he's the man you want to share this moment with?"

I stare at the beige tiles beneath my feet, most cracked with age, and twirl a stray piece of thread between my fingers. "Would you?"

"Do you like him?"

I *like* Georges. I think I might be lusting after Joe, though. I did lust after Georges, too, but that might just be because of this heat getting to me. . . . Is it the city, the mood, all those taut bodies along Ocean Drive today, or am I just a repressed skank at heart?

"Maybe. . . ."

"Ranya, just remember one thing: You're a woman-woman, not the child-woman you were conditioned to be all your life. You did your best, and now it's time to live your life. If you like him, what's the harm in it?"

"What if he's diseased?"

"Make him wear a condom."

"What if he's just using me for sex?"

"Isn't that what you're doing to him?"

Oh my God. She's right.

I slide over to her and wrap her in a tight hug. My first real human contact in weeks floods me with another wave of emotion. I think I might erupt in tears again, but at the sound of rustling at Reception, Priya jumps away from me and rushes to the front.

"Hello, darling," I hear her say, her words muffled by the walls between us.

"What are you still doing here? The store is supposed to be closed!" a man's voice bellows.

Mumble, mumble, mumble. . . . "I'm sorry . . ." *Mumble, mumble.* "I was talking to a customer—"

"A customer?" the man's voice counters, rising and getting angrier. "Where is he?"

The next thing I hear is heavy footsteps crossing the same richly decorated hallway I'd crossed just about an hour ago, and before I know it, a large, burly man, barrel-chested, fat, and a good twenty years Priya's senior, is holding the door ajar.

He spots me in the corner against the treatments chair, bewildered, and stumbles back. "Sorry," is all he says by way of apology, and he retreats, shutting the door behind him and leaving me to collect my things.

Rio

I want to get drunk. No, I need to get drunk. On second thought, I need to get laid. By anybody except Joe.

¿Deseas algo más?

I lift my eyes, heavy with melancholy and cheap Puerto Rican rum, at the bartender, another suave, slender, sexy man the likes of which are a dime a dozen in this town.

How 'bout a little bit of you right here on this counter? I want to say, but I wisely stick with, "I'll have another Cuba libre, *por favor.*"

I'm too sober to proposition anyone yet. Too mortified

by this morning's scene. Too weak to push the incessantly running instant replays of it out of my head.

Joe, it seems, has finally found "the One" and thought he'd share the news today.

"What the hell do you know about *the One*?" I spat at him, once again, behind the safety of my office walls. If those walls could talk, *m'hija,* they'd be having a *cafecito* with my mother right now, telling her to come get her daughter, that she was on the verge of losing it if she hadn't lost it already. *I don't care,* my *mami* would say, probably. *I lost her a long time ago anyway.*

"What the hell is the matter with you? Since when do you care who I fuck?"

This is different, I wanted to whimper. But I couldn't. That would have only succeeded in repelling him even more.

"What the hell is wrong with *you, pendejo*? Who decides they've found 'the One' after one meeting? Have you even gone out with her yet?"

"Why do you even care? You think I'll stop giving it to you? Maybe at first. . . ." He came around my desk to wrap his arms around me.

I pushed him away. "You're disgusting! What kind of person are you?" I heard the words and I had a hard time believing they were coming out of my own mouth. I'd managed to be with Joe, albeit in a completely messed-up, dysfunctional, and masochistic way, for almost five years now. Nearly as long as I'd been with the company. I had no idea what I was expecting, But then again, it had been a long time since I thought about marriage, or kids, so who cared what kind of man Joe was? All these years, what had I been after? A loving relationship? The only loving relationship I'd ever had was with this magazine.

Ay, Dios mío, where had my parents gone wrong?

"I'm disgusting? *Me?*" Gone was the twisted, sardonic smirk from his face, replaced with a kind of bitter, ugly venom. It was all going to fall apart, I knew it. I know it's not Ranya's fault, I knew what he was about to say; it was written in the stars from day one. I just couldn't help needing to hear it, and I couldn't help wishing she would just drop dead. Disappear back to wherever she had come from.

"Did you seriously think we were going to have the house in the burbs and white picket fence bullshit? Huh? Did you?" He swung me around and shook me, like the way he used to as a prelude to a roll in the hay. Or, in our case, the proof stacks.

I didn't answer. I just stared at my shoes, a Payless version of a Dior black-lace-on-nude-leather number I featured in last spring's issue. The salary attached to my job had never matched its supposed glamour.

Maybe it's time to ask Georges for a raise. If I wasn't tossed out on my ass first.

I take a slug of the rum and Coke on the bar in front of me, trying to drown out the memory of what I said next.

"Yes."

That's right, *chica*, that's what I said. The humiliation of it all comes back in hard-hitting waves. Yes.

One day, when he was done running after tight young *culito,* he would be ready to settle down, I reasoned. He was already pushing thirty-five; why wouldn't he? I gave him another five years. By then *Suéltate* would be a raging success, I would make the cover of *Time,* or *Newsweek,* or whatever gringo self-validating bullshit rag, and he would say he was proud of me, because *mami* and *papi* sure as fuck weren't going to say that, and we would look at each other and realize how stupid we were, running around all those years when we were only perfectly right for each other all along.

He just laughed at me. He laughed as I stood there, slumped against the smooth wood of my cheap desk, the desk Georges was never going to replace with one befitting the editor in chief of *Suéltate* magazine. Just laughed and said I was one crazy bitch before heading over to the door and closing it behind him.

I wasn't even worth a proper, self-respecting *slam.*

I couldn't blame him, though. Yes, one day he would get tired of chasing skirts. When, no one can say, but they all do eventually, don't they? Otherwise they just end up becoming the pathetic loner at the far end of the bar, his wrinkles and bad tan apparent even in the dark shadows of the teenybopper club he's way too old to be at but is at anyway, his sleazy old-man outfit even more conspicuous than his age. I know men like that. I have never-married uncles who are men like that. I bet Joe has them, too, and their patheticness would never be lost on a guy whose mere existence embodies cool, like Joe. Even Joe, with all his philandering, knows that when you get to a certain age, it's your wife you should be cheating on, not your girlfriend, friend with benefits, booty-call girl, or however the hell he thinks of me. How fucked up is it that he doesn't even want me as the wife he's planning on screwing around on anyway? Even more fucked up—why am I so hurt that the girl he wants to marry, the girl whose best friend he is destined to be banging one day in her laundry room while she's at a PTA meeting or a park playdate with the other designer mommies, is Ranya?

I slam my drink against the counter and signal the bartender for one more.

I'm at one of those ghetto bars you find on the rough streets of downtown Miami, far away from the Beach scene, where you'd sooner run into a polar bear than a house mix. Reggaeton is king around these parts, which is exactly the way I like it. If I close my eyes shut or, better yet, keep them open and fixed on the beautiful *tigres* who haunt these hangouts, I can almost pretend I'm in La Casona in Honduras, the biggest club in La Ceiba, where I'd danced summers away as a teenager, a million miles from the glitzy, glamorous hollowness of Miami.

I watch the *tigres,* nineteen- and twenty-year-old boys with slinky tattoos circling their bulging biceps and small gold hoops in their ears, buzzing around any skinny little thing in white spandex and black lip liner who's happy to give it up in a not-too-dirty corner of the men's room without too much trouble or expense.

I am alone at a bar full of young, horny men who won't stop looking at me out of the corners of their tar black eyes, and no one will talk to me.

I wonder if my important-magazine-editor outfit of pin-striped trouser jeans and floaty tunic top is intimidating them. I should have dressed more like those girls I put on the pages of *Suéltate*—leggings, tight dresses in colors like sunset and saffron and "bronze goddess." Maybe then I can land one of those young, strapping things.

Who's the tigre *now*? I chuckle into my third rum and Coke of the night. Maybe not a *tigre* . . . maybe "cougar's" the word.

The song "Maneater" comes on, which gets me thinking about work and if maybe we should feature Nelly Furtado on our next cover even if she isn't strictly Latina—I mean, would I put a *brasileña* on our cover? Sure I would, so why crap all over this *portuguesa canadiense*? But that just gets me right back to where I started, thinking of Joe and what he's doing with Ranya right now, as we speak.

The lyrics ring loud in my ears.

Maneater.

Is that what I am?

Why the hell not?

Since Joe made it clear I wasn't the marrying type anyway, why not enjoy being loose to its fullest?

I stand up but have to grip the edge of the bar to hold my balance. I spin around and survey the room for about sixty seconds, scouring dark corners and spotlight-lit dance-floor nooks where couples are going at it with the ferocity of hunger and raging hormones.

And then I spot him, leaning at the other end of the bar, with a friend. They're both young and handsome in that Latino way of *café con leche* skin, sexy chin stubble, and creative body art. Their bodies look ripped under their snug T-shirts and low-riding jeans, gleaming white sneakers with the laces undone poking out from beneath the frayed cuffs.

I make up my mind right away. The shy-looking one who hangs back while his friend hits on one hot girl after the other, waiting to see which one will bite. He finds one—black, with thin blond-bleached braids down to her ass and a purple tube minidress that doesn't leave a damn thing to the imagination.

Shy boy is now alone. Maneater. Easy prey.

"You're not dancing?" I try very hard not to slur as I saunter up to him.

"I'm taking a break," he says casually in Spanish.

"With all these hot girls around? You a *maricón* or some-thing?"

He laughs and shakes his head, embarrassed. "No, I'm not gay."

"That wasn't very nice of me to say. I'm sorry."

" 'S'okay. You thirsty?"

"You offering?" I manage before lurching forward. He

steadies me with one very strong arm. I can actually feel his biceps tensing as he grips my own, gently but firmly. I wonder if that's the only muscle tensing in his hot body right now, and a flush floods my insides.

It's a huge relief to know Joe isn't the only one who can do this to me. It's amazing, but in all these years of that asshole dipping in and out of my life, I never strayed. Not once. Can you believe that *mierda*? A lot of good that did me.

"You live around here?" I slur.

He just erupts into a crazy fit of laughter. Again. Uh-oh. What kind of *tigre* is this? He should have been all over that. It must be the outfit. That or he's holding out for a *gringa* blond bitch with a flat *culo* and big plastic boobs. That's the problem with some of these boys. Greener—or, in this case, blonder—pastures and all that jazz.

"What's the matter? Why are you laughing?"

"Don't you want to dance first?"

I can't believe it. A roomful of horny, skanky man-whores, and I had to pick myself the one romantic of the bunch.

"Dance?"

"*Sí, bailar. Así, ¿sabes?*"

He closes the already narrow space between us and starts moving his hips to a sultry reggaeton beat, dipping and flowing along with the music, dragging me and my budding buzz along for the ride.

God, this is almost as good as sex.

The truth is I'd lost touch with a lot of girlfriends over

the years, lost some to marriages and the ensuing kids, and jobs on other coasts or in other countries altogether, not to mention that I was never one for female friendship anyway. They were few and far in between, my girls. And when my best friend moved back to her native El Salvador to join her fiancé, I ran out of friends to go out with. Of course there were still the PR gigs, professionally orchestrated affairs with shrimp canapés and pomegranate martinis, or whatever the exotic antitoxin fruit of the day was, but this, *this,* was a thing of a distant past.

The beat dips even lower and down we go with it, in perfect synch. Could Joe move like this? I don't know. We would have never gone on something as normal as a date. That would have been way too semi-functional-relationship-like.

He's getting excited, and I increasingly intoxicated.

"Wanna go to the back?" I give it another shot.

"Aren't you having fun?"

Oh my God. He really is gay. He lied. Or else he thinks I'm disgusting.

"Look, if you don't like me, just say it to my face!" I yank my arm away from him as he is performing an elegant, swirly hip shimmy.

His face twists up in confusion. "I like you!" he says. "*Estás preciosa,* if you want to go we'll go, but I'm having a good time here . . . you really want to go?"

I give up. Besides, I'm getting too woozy to protest.

"No . . . let's stay."

One hot reggaeton after the other, interspersed with a few pop dance songs, follow each other into the night and then the early hours of the morning. I dance until I realize I've lost my shoes. I must have taken them off and stashed them somewhere, too drunk to realize. I tell the pretty shy boy with the gelled black waves and the gold hoop earring, and we laugh together like it's the most hysterical thing since pantaloons.

Suddenly we're kissing. I don't know who started it, but it feels amazing and exciting, and new and natural all at once.

We don't even make it up the stairs of my apartment. He yanks my top over my head right there against the raw concrete of the staircase. I wrap my legs around his hips and start working on his buttons with the one free hand while he kisses me, our tongues dancing the tango together in salty wet embraces. I slip my key out of the zipped side pocket of my bag and hand it to him, vaguely thinking that this might not be such a great idea but too far gone to care. He fumbles with the lock while the rhythms of the club echo in my head. I giggle as I feel a rush of air against my nipples—he's snapped off my lacy black bra, the expensive French one with the intricate meshing. We're inside, on my bed, having fallen back against the same sheets Joe and I made love on so many times. I breathe him in, pungent cologne mixed with salt and sweat, close my eyes, and wonder why I had waited this long to do this.

Zahra

Ranya is getting dressed for a date. A date with a multi-millionaire heir to a family fortune, a fortune he has never had to do a thing for, and I am here, sprawled on my couch, on my second tub of cookie-dough ice cream, two empty chip bags at my feet.

I should at least have the decency to turn bulimic, but I don't have the energy.

God works in mysterious ways.

You do nothing worthwhile your whole life, accomplish nothing at all, and you get a date with one of Miami's most eligible bachelors.

You slave your youth away at school, let yourself be at the mercy of one set of relatives after the other, all so you can get a decent education, then put in hours at a job that treats you as if you were a machine, make one mistake—*one*—and you end up on your couch alone on a Friday night eating yourself into an early grave, or at least obesity, ensuring that no man will ever look at you twice. What's the point? It's not as if potential husbands were ever clamoring at my door. I might as well have the only kind of fun available to a girl like me.

"How does this look?" she calls out from what used to be my guest room.

She walks out in open-toed black heels and a shockingly tiny minidress covered entirely in sequins. She's also done something to her hair, I'm not sure what. Where she looked sulky and somber when I first saw her in London, now she radiates energy.

I see the way she looks at me, the way her head cocks just a little to the side, as if to say, *You poor, ugly, unwanted thing . . . how I wish I could fix you.*

"You did something to your hair." I glance at her briefly and then turn back to the TV. It's a reality show—*I Love New York.* Reruns. I'd already seen it the first time it aired. I also used to watch the Flavor Flav show it was spun off of, and the one about correction school for potential Flavor Flav contestants as well.

You might call me pathetic, but then you'd have to tell me something I didn't already know.

"What are you doing tonight?" she asks.

"Oh, you know, I have a hot date in an hour."

She crosses her arms.

"Do you want anything?"

She edges closer and carefully lowers herself onto the easy chair next to the couch, as if my patheticness was catching and she didn't want to get too close.

We sit in silence for a few minutes, her trying to figure out how to tell me, nicely of course, how much of a loser I am, and me taking perverse delight in watching her squirm.

"How was your trip?" she finally says. "I didn't get a chance to say bye before you left."

Now that was unexpected. She must know I slipped away surreptitiously so I wouldn't have to run into her and answer her billion annoying, intrusive questions before I left. Right?

"Shouldn't you be getting ready for your date?"

She purses her lips.

We go back to silence, but for some odd reason she still doesn't leave.

"Do you know Joe?"

"Do I know him? Of course. I'm the CFO of the company his family owns. What do you think?"

"No, I mean, do you *know* him. What he's like, if he's a nice guy. He's Georges's brother, so he must be nice."

Now she has my attention. Is she really that clueless?

Then I remember she mustn't have been around the Golden Boy long enough to see through him, and besides, she seems sheltered enough not to be able to tell anyway.

But even for someone that shallow, how could she miss the simmering fizz between Joe and Rio? They pretend to keep it under wraps, but everybody knows. Haven't they told her? And it's one thing for Rio to turn a blind eye to Joe's dalliances with models and C-list actresses, but with her lowliest underling?

I feel a faint tinge of responsibility. I should tell her. She's never done anything to me, at least not in her adult life.

But then I take a closer look at her. The long, lean legs, the hair I now realize has been layered and lightened up to a more sun-kissed, beach-friendly hue, the clothes that fit like they were cut especially for her body. I think far, far back to our school days, to how much the teachers loved her. She was pretty *and* bright. What was there not to love? And then I think about her husband, and how maybe she's not as naïve as she looks.

"He's great. How's Georges?"

I try to read her, but I can't. That might just be my poor people skills, though.

"He's fine," she says, averting her eyes.

We both turn back to the TV.

"He seems changed from London . . . less, I don't know, carefree. I don't know if that's just me."

Since it's none of my business, I don't tell her that

Georges is always uptight around his family and relaxed abroad. They are like a dysfunctional, Arab Brady Bunch, with the mother cutting enough of a personality to make up for a deceased father. Neither do I say that for all of Georges's qualities—his kindness and consideration, warmth and quick wit—he'd never had much of a backbone. A sensitive bent isn't the kind of trait a man groomed to take over the family business—more like an empire—should possess. His father didn't like it, and his mother detests it.

So I just ignore her in favor of another spoonful of ice cream.

"Zahra . . . it's Friday night, are you sure you want to sit here watching TV all by yourself?"

I stare at her incredulously. *Who told you you could judge me out loud, Miss Perfect?* I want to say. But I've never been able to look anyone in the eye and tell them exactly how much I didn't appreciate what they're telling me, and how dare they judge me, and that I didn't care what they thought because they'd never had to go through a day of their lives being me.

"And what do you suggest I do?"

"I don't know. . . ."

Don't I have any friends who'd take care of me, she wants to ask. And maybe if I didn't stuff my face like this so often, maybe I might actually have some decent prospects. I think about Rodrigo. Maybe I should call? I said I would after the last time—I couldn't stand his vapid stupidity for one more second, let alone an entire date, but seeing Ranya all dressed up and excited is like pouring acid on the open wound of my soul. I am alone, and bored, and lonely, and craving some sort of human contact. If my best option right now was a neo-wannabe Che Guevara with bad acne and high on weed and sloth, then maybe it was better than sitting here by myself, wallowing in self-pity.

Or maybe I should scrub myself clean, slather on some makeup, pour my bloated body into something halfway decent, and go out in the hopes of nabbing someone a bit more palatable than Rodrigo.

Then again, if girls like Ranya are my competition, maybe I should just stay put.

"There's something else I wanted to talk to you about," she says, looking even more nervous than before.

I rub my nose and scratch my scalp, waiting for her to speak.

Waleed comes out of nowhere, and instead of running to me, the inconsiderate fur ball leaps onto Ranya's lap. Even the cat likes her, for God's sake.

"About rent . . . ," she begins, "I did my budget and I don't think I can afford what you're asking for. I really like having you as a roommate, but unless you meet me halfway, I'm going to have to move out."

I should be elated. This is my out. But if I throw her out, will Georges be angry with me? Does it matter? He did say it would be temporary, and how great is it for me that it turned out to be even more temporary than I thought?

Except I'm not elated. I'd never admit this to a living soul in a million years, especially not Ranya, but there was a sliver of comfort in coming home after the devastating few days in Boston to something other than an empty condo and a fat orange cat. I'd lived much of my life in crowded quarters, amongst the dirt and sweat and loud and nosy presence of people—people everywhere, in the beds where we slept two to a corner for lack of space, on the few chairs we took turns sitting on for lack of money to buy more. And then more crowding when I was a poor recent grad in Boston. I thought I craved big open spaces, so when I had the chance I bought the biggest, nicest condo I could afford. It was my only indulgence in a life of austere deprivation. No one told me that open spaces could feel like prisons, too—shackling you with their lonely emptiness.

And besides, Ranya paying whatever rent she could pay meant more money to send home to my family.

"Pay what you can for now, and we'll talk about it again in a couple of months, okay?"

From the elation on her face, you'd think someone just told her she'd been crowned Miss Lebanon. She leaps over to me and hugs me.

"Thank you thank you thank you!"

I want to tell her not to get too excited, that just because I'd decided her presence was slightly more entertaining than Waleed's it didn't mean I hated her any less. But I don't know how.

Waleed, who'd been startled off of Ranya's lap when she

lunged toward, voices his annoyance with a loud meow. Ranya picks him up off the floor and nuzzles his whiskers against her nose.

"You never did tell me how Waleed got his name. Aren't cats usually called Sprinkles or Oreo or Spot, or some silly name like that?"

"Not when you're Palestinian," I say curtly, and turn up the volume on *I Love New York* louder, just as New York's mother launches into a huge catfight with her daughter over her latest mate selection. I love this stuff.

Ranya gets the message and goes back to her room, taking Waleed with her.

Waleed was my cousin.

He worked at the neighborhood coffee mill, which, in the West Bank, was akin to running a gas station—just like everyone needed gas for their cars, people needed to get their coffee, and not just any coffee, but the best beans they could get their hands on. Not even air strikes could keep that little shop from rolling up its metal shutters every morning. Coffee, after all, came from Arabia, so people took pride in their beans. Waleed stocked some of that instant stuff like Folgers and Nescafé of course, but he liked to say that it tasted like the water from dirty socks left to soak overnight and how there was no accounting for people's tastes, especially those crazy Western people with their strange lack of taste buds.

As at most self-respecting coffee mills, Waleed also stocked all kind of nuts—walnuts, hazelnuts, cashews, peanuts—and all their derivations, like nougat and peanut brittle and sesame bars and candied almonds, which he roasted in a big old hot oven that heated up the whole store.

The smell of fresh roasting coffee is probably the most unshakeable memory of my entire childhood.

For some very odd reason, maybe because he wasn't terribly good-looking himself and hadn't managed to find a girl willing to marry him by the very old age—by West Bank standards—of thirty, he was as nice to me as could be. His shop was the only place in the whole world where I was the princess and everyone else was the nobody.

"Ahlan b'el helwy," he would announce when I skipped onto the broken tiles of the store, giggling and pressing my nose against enormous glass bins full of treasures.

Good day to the beautiful girl. He said it like he meant it, with pizzazz. I'd tell him about what I was learning at school way over there in the gilded city of Riyadh, careful to edit out details of how mean and filthy rich the other girls were and how they didn't think I was beautiful at all, as a matter of fact, and treated me like the poor castoff that I was. He would tell me he was so proud of me and hand over a paper cone of assorted goodies that he'd twisted and filled himself with delicious surprises. Then he'd grind me a kilo of the house special, seal it tightly in green and white paper, and tell me to give it to my parents and say hello.

There was a small splinter group no one had really heard of back then. They called themselves Hamas—a party with a new twist on old aspirations. They would deal with the problems of the Occupation, the checkpoints, the arrests that came in the middle of the night, the unemployment, the humiliation—the Islamic way. Their interpretation of it, anyway.

Then there was a suicide bomb in a crowded outdoor West Jerusalem market that claimed the lives of eleven and wounded more than thirty.

Was it Hamas? Was it another group? Nobody knew. Nobody seemed to know anything, but everyone had their theories. I didn't understand very much about peace accords or political factions back then, but I knew there was enough misery going around that no one could tell what would happen next.

Three days later, Israel retaliated.

A moving vehicle that apparently carried one of the masterminds of the attack was targeted and bombed. The blast blew away the storefronts of half a dozen businesses that lined that section of the street—*sheesha* cafés, a barbershop, fruit and vegetable stalls. They said some of the charbroiled carcasses were found still clutching bits of the water pipe tubes they had been smoking. And one coffee mill had burned to the ground, the big wooden oven in the back having gone down in an Armageddon of flames.

Like I've said, we had a tradition of disaster in our family. We took the news in stride.

I think I'm going to call Rodrigo after all. I don't want to be alone tonight.

Ranya

It's incredible how easy it is to forget you're married. In my literature classes we would read about French ladies and courtesans who married rich and powerful men and then all but abandoned them in favor of dashing dukes and a life of intrigue, whether at court or in high society. They would keep separate wings of a house, sometimes even separate houses in separate countries altogether, and yet they would still be Madame This or Madame That.

Marriage, it seems, had been a sort of ticket to freedom. An easing of parental and societal reins that allowed women who were so inclined to carry on with their lives as they pleased. And if the husband in question happened to die, then so much the better.

A jolt of guilt stabs my chest.

I don't want Dodi to die.

Priya was right—it can't be easy to be him. I couldn't possibly have seen that all those weeks ago when I left, but something in me had changed. The icy bitterness and resentment that had such a tight grip on my heart had begun to thaw, and with them my anger was melting..

I didn't even mind so much that I could hardly afford anything anymore—I was too busy these days to shop anyway.

Now if I could only muster up the courage to call my mother, and figure out what I was going to write about in my column, then I'd be happy to melt into this role of absentee wife forever. I could have relationships free of in-laws and routine, of predictability and the crushing weight of sameness.

But I'd have to start by seeing if I could manage *one* such relationship first, before deciding if I could handle that kind of life. Plus, at one point or another, I'd have to face up to Dodi.

"Where are we going?" I say to Joe brightly. I'm on a date. A real, honest-to-God date. A date I am not hoping will end with a call to my father and a request for my hand in marriage. It's exciting and terrifying both at the same time.

Joe shoots me a look that sets my insides on fire.

Would it be so bad to give in? And exactly how do you

go from never-been-kissed to one-night-stand slut in one grand swoop?

"Baby, you know that wherever I'm taking you is where it's at. Don't worry." He pinches my chin gently in that quintessentially Arab-man come-on gesture, and I have to suppress a laugh. No matter how he dressed himself up on the outside, his essence would invariably seep out of his skin in little details, invisible to most people, even to himself.

The fire-engine red Alfa Romeo saddles up to a sleek street mobbed with beautiful people, each one taller, fitter, and better dressed than the next. Never in my life, even at my own wedding, had I seen so much shine, shimmer, bling, and bronze. From skin glowing with a fresh tan to rhinestone-studded fake eyelashes, it's almost too much. But it's also so much fun, it's positively seductive. All around us, Spanish house music blares—from cars and restaurant fronts—making me feel like I've landed on a tropical Latin island, not in the United States of America.

A valet in uniform takes Joe's keys, and we're ushered into a huge dining room decorated entirely in white leather, wall-to-wall mirrors, and vaulted dark wood ceilings.

We're seated quickly, the waitstaff fawning over Joe. He soaks it all up, not unlike how Dodi enjoyed commanding attention when walking into a room. Except he usually got it with arrogance, obtained because people wanted him to shut up and not blast them to smithereens with his loud, obnoxious complaining.

The restaurant is more of a club than a place to eat, with patrons obviously dressed to be seen, the menu emphasizing body-friendly foods like fish and salads and *tapas*. It's hard to talk over the music and the noisy chatter of the clientele, glasses chinking, and laughter that sounds more like shrill shrieking than anything else.

A bottle of red wine arrives at the table, compliments of the chef, and Joe motions the sommelier to let me taste it.

For a second, I panic. I don't want to tell him, to spoil the moment. What's more, I'm not so sure I *don't* want to taste it. My deference to religious dogma had had its ebbs and flows in the past, and this was definitely an "ebb" moment. The problem is that I'd never gone quite so far in the other direction before.

I let the man in the white shirt and the burgundy vest pour half an inch of rich, velvety liquid the color of dried blood.

I swirl it around just like I'd seen in the movies so many times, close my eyes, and sip. The intoxicating smell assaults my senses before the taste does. I spit it back into the glass, look up at Joe, and smile "perfect!" hoping he won't notice if I drink really, really slowly and only in between big bites of food.

I find myself with not much to say over our orders of ceviches and mashed yucca, and Joe isn't helping. He doesn't ask about what brought me to Miami, and to be honest, I'm glad, but it does make for some pretty dry dinner conversation. I ask him about his job and he's equally evasive.

"Is good for now, something to do, you know? But the future isn't in print. It's all about the Net, about entertainment."

What?

I'm not sure I understood the link between all that, but I smile sweetly and think about how sexy his chest looks with the three buttons of his black ribbed shirt undone. Then I think about how if Georges were here I'd tell him about what I'd read in my new guidebook about Miami architecture and how I'd love to check out the lobby of the Eden Roc hotel, the glass façade of the Bacardi building, and the Living Room installation in the design district.

"Have you ever seen the Rubell Family Collection?" I say, referring to something else I'd read about in my guidebook.

"No."

Joe continues chewing on a piece of spinach and I'm not sure what to follow that up with. Is this what a date is like? No wonder people couldn't wait to get the whole mess over with and just get married. Would it have been like this with Georges?

But again, Georges wasn't the one to bother taking me out on a proper date, even if he did ask about me a lot, making sure I was comfortable at Zahra's and that Rio wasn't treating me too terrible. Still, he'd made no attempt to move our easy friendship to the next level, so I have no business wondering if I would be feeling this kind of heat, these heart palpitations that are overcoming me once again, commingling in a cocktail of fear and anticipation, if Georges was sitting across from me instead of Joe.

The chef eventually comes out to greet Joe, slapping him on the back as if they were old buddies. They make small talk for a few seconds, and Joe looks pretty pleased with himself, before the chef goes to sow his good humor at some of the neighboring tables.

"You're still up for going out, right?" Joe says after a shared dessert of the most exquisite chocolate mousse I've ever tasted, and a violent game of footsie.

As we wait for the valet to bring the car around, Joe snuggles up behind me, clutching my sequined hips in his hands and running his thumbs along the length between my waist and my thighs. I'd never let anyone touch me like that before, and I have no idea if this is what I want. The only thing I'm sure of is that I don't want him to stop doing what he's doing, to laugh at me if I tell him how inexperienced I am, and to stop paying attention to me in favor of the hundreds of gorgeous women in fifty different shades of stunning that file past us along this busy nightspot.

So I just let him.

He takes me to a place called Tantra where a bouncer leads us beyond a grass-strewn entrance and a packed dance floor to a cordoned-off VIP area where Joe's friends are waiting for us with several bottles of clear liquid cradled in frosted buckets on the table in front of them.

He introduces me, but the eighties house mix is too loud for me to make out anyone's name, and they all seem to be halfway drunk anyway. Joe squeezes into the booth next to a man who's a darker, goateed version of himself and they launch into an apparently hilarious conversation I'm not invited to join. Meanwhile, under the table, Joe's fingers knead my thigh absentmindedly while one of the girls, a raven-haired and pinched-nosed beauty who looks like one of those Miss Venezuelas who'd invariably claim the Miss Universe crown every few years tries to strike up a conversation with me in indecipherable snippets. She gives up all pretense of being nice after about five minutes and turns back to a thirtysomething girl next to her with hair pin straight, razor cut, and dyed the color of blanched corn.

The house mix bores me. I yawn, but no one notices. When the music finally switches to a vaguely danceable Spanish pop mix, Joe nestles his nose into my neck and asks me if I want to go home. I don't really, but neither do I want to stay here with these cold strangers. Plus I'd helped myself to some of that clear liquid on the table and mixed it with soda like I'd seen the other girls doing. I'm now dizzy, and sleepy, and not up to partying at all. If this is the "getting shitfaced" Behnaz rants and raves about all the time, then I must really be out of tune with the world.

"Are you sure you can drive?" I say unsteadily.

"Of course!" I think I might have offended him so I don't press the issue, plus he doesn't look drunk in the least, and with the free-flowing booze I couldn't tell how much he'd had to drink anyway.

We climb into the red Alfa Romeo once again, and it

purrs all the way over the causeway to Zahra's building, one of the dozens upon dozens cutting sleek figures across Miami's night sky.

He parks it in a guest spot downstairs, shuts off the engine, and we're plunged in silence, and me in awkwardness.

He's going to kiss me.

Of course he is. He'd only been pawing me for an entire evening. But is he going to more than kiss me? And at which point exactly do I confess my utter ignorance in these matters and ask him politely if we could just call it a night?

Before I can formulate a plan of action, he's lunged over to my side, squashing me against the windowpane of the car.

His lips are on mine, his rubbing-alcohol-tasting tongue all over my mouth, inside and out, and while I can't say I'm loving it, neither can I summon enough willpower to tell him to stop. Nerve endings all over my body start to fire, like a machine going in overdrive, ready to take off. This is it. This is how it should have been with Dodi, if he'd ever bothered to romance me properly, bringing me to the point where my brain was too overtaken by physical impulse to think, to be afraid.

"Can I come up?" Joe gasps.

Uh-oh.

"I'm not sure that's such a great idea. . . ."

"Why not?"

"I . . . I don't think I'm . . . I'm not . . . I'm not a one-night kind of girl," I say, hoping it sums up my situation so as to cut off further inquiry at the pass.

"Ranya," he lunges again, "you're a hot chick. . . . What's the problem? You need to loosen up a bit." He emphasizes his point by reaching under my skirt.

Oh. My. God.

Is this what I spent all these years worrying about? As much as I want him to stop, the rush is intoxicating.

"Come on . . . let's go upstairs," he insists.

"N-n-n-o. . . ."

"Why not? I know you want it. . . . You have no idea how much I want to pleasure you if you just let me. . . ."

Oh. My. God.

I break out into hysterical laughter for a second before trying to camouflage it behind a coughing fit.

And this is supposed to be the Rico Suave of the office?

"What's so funny?"

"Nothing! Absolutely nothing. I'm just not sure I'm up for any, um, pleasuring," it's so, so hard to say this and keep a straight face, "tonight. But maybe another night. Definitely. Another night."

I try to free myself from his grasp even as his experienced fingers and hungry kisses collude with hormones that have been simmering under the surface for way too long, keeping me firmly planted in the passenger seat.

It's like he can't even hear me.

"Joe . . ."

"Mhhmm?" He's moving down to my neck.

"Joe . . . ooohh, noooo. . . . No, that's so wrong. . . . Oh! Yes, right there. . . ."

"See," he breathes huskily into my ear, "I told you."

"No, Joe, it's great, but seriously, that's enough."

"What's your problem? Are you a virgin or something?"

My breath catches in my throat. How did he . . . He doesn't know. He can't know. He's just being an asshole. I need to get out of here.

"Get off me!"

Even in the semi-darkness I can see the bewildered, I-can't-believe-this-chick-is-for-real smirk on his face.

"If that's all you want, there are plenty of women who'll give it to you, especially with your money. Good night."

I unlock the door and smack one foot against the pavement.

"No, wait, stop—I'm sorry, I . . . I didn't think you were serious."

"Good night, boss," I say. "And thanks."

"For what?"

For handing me my first article on a gleaming silver Tiffany tray, I think, and slam the door behind me.

DO YOU REALLY WANT IT?

In a day and age when Latinas all over the nation are empowered enough to cast off once-valued labels like "meek," "quiet," "obedient," and even "good cook," why can't we shake off the capital offender—Guilty with a capital *G*—while we're at it? Whether it's the guilt of seeing your mother's face in the shadows of your imagination when you're about to get down and get loose, or the guilt associated with telling an over-eager date where he can stick his groping paws?

Here are *Suéltate's* top five lines that should send every self-respecting woman running as far away in the opposite direction as her Manolos can carry her:

- What's your problem?
- You need to loosen up.
- I know you want me.
- Are you a virgin or something?

. . . And the #1 line that should send you sprinting for the hills is: I just want to pleasure you.

There you have it, ladies.

Remember, you're free to get it on whenever (and wherever . . . just make sure no one's watching) you please; just ask yourself—do you really want it?

Ranya

"Did you do it? Tell me tell me tell me!"

"Priya!"

"What?"

She lays a hand at her chest in mock befuddlement, interrupting the smooth back-and-forth dance of the nail file across my outstretched hand.

"You're going to have to do it if you're going to have material for your next article, you know."

"That, or I could ask you to write it for me, since women come in here all the time and spill their juiciest, darkest secrets, right?"

She throws her head back and laughs. "Seriously. The things these freaks have told me. Of course most of the time I'm a little jealous of all the fun they seem to be having while I'm stuck in the marriage from Hell, but there's not much to be done about that, is there? Maybe you should put that into your article. . . ." She lowers her head and attacks my nails with renewed vigor.

It's been a few days since I handed in my first real article to Rio—a whole page, with special artwork and layout, with my work on it. Rio even wrote a few words introducing the new feature as a "bold, brave, and thoroughly honest look at this important facet of modern Latinas' lives."

I was still aghast at the prospect of coming up with a new article for next month.

I've been in hiding for nearly two months now. How much longer will they allow me to stay in this state of limbo? When the storm comes, it will hit hard, I'm sure of it. After all, if Dodi had the gall to report our joint credit cards stolen, what can I expect from him next?

And then there's my mother.

I finally summoned the nerve to call, to tell her I would come home soon but wasn't quite sure when yet, that I still had some thinking to do. I also wanted to assure her I hadn't made anything up—okay, *fine,* maybe some teeny-tiny details about how I found out about Dodi's abominable offense—but that I essentially hadn't lied, and should be given some space to sort out my feelings.

Not to mention that—God forbid—I was actually having

fun in Miami. Now this is against all supposedly grieving soon-to-be-Arab-divorcée rules.

I love the fact that my life is now filled with some higher purpose than making sure that the baked squash and roasted lamb dish was ready and piping hot when Dodi came home from work. Even if that higher purpose is deciphering coded orders from a hurried and PMSing Rio as she rushes between meetings with freelancers and ad execs, and Georges and Zahra, and photographers, and models, and publicists. . . . And in spite of her never warming up to me, I am in awe of her professionalism, her inspiring determination, and her razor-sharp business sense. It shames me to think of how blessed my life was, and what little I did with it.

I hadn't gotten past "hello," though, because my mother, after nearly two months of not hearing my voice, hung up on me.

It was the most brutal blow of my entire existence—and enough to make me seriously reconsider what I'm doing here.

I ended up getting the story from my cousin Aline— thrilled as she was that I was finally "living it up on my own" and how it was about time, and was I dating anybody. Of course my face nearly melted off with shame at the thought that someone back home—even Ali—might think I was being adulterous. It doesn't matter one bit what Dodi did—or does, now that I'm not around. I wasn't going to compromise my principles. And one near slipup with Joe only served to steady my resolve. I was going to do this with my head held up high, with nothing to hide or regret. Which was going to be difficult to do once I got back to Montreal after months in Miami, after my parents had told everyone I was away visiting family in Lebanon. . . .

That's right. Ali spilled the beans.

My mother's friends would surely raise their daintily arched eyebrows at the news: a newlywed of one month taking off to see her family in Lebanon?

Surprising . . . but not entirely unheard of. In a society where people looked down on dating as something only Westerners and shameless Arab girls indulged in, it happened once every few dozen marriages that things simply didn't work out. Like Deema, a girl I'd heard about through friends—who came back from her honeymoon in the Maldives after a hundred-thousand-dollar wedding demanding a divorce. No one really knew why *for a fact,* but it was rumored he tried to . . . er . . . include a third party in the honeymoon celebrations and, apparently, either overestimated his new bride's eagerness to please or else underestimated her virginal reserve. In any case, that was one extreme example of things not quite working out, things that are quietly swept under the rug, never to be referred to in polite company.

And so I would join those nameless, faceless girls whose shadows hint at the cracks in the gleaming façade some people still hold up to each other to convince themselves the same thinking that worked just fine in another part of the world, in another era, works just as well here and now.

Still, the proverbial shit was bound to hit the fan soon.

"Priya? . . ."

"Mmm-hmm?" She's too concentrated on not bleeding the near-black Chanel stain onto my skin to look up. "I don't do much of this color down here," she says. "We're more of a pink or coral city."

"Why don't we go shopping on Lincoln Road after this? Maybe grab a bite to eat?"

"And what would I do with the store?"

"Shut down a little early today. . . . It's almost closing time anyway, and besides, you're always here. Why don't you get someone to help you?"

Priya shakes her head. "My husband drops me off here every morning and picks me up every night, and the bastard is too cheap to hire me a girl to help, even though I keep telling him we're losing customers from the lack of staff. I even drew up some calculations and everything to show him, and he still wouldn't listen. I could kill that man."

All this spills out of her in a stream of accented annoyance, bordering on hatred. Still, she caps it off with a resolved sigh, leaving me to wonder at where it all came from.

The one brush I had with her maniacal husband left me a little cold, to be honest, but a repeat victim of stereotyping myself, I refused to indulge the questions that were burning inside me since that day he came storming into the back room, convinced Priya had some man hidden between the supplies in the closet. I now feel slightly more emboldened to ask.

"Priya . . . you don't have to tell me if you don't want to, but how did you get yourself in . . . ," I try to be as delicate as I can, "a marriage you're not entirely happy with?"

"Not entirely happy with? You're joking, right? I'm not *at all* happy with my marriage. I just didn't have much of a choice!"

"It was arranged?" I say tentatively, scared out of my wits of offending her.

"Of course, darling. What do you think? I come from a town a few hours north of Karachi. My husband's extended family does business with my father. Their son—my husband—had gone off to the States to find work. After a few years here, his mother wrote to her sister asking her for a suitable girl for Rahim and I was offered up. So here I am."

"But . . . didn't you have any say in the matter?" I look at the bubbly, sweet, and incredibly bright girl in front of me and wonder how such a fate could have befallen her. Of course I know about arranged marriages and small towns in India where women still fling themselves into flames if their husbands happen to precede them in death, and girls in Egypt and Saudi Arabia and parts of Africa who had awful, unspeakable things done to them for reasons no religion condones and no one really understands. But it's another thing entirely to be staring into the eyes of one such unfortunate woman.

"Choice? Ha!" Priya cackles an embittered, hollow laugh. "I'm lucky I was able to go to school for as long as I did, and that I had a wonderful teacher who believed the key to undoing centuries of backward thinking was education. I'm not so sure she was right, mind you—Rahim is plenty educated but still as dumb as a deaf mule. Still thinks that if a woman he's in any way related to so much as coughs out loud in public, it will stain his good name. What is there to educate in a man like that?"

The militant Muslim girl inside me cringes. My parents were not like that. My friends' parents weren't like that. I thought Dodi was a bit much with his outward conservatism and traditional ideas of male-female relationships, but now I know what that was all about—putting up a solid front to hide the double life lurking behind. But Priya? Why was she putting up with it?

"You don't have to do this, you know," I say carefully. "You can pick up and leave. . . . He can't touch you."

She just smiles and shakes her head, looking at me that same wistful way someone does when they know what they're about to say will go totally over your head.

"And where would I go? This place belongs to his mother, and she pays him, not me. I don't have any of my own money, I don't have a degree of any kind—you think Pakistani high school will get me anywhere?—and Rahim is more afraid of having his honor stained than of the police.

It could be much worse, you know. I get to mind this place pretty much unsupervised, so if I wanted to be really, really naughty, I might just get away with it. And Rahim and his mother being as dumb as they are, they don't understand the things I read about in books and newspapers, and don't bother to stop me. He's not a dictator, you know— takes me to the library from time to time, the shops when I need something. It's just that . . . well, we're just very different and he's very stubborn in his ways. I'm not sure we'll ever grow to love each other, and God knows I might never respect him, but he puts a roof over my head, and who knows, God may bless us with children one day."

I stare at the long-sleeved shirt under her sari and I'm suddenly gripped by all kinds of fears—does he hit her? Is she hiding more than she's letting on? Why didn't I see this sooner? Should I call the police? Or would that just make things worse?

She takes one look at my crestfallen face and sighs, a long, sad sigh she must have been carrying in her heart for years and years.

"Not everyone has had it as easy as you, Ranya. Look at you, pretty and educated at the best schools, and no matter how much your family disapproves of what you're doing here, they won't harm you. They love you too much. Remember to count your blessings."

She pats my hand with the kind of warmth only the

truly good have, people who've seen it all and have still managed to come out smiling.

Tears spring to my eyes and I dissolve into a bawling mess even as Priya rubs my back and tries to laugh it all off, saying things like "shouldn't I be the one crying, darling?" and then laughing some more.

Rio

Not bad. Not bad at all. The writing is a little amateurish, but I love the angle. This is exactly the kind of mood I wanted to cover—one step spicier than the agony aunt feature, but not a *Cosmo*-type piece comparing different brands of vibrators, either. Plus the header would look good on the cover. Who knew the little boyfriend-snatching bitch had it in her? Not that Joe was ever my boyfriend, strictly speaking, but you know how it is.

I take a red gel-point pen to the piece and replace "mother" with *"abuelita,"* "an overeager date" with "your *muchacho caliente,"* and "ladies" with *"chicas"* just to give it that *Suéltate sabor* it needs to fit in with the rest of the editorial copy. Then I tighten it up and check for glaring grammatical errors just before sending it over to our off-site copy editor.

Good. One less thing. I can now kick back and think about what I'm going to do with the *tigre* who turned out to be somewhat of a kitten.

I didn't think he would stay, unless he happened to pass out from the 357 rum and Cokes we knocked back that night. At least that's how many it felt like.

My stomach churns—not from the ten o' clock munchies, either—when a memory from this morning flashes in my brain. His touch, creeping under the covers and over my naked skin.

He'd stayed. Not only had he stayed, but he woke me up with a few strategic kisses strewn all along my back like rose petals. The sheets smelled of me and him and last night, and nothing like Joe.

Then I got a grip. I didn't even know shy boy's name. And I had no intention of finding out.

"It's late. I have to get to work." I got up and scoured the floor for my underwear.

"Isn't that my line?" He arched his back and stretched out like a *gato* in the sun. A hot, studly *gato* with young, sculpted arms and the whisper of a six-pack. Or at least a four-pack.

"Do you really have to go now?"

I took this as evidence that he had no job to get up for. Not good. But wait a minute—why did I care?

"Look, er . . ."

"Diego." He crossed his hands behind his head and looked at me as one does at a questionable piece of meat.

"I'm sorry, but you really have to go. I'm going to hop in the shower now," *and when I come back, you'd better not be here,* I felt like adding, but the good little polite Latina in me, or what was left of her, wouldn't let me.

"Aren't you the boss? You could go in late, or maybe even take the day off?"

The boss? Where had he gotten that from? I wondered.

"Where did you get that from?"

"You told me. Last night. You said *Suéltate* was your magazine, and you were the boss, and you weren't going to let some no-good dirty *árabes* shut you down."

I stood there frozen, my mouth gaping open like a half-busted piñata.

I said that? What kind of drunk was I?

A hit-below-the-belt kind, apparently.

He just laughed at me and stood up, exposing himself in his full glory before sneaking up beside me, nuzzling his stubbly chin into the back of my neck, and leading me toward the shower.

"You should start getting ready," he whispered.

"How old are you anyway?"

"Twenty-five."

Ay, chica.

Ranya

How did you know I like a sense of humor in a woman?"
Joe slaps a proof of my debut article, marked up with scribbles and slashes of red ink, on my desk.

"You read it?" I don't look up from my screen.

"Those weren't nice things to write about your boss." He drums his fingers on the desk in front of me and tries—unsuccessfully—to suppress a smirk.

"Those weren't nice things to do to a nice girl in your car that night. . . ."

"Really?"

"Really."

"Huh, no one's ever complained before."

"'No one' wasn't me, and isn't there a first time for everything?"

"I could have you fired, you know."

"I would have sued," I say, only half-kidding. "And I still can. . . ."

"Jesus, right in the 'nads. Moving on . . . are you busy this weekend?" he says.

Oh, no. I don't think I'm up for round two of dodging blue balls and raging hormones.

I make a face to say "thanks but no thanks," but Joe throws his hands up in mock surrender before I have a chance to formulate one syllable.

"Not like last time, scout's honor, though you should have trusted me on that one; it would have been the most memorable night of your life, you know."

"I'm sure." If only he knew I meant that without even the slightest tinge of sarcasm.

"Thank you; I'm flattered by your confidence."

I find myself laughing breezily. This Joe seems different from the pushy, showy jerk of the night before. Maybe he'd just been having a bad night. Maybe I shouldn't be so quick to write him off—as a friend, naturally.

"What'd you have in mind?"

"I'm having dinner with a guy in the restaurant business—huge, right now. He's behind some of the poshest resto-lounges in the country."

"And you want to open a restaurant?"

"Maybe. It's just a . . . an exploratory meeting, as they say."

"But what about the magazine?"

He looks toward Rio's office furtively. Her door is closed.

"That's up to Georges. I'm not too sure I belong in this business after all."

I open my mouth to protest, at least to point out the tiny detail that he might be slightly more interested in the business if he actually spent any time managing it. He cuts me off before I have the chance.

"It's this Saturday and I'd like you to come."

"Me? Why?"

"Because I invited you."

"You mean as your date?"

"No, as my girlfriend." He winks and disappears down the hallway.

"Your *what*?"

Too late. He's gone.

Georges is being weird, and I hate it. I can't help but feeling it's my fault somehow, not because I have an inflated sense of self-importance (okay, yes, it's true, but at least I'm *aware* of it), but it mostly has to do with how . . . well, *stiff,* he's been around me lately. No more kind looks from across the room on those rare occasions he happens to be in the office, no more impromptu coffee breaks or phone calls to make sure I'm getting along okay.

It's time, I decide, to do something about the situation. Especially since besides Priya the wonder waxer, I don't have a single friend anymore. Not the girls I'd left behind in Montreal who would have sided with my family in thinking me insane, or Rio or Zahra, no matter how hard I try to get them to like me.

When he calls the front desk at four this afternoon—Rio still has me on receptionist and coffee girl duty in spite of my newfound way with words—I take a moment to talk to him before putting him through to Rio.

"Hey there, stranger."

"What's up?" he says.

"Nothing. I just . . . Are you sure everything's okay?"

"What do you mean?" His voice comes across the line clipped, even slightly annoyed.

"I've been doing some reading—you never told me what an artistic hotbed this city is. You didn't tell me about the design district, or Calle Ocho, or anything. All I've done so far is window-shop in Lincoln Road Mall and tan on Ocean Drive."

"And whose fault is that?"

"Yours, of course."

A laugh, finally. More of a snort actually. At least it's something.

"You'll never guess which street I absolutely fell in love with . . . ," I continue.

"Shock me."

"Española Way. Do you know it? It's right between—"

"I know exactly where that is, don't worry. Is it all that salmon pink you fell for, or was it the boho jewelry market?" he mocks.

"Neither. Do you think all it takes is a splash of pink and kitschy Virgin Mary earrings to impress me?"

"Absolutely."

"You'd only be half-right."

"Oh, yeah? What else do you like about it?" he teases.

"Why don't you take me out for an iced coffee and I'll tell you."

What if he thinks I'm asking him out?

Am I?

Of course not! I'm married! I kissed his brother! It's totally, completely, utterly out of the question.

"I'm so sorry," I stammer. "I didn't mean that. . . . I mean, yes, it would be really nice to catch up, you know, properly, but that's it," I backtrack.

I bang my head against the scratchy surface of the desk as my foot squeezes further in my mouth. What's the matter with me?

"What do you mean by 'that's it'? What else did you have in mind?"

Thankfully he starts laughing again before I have to think of a way to dig myself out of the mess I'd made of this conversation.

"Why don't we meet up there after work today? Deal?" he offers.

"Only if you're free . . ."

"Don't worry about me, I'm ashamed of myself for not asking you sooner myself. I'll pick you up at five."

I hang up the phone, feeling warm and fuzzy, and like maybe, just maybe, my life wasn't the complete mess it appeared to be most of the time. At least not all of it.

You haven't answered my question yet," Georges says, and licks the back of a spoon dipped in pistachio ice cream enthusiastically.

I smack my hand against my mouth in an attempt to suppress a snort.

"What?" He raises his eyebrows in mock confusion. "Am I bothering you?"

"I've never seen a grown man enjoy ice cream the way you do."

"Let me tell you something." He leans over the wood table, old and splintered, close enough that I can feel the chill of his iced breath. "First of all, this is gelato, not ice cream. Gelato and ice cream exist on different planes of the universe. Don't let me catch you making that mistake again, young lady. And secondly, don't ever let anyone tell you you're too old for pistachio gelato."

"What about chocolate gelato?"

He shakes his head, straining to look exasperated. "Sorry. You clearly have the palate of a six-year-old. I'm not sure we can be friends. It's too bad, you're really nice, but it's important to have standards, you know?"

"Ha! You're lucky I have no standards to speak of; otherwise I wouldn't be here."

"Not bad." He nods approvingly. "Feistiness becomes you."

For the next few moments, we sink into a comfortable silence, him lost in his gelato and his thoughts, while I listen to the sounds of the street all around us, of traffic and waiters clearing tables and cars honking, of backpackers descended from the hacienda-style network of intertwined little buildings that make up the Clay Hotel and Hostel, debating which clubs would be best tonight. The street is a hidden little wonder of kitschy charm, a splash of bubble-gum pink against the concrete gray of surrounding avenues, where Old Seville meets Al Capone. Gaudy red velvet love seats share the cramped space of outdoor cafés with faded teak patio chairs where Georges and I are sprawled, taking a break from sightseeing. In the strip running along the middle of the alley neo-hippies in tie-dyed boho skirts and Jesus sandals are slumped lazily on the sidewalk, chain-smoking, chatting, watching passersby peruse homemade charm bracelets and beaded necklaces.

"I can't believe the Delano is just a few streets away from here. I feel like we're in another world."

"We sort of are. A lot of the people who you find at the Delano lounge on a Friday night wouldn't be caught dead in a place like this."

"Hmm. It's too bad."

"What?"

"I don't know. . . . It's just funny how narrow-minded people can be sometimes. Judgmental."

"Miami's a bit of a see-and-be-seen city, or at least that's what it wants people to think."

"Miami has an opinion of what people think?"

"Of course it does. Cities have personalities, too, you know. Are you going to tell me Miami is just like New York? Or London? Or even Beirut with its beaches and bon vivants?"

"Well, no . . . of course not."

"There you have it. Personality. That's what it is. Miami is like New York's hotter, more fun but shallower cousin."

"And what, may I ask, do you know about Beirut?" I cock an eyebrow.

"What my great-grandfather told my grandfather, who told my father, who passed it on to me." He chuckles.

"So you've never been?"

"No."

"Why not?"

"I don't know. . . . I feel so . . . *removed* from it, you know?"

"So you never feel a pull?"

He sighs and looks away. "I feel something, but I'm not sure I'd describe it as a 'pull' per se. How do you feel pulled toward a place you've never been?"

I drum my fingers on the splintered wood of the table, pondering his words for a moment. I'm not nearly as out of touch with my roots as Georges is, and yet what I feel is so difficult to get a handle on, a whisper of a feeling rather than a full-blown emotion.

"I didn't know it at the time," I say carefully, "but leaving the Middle East behind for good was like having a limb amputated. I can't see it anymore, but the memory of it is always there. . . . It's like an ache, only worse. There's no medication for nostalgia."

"Maybe not," he says without looking me in the eye, "but do you think nostalgia might be casting an overly rosy glow on something that maybe wasn't so rosy, and keeping you from enjoying what you have right now?"

Sure it was rosy! I want to scream. *Don't take away my memories! They're all I have left.*

I think about what it is that I have now, today, in my life. A job, for starters, an honor I couldn't have claimed even a mere month ago. An apartment—sort of. Even if my roommate hates me, even if I had no say whatsoever in its setup, even if nothing in it is mine. Yet it still feels more "mine" than any other place I've ever lived in before.

Then I think about what I don't have—my parents' support, which tugs painfully at my heart every time I'm reminded of it. A loving relationship, something I thought I had with Dodi. And money. I hardly had any of that these days, but what little I do have I'm free to spend as I see fit.

That's something, at least.

"Ready for round two of Big Georges's Miami Tour Bonanza? We'd better get going if we're going to have the best flan this side of Cuba in Calle Ocho, and then dinner at a little hole-in-the-wall Bahamian restaurant I know in Coconut Grove. Let's go, I'm sure you've seen enough of the Beach by now."

"Georges . . ." I swirl my spoon into a lake of goo at the bottom of my bowl that was once ice cream. He's looking at me. The sun is slowly sinking behind him, casting a glow around our little table, coating everything around us in a thick spread of saffron sunlight.

"You want another round of gelato?"

"No."

"What is it then?"

"Why did you hire me and make Zahra take me in?"

"Don't let her get to you—she needs someone in that big place with her. Someone to show her how to lighten up every once in a while."

"Why isn't that someone you?" I bite my bottom lip and smile coyly, hoping it'll take the edge off my freakish intrusion. It isn't any of my business . . . but I like Zahra, in spite of everything. She can yell at me all she wants for falling asleep with all the lights on or sneaking tuna bits to Waleed, but I know she's kind, and considerate of other people's needs. Just maybe not their feelings. Nobody's perfect.

Georges looks like I just proposed he strip down to his boxers and dance a *dabkeh* down the middle of the street.

"What are you talking about?"

"Please . . . Do you really think I'm that blind? Or maybe you're the one who's blind."

He sighs, looking positively deflated.

"There might have been . . . something . . . a long time ago, but it just . . . it didn't happen. That's it. That's the whole story. Seriously."

"Why not?"

"Look, it's a really long story."

"We can skip the flan." I grin.

"Not the flan!"

"Can you be serious for a second?"

"Okay—you want to be serious? Let's be serious then."

Oh, no. He's going to ask me about my past. My family, where I came from, and how I popped up along the banks of his gilded life, all pathetic and street urchin–like, even if we were in one of the swankiest hotels in one of the swankiest cities in the world, not quite the Dickensian backdrop for where you'd normally expect to find the helpless, hopeless, and hapless.

"What *the hell* do you see in my brother?"

What?

"*Excuse me?* What kind of question is that?" What I really want to say is that he had every opportunity to ask me out and never did and why should he suddenly care if Joe's paying attention to me? Besides, if Joe has it in his head that we're a couple, it's not *my* fault, is it? Does one measly, drunken kiss mean we're an item?

I'm shaking with fury and rage and fear and . . . the first twinklings of *hope*?

"Forget it." He's suddenly turned a scary shade of scarlet. "You're absolutely right. I'm sorry I said anything."

"Are you okay?"

"I'm fine. Let's go."

"Go where? What do you *mean*?" I shriek. People look up from beers they're nursing and away from eyes they were gazing into to stare at us. For once I could care less. "I don't have anything going on with Joe. He asked me out to dinner, and we went, and that was it."

Which is more than I can say for you. But I don't say it. I can't say it. To say it would be to release it out into the universe, a place where it would no longer be mine. To say it is to not be able to take it back, and with my family, my situation, with Dodi, I just can't do it.

Not to mention it isn't strictly true nothing happened. Not that it was my fault, but it happened, and I can't take it back. I can only lie about it. Or change the subject.

Suddenly I hate Joe. And Georges. And Dodi. And all of them. Maybe Rio and Zahra had the right idea all along— perfectly content on their own, confident career women that they are. Because just when you start to care, someone tries to jump you in a car and his brother ends up hating you for it, or someone turns out to be gay or some other crazy thing you have absolutely no control over, and then where are you? Maybe it's better to just detach from the whole

thing altogether—understand relationships as the dispos-
able, flimsy things that they are, or else just let your parents
pick for you and wash your hands of the whole mess.

"Ranya, I'm sorry. Really." He reaches for my hand and
holds it for one piercing, heartbreaking second. And then
wrenches his hand away. I want to jump out of my seat and
reach for him, but I can't. If my own inertia weren't enough,
the steadfast look that's crept its way into his eyes bolts me
in place. "You asked me why I helped you. . . ."

My heart lurches. What is he going to say?

"I don't know . . . you have this thing about you that . . .
that sucks people into your orbit, or whatever. . . . I don't
know what I'm saying." He shakes off a laugh and sighs. "I
think you make people want to wrap you up and shield you or
something. I know it's really odd to say, but it didn't feel like I
was doing anything strange at the time. It felt . . . natural."

I'm a little stumped at the confession, not sure how to take
it. I know I've often thought of myself as a little fearful . . .
okay, spineless if you were going to be mean, but I didn't think
I was so . . . *transparent*.

"I didn't need your help," I say too briskly, and notice
the flicker of hurt in his face. Too late.

"I know you didn't. You would have been fine."

Would I?

"It just felt nice to help, and even nicer to be able to
chill out like this from time to time." He pauses. "Joe is my
brother, he's my blood. One thing my mother and father

drilled in our heads our entire lives is that family always comes first. Before money, before . . . women." At this he colors slightly. "But Joe can be a little . . . careless. With work and with his personal life. I'm not saying he's a bad guy. . . . I just know how Arab girls are sometimes—maybe you shouldn't expect a long-term commitment until you guys get to know each other better."

My mouth drops open. *Does he think . . . ?*

I just know how Arab girls are sometimes . . .

I narrow my eyes at him and tilt my head sideways, trying to figure out exactly what to say.

"Do you think I'm some kind . . . of *gold digger*? You think I'm trying to land Joe as a *husband*?" I don't try to contain myself anymore. I burst out laughing and make a grab for my purse.

As if putting up with Zahra's annoyed airs and Rio's complete bitchiness weren't enough, here was Georges calling me a gold digger. *Me.*

I grab my purse and bolt out of the chair. If only he knew.

"Ranya—don't! Shit, that came out all wrong." He runs a hand through his hair, sending the usually smooth blue-black waves jutting out in all directions. "Ranya, sit. *Please.*"

"No." I swing the purse strap over my shoulder. I'm done with men thinking they can tell me what to do. I was done with that the second I stepped on that flight to London.

But even as I spin on my ankle-booted heels, ready to dash off the patio, Georges's words reverberate loudly in my ears.

I just know how Arab girls are sometimes . . .

Of course we're always on the prowl for a husband. In that sense we're no different from most other girls around the world, even the ones who pretend they don't care, or those who say they'll settle down when they find the One.

Funny how criteria for the One seem to shrivel and dwindle as one gets older, evaporating altogether in some cases.

The problem isn't in our hopes—it's in the pressure we pin on the men who are supposed to deliver us our hopes, all ready-made and packaged for us to unwrap. No wonder Georges is cautious. Any girl would kill for one of the Mallouk boys.

Maybe under different circumstances, I might have, too.

Zahra

I fucked up."

Georges is slouching forward on my living room sofa, his head in his hands, and almost on the verge of tears.

I sit farther down, careful not to accidentally rub any part of my body against his, my back upright, my legs crossed primly at the ankles, not having any idea what to do. What do you say to the only man you ever really loved, when he's heartbroken over another woman?

"Where the hell is she?" He falls back hard against the cushions, sighing and looking up at the heavens as if someone up there might hold the answer. His eyes fall on the

portrait of Jesus I have hanging above a console. The decorator had wanted to put a mirror there—so I could give my
makeup a final touch-up, check my clothes are hanging the
right way before walking out, apparently. I let her talk, ideas
spilling out of her like water from a gurgling fountain.
When she left I took my Jesus and put him up where I could
see him, where I could ask him to watch over my family in
life, and Waleed in death.

"She's been spending a lot of time at this little spa on a
street off of Collins, close to the office. I don't know where
it is exactly," I offer meekly.

Ranya had only tried to tell me about her new friend a
half a dozen times. That girl couldn't sit still and quietly for
ten consecutive minutes if her life depended on it. Of course
she might have just been talking nonstop in an effort to
draw me into conversation, as though I were some miserable
charge she took pity on and wanted to help. Even made a
few well-intentioned but ultimately unsuccessful attempts
to improve my fashion sense. I listened. Patiently. And when
she was finished I would tell her about children chained to
workstations who made her precious clothes for a pittance,
of people locked in factories overnight to meet production
quotas, of villages that weren't allowed to collect rainwater
because the rights to water had been acquired by a
monster-sized conglomerate, and did she still think bad fashion was the biggest issue facing the world? Most of the time
she just slunk away, sorry she'd brought it up, but once, she
stood in front of me, thought for a moment, and said, "That's

why it's important that in a world full of ugliness, people still have a right to beauty."

I'll admit she had me surprised. Less at the assertion and more that something halfway intelligent had escaped her lips.

"Have you tried her cell phone?" I say, for lack of a better idea.

"She's not answering."

Georges looks up at me, except not *at* me but *through* me, as though I were a hologram.

Where's the beauty in my *life?* I would ask Ranya if she were here. The poetry, the magic of having someone like Georges love me instead of seeing right through me?

It's not fair.

A noise outside my front door startles us. Georges lifts himself out of his seat, hovering for a few hopeful seconds over the sofa, waiting to hear the lock turn. It doesn't. He sighs again, defeated. False alarm.

"Do you mind if I wait here a little longer?" he asks.

"No."

"Thanks." He sighs, then gets up and lets himself out onto my balcony. I watch him as he leans over the railing and stares out at the calm waters of Biscayne Bay below, ink-blue in the darkness.

Sometimes I wish I knew how to speak to people so they would know I wasn't ice on the inside. I watch them, all of them, Rio, Ranya, my sisters, and I'm in awe of just how they always seem to know what to say, how easily they can chatter on about how they're feeling when every word for me feels like forced labor. I'd chalk it up to a recessive gene, except it's not always this way. I've had my moments. One very notable moment in particular.

I was in Boston, in happier times, my fourth year at Morrison, doing what I loved, even if the hours were brutal and the bosses thankless. Not that it mattered to me—my apartment was a claustrophobia-inducing box, I didn't have any friends beside those activists I was still in touch with from college, and even those few relationships started tapering off.

I'd almost managed to forget about Georges, to move past entire undergrad years spent living for the day—however unlikely—that Georges might see past our pretty, polished classmates, who juggled higher education with landing suitable husbands and perfect grooming, and maybe, just maybe, look at me instead. What I thought he would see in me, I had no clue, but I hoped anyway.

One day he called. Just like that, out of the smoggy city mist. He was in town on business and was hoping we could catch up, have a drink, maybe dinner. I was at work, waiting on some important trade confirmations to come through the fax machine. Sometimes it would take those damn things hours to transmit through Stone Age machines, blipping and bleating like noisy farm animals. Georges was only in town for the night, so I had a choice to make. Sneak off for a couple of hours, or possibly never see Georges again. I decided to come back to the office after dinner. No one would miss me, and the fax machines weren't going any-where.

No matter how much I tried to temper my expecta-tions, something inside me was saddled with the utterly unrealistic idea that if he called me after four long years—years when he ostensibly should have forgotten all about me—then maybe it was okay to still hope.

I took him to Cheers, where we laughed at the cheesi-ness of it all and he told me if I thought that was cheesy, then I should see some of the touristy places in Miami, and drinks turned into a long, slow dinner of king crab legs and clam chowder and lobster rolls, and I joked about how I thought that one meal was going to make up for all the weight I'd lost since I started with Morrison.

He offered to walk me home afterward, and we laughed the whole way there, drunk and cold, and just happy to be alive. We reached the foot of my building and stopped, the easy laughter dissipating with every hot breath we blew out into the frigid air, every shuffle of our feet, each waiting for the other to say something.

"I forgot how cold Boston gets in winter. Geez, how do you live here?" He was the first to break the silence.

"I like it," I blurted unsteadily, the night fading into the fog of intoxication. How much had we drunk? I didn't know. Neither did he. We just laughed and held on to each other to keep from stumbling.

"You look good," he said.

Is he talking to me? I remember thinking. *Or am I just*

drunk and hearing things? So I just burst into another fit of giggles, except this time on my own. He wasn't laughing, and he hadn't let go. Suddenly my fingers weren't freezing anymore, our joined bodies forming a bubble of cozy warmth around us.

And then he kissed me.

Slowly and suddenly at the same time.

No kiss that had come before, not one, had ever felt as right.

Then he said something I'll never forget. "I'm sorry."

"Why?" I asked. "I didn't mind."

He didn't answer, just cast his eyes down at the frozen ground. So I kissed him back. All the way up to my little shoe box of an apartment. We made love on my couch, too lost in the moment to pull the bed out, or to get sheets and pillows. Among the scattered empty containers of Chinese takeout, my big pile of laundry and even bigger pile of books, he gently pulled my thick sweater over my head, kissed my face and neck and shoulders, and made me feel beautiful. As beautiful as Waleed used to when I skipped into his shop, an awkward little girl with knobby knees and scraggly, unkempt hair.

I could have sprouted wings and flown at the moment. Georges was here with me. I was with Georges. Anything was possible.

Which is why the blow hit doubly hard the next day when he explained how what happened was a mistake, how he cared so much about me but didn't think we were right for each other, that he didn't know what had come over him last night and that I was the last person he wanted to hurt.

It wasn't that he was cruel—only that he had no backbone. His mother, a staunch Lebanese Maronite from a long lineage of proud Lebanese Maronites, would have never allowed her eldest son, the man who would take his father's place at the head of the family empire, to be with a Palestinian girl. A poor one at that. Too many massacres had gone down in our histories, too much anger and venom, and Georges didn't have the stuff it took to stand up to it all.

Or maybe I just wasn't worth it.

I lost all the respect I had for him that day, even if my heart still stubbornly clung to its feelings for him, even in the face of abject rejection.

I also lost something else that day.

My job.

I'd never made it back to the office, and the confirmation for an important fax detailing vital trade instructions had come in busy. As in it was never received by the traders on the other end. The stock had plunged in value soon after, with my client still holding a majority share.

And Morrison was out nearly $10 million.

Do you want something to eat? It's just about dinnertime. . . . We could order in if you want." An onlooker might mistake the easy intimacy that's blossomed between Georges and me since that cold Boston night five years ago for an undercurrent of love, or at least affection.

But in reality, what's happened between us is as subtle and ordinary as what happens in the most common of marriages: Time and proximity, responsibilities and routine had snuffed out the last of the stubborn, feeble flames we'd nursed for each other. Once I accepted the position of CFO at Mallouk Enterprises—I had no choice but to get out of Boston and had nowhere else to go—I decided the best way to move forward was to leave what had happened exactly where it belonged: in that dreamlike fantasy place where things happen, or don't happen, when you're drunk and reality eludes you. I met his mother and hated her on the spot, as she hated me. A woman who peppers her speech with French and Italian just because, who makes plain her disgust for those who weren't lucky enough to have been born into money, and who has a thousand and one ways to make you feel small and unworthy. It was clear who Joe took after.

"No thanks, Zee. I think I'm going to head back." Georges gives the balcony railing one last tap for good measure, casts a last forlorn look at the bay, and heads back into the living room.

"I'm such a dick, do you know that?" he blurts suddenly. "Do you know I just about called her a gold digger? I mean, shit . . . *shit!*"

I can't help a little jolt of inner glee. Ranya. A gold digger. If I weren't feeling just a bit bad for Georges's apparent misery, I'd break out in laughter. If only he knew.

He shakes his head and knits his brows, pacing furiously

in front of me as if he was deciding whether or not to punch himself out.

"I told her to watch out for Joe, just in case, you know, he broke her heart or whatever." He cringes at the memory of his words, the whole sorry scene playing out all over his face. "I was just trying to warn her in case she . . . thought maybe he might be serious about her. She just blew up!" Georges looks like he's going to punch a hole in my wall. "All I was trying to do was spare her feelings!"

Like you spared mine?

I don't say that. I couldn't. Not ever.

"Why are you so worried about her?" I manage to whimper.

"Because I like her, Zee, okay? I really like her. I think I more than like her actually. I started to when I first talked to her in London. I thought she would be like all those women I meet all the time, always on the hunt, angling for husband material without the smallest thought as to how much they really cared about the guy behind the suit and the money. You look at her and she's this . . . this little package of perfection and you think how is this girl single? She must be a class A bitch, or at least a snob, but you talk to her and shit, Zahra . . . it's like the more I get to know her, the more I'm convinced she doesn't have an angle. She loves that crappy job I got her at the magazine, and defends both you and Rio even though I know you both treat her like shit."

He pauses for breath as I sit perched on the edge of the sofa, silent as the sea below my window, waiting for this wave of emotion to pass. I haven't heard this kind of anguish in his voice since that day he told me, whimpering and spineless, that we couldn't be together. And here he is all these years later, all these circles round and round, and then back to the same spot. Impotent. A clap of thunder in the deepest depths of the desert where there's no one to hear it.

"You know what else?" He chuckles sardonically. "I saw her first." He hangs his head and then throws it back again. He looks like he might explode. "I did everything I could to help her; I would have done anything."

Except tell her how you feel.

"And Joe swoops in, throws her one of his golden-boy smiles, takes her to a couple of fancy parties, and that's it? Joe, who, ironically, is going to toss her to the curb at the first sign she's getting attached. And then she'll be just like everyone else. Jaded. I know I sound completely pathetic, but . . . it's just not fair."

How funny. My sentiments exactly.

I'm not a bad person. Never set out to hurt anybody. In fact, everything I've ever done I've done selflessly and with conviction. I don't help my parents because I have to; I do it because it's what you do. Everything I did in college, the protests, the activism, the holding out a night-light of hope against the torrential wind of war and fury that took Waleed away—I did it because reaching out was the only way I knew of feeling human.

But what had it done for me? Five years of being Georges's little handmaiden, fed scraps of his attention, not able to stay but terrified to leave—so he could fall in love with a little ray of sunshine who'd never known a day of hardship her entire life?

"I wouldn't worry about Ranya being a gold digger. She's not after Joe."

This time I look him straight in the eye. "She's married, Georges. She's just in Miami to hide out from her husband. She's married."

Ranya

I didn't go home after my fight with Georges. I went to the office. I'd had what they call an "epiphany." Georges's completely mistaken—and yet not surprising—accusation mingled with Priya's heartbreaking words in my head.

Suddenly I didn't want to write a stupid sex column, not least because I didn't have a damn thing to say. I wanted to write about holes. Black holes people like Priya fell into, never to be seen by people like me. I also wanted to write about Georges, and what he'd said.

I just know how Arab girls are sometimes.

It makes my blood boil all over again just to think about

it. I saw myself storming across the street and hopping into the first taxi I saw, all the while a humiliating chorus sounding in my head, playing in a twisted loop, over and over again. *Is this who people think I am?*

Not knowing the truth of my situation, that I was actually just taking time off from a farce of a marriage, were people just assuming that I was out to land the first suitable man who came my way? Is that what I'd been reduced to?

I just know how Arab girls are sometimes.

What? Manipulative? Fearful of going with the flow to see where it takes them? Always thinking ahead instead of being happy in the here and now?

Is that how I ended up marrying Dodi? By keeping my eye on the prize, overlooking all the tiny little details of everyday life and intimacy and connection that might have tipped me off to who he really was?

Why had both Priya and I turned out to be victims, in spite of our phenomenally different worlds? Who was the Great Satan at work here?

The instant I articulated that thought in my mind, the obvious answer sprang to me. It would be too easy to blame religion, or a traditional upbringing, or any of those thorny cultural issues everyone, Middle Easterners and Westerners alike, loved to dance around. There was something else going on, something infinitely more insidious.

I asked the driver to turn around, saying that we'd be going to the *Suéltate* office on Collins Boulevard, South Beach.

And now here I am, on the Saturday evening before my date with Joe, my fingers poised and hovering over the keyboard of my workstation.

The idea is muddled and unclear at first, and then starts taking shape, slowly, like a familiar figure emerging from a careless cluster of clouds. I scribble notes until my joints cramp. I outline, come up with questions, and make lists of names and phone numbers, filling the holes with online searches.

The first name that came to me was Diana Shalhoub. We did our poli-sci undergrad together in Riyadh, and I always thought of that girl as a future UN delegate in the body of a Miss Lebanon contestant. Through the wonders of Google, I find out she became a human rights lawyer, active in the negotiations between Israel and Lebanese detainees.

My stomach in knots, I pick up the phone and dial.

To my amazement, she picks up.

"Diana?"

"Yes?"

"You're not going to believe this, but this is Ranya . . . Ranya Hayek from—"

"Ranya Hayek? Are you serious?" She cuts me off with an eardrum-piercing shriek. "How are you? I can't believe I'm talking to you after all this time. . . ."

We chat about everything and nothing, catching up on everything we'd done since our school days. Unsurprisingly, Diana has a lot more to say than I do. On top of being a female attorney in a tough, macho field, she's also a mom to twin girls. When I think I've summoned up enough courage, I ask her the big one: Is she happy with the way her life turned out?

It would seem that at least in Diana's case, she is. Her line of work has its debilitating frustrations, moments of powerlessness and despair, but overall she's proud and supported in everything she has done. I tell her about my project and she congratulates me, saying the time is ripe for such a thing, that people needed to take the spectacles of bias off of their eyes and see things for what they really were. The good, the bad, and the ugly.

She gives me the names and numbers of classmates she'd kept in touch with, and friends she thinks I should talk to. She even promises to e-mail me a picture of herself in her office.

By nightfall I have over a dozen promising leads and the skeleton of a real story.

Rio

"They call this steak? Your mother should teach them how to cook." My father doesn't speak. He grunts. "How much are you paying for this?"

"It's okay, *papi,* how often do we get to see you and *mami*?" Always the smooth talker, my baby bro. The same baby bro who's now a strapping six feet, three inches of lean, lanky muscle and who makes more heads turn than I do in my tiniest tube top and hoochie-mama jeans. How did he end up with all the hotness genes in the family? Sigh. The Universe has been colluding against me since the day it put me on the losing side of the great DNA divide.

"Did you know I once almost ran into Gloria Estefan on the street just outside of here?" he continues, in between scoops of gooey guacamole with the greasiest tortilla chips this side of a mechanic's work rag.

"*Ah, ¿sí?*" My father cocks an eyebrow, impressed, while I roll my eyes. Why do they always have to act like such *montunos,* my parents? People evolve, their tastes refine and their experiences expand; my parents regress. I expect they will forget how to use a touch-tone phone any day now. And let's not talk about computers. What do you expect from people who think Gloria Estefan is royalty?

I look at my watch. Luckily we're not big talkers in this family, so I don't foresee I'll be in this hell much longer. And tomorrow, they go back to Honduras, where they retired to the same little house my father and his brothers built before I was even born. Under-the-table laborers don't get a pension, you see, and a dollar goes a lot further in the Third World than it does over here. Not that they lost too much sleep over the move back—I suspect the Vargases had had their fill of the American Dream, thankyouverymuch, and were ready to enjoy what was left of their lives in peace, or if not enjoy, then at least not risk a stroke wondering if they'd be able to make next month's rent. But a small part of America's spell on them must still linger in their hearts—at least that part of them that had learned to worship at the altar of the Mall—and so they still come up here once a year to indulge a little, and to make sure their kids aren't dead.

Rafa and I had a fight over where to take them on their one night out on the town. (*Papi* still thinks it's a waste of money, even when someone else is paying. Don't ask him if he thinks betting on dogfights in the slums of La Ceiba qualifies as a waste of money, though.) I was pulling for Karu&Y, *the* place to be in Miami right now. It seemed only celestial connections and sneaking off into a darkened alley with a member of the velvet-rope mafia could get you in. That or promising the owner a profile in the next issue of your magazine. The owner being none other than the totally delectable Cesar Sotomayor, Brazilian-born, European-bred polyglot (he can speak five languages, *chica, five*) son of a diplomat. And surely gay. He has to be. But then again, maybe not—Joe isn't. And from what I'd heard of the ex-pilot-turned-restaurateur, he's like a Brazilian clone of the current fickle-minded man-whore asswipe who shall no longer be named. It might be a little difficult working with the guy if I won't let myself say his name anymore, though. Thankfully, it really looks like he's just about had it with "running" a magazine (as if) and might be ready to jet off to Europe, or Argentina, or something.

Maybe with Ranya in tow, the lovely, ice-queen arm candy, the two of them cutting the figure of the most exquisite couple since Brangelina. So what if the girl looks like she'd be as imaginative in bed as your average celery stalk? That's not why he'd marry her. Just like Latinos, these *árabes*. Fuck the whores, marry the Madonnas.

Ay, just the thought of them together is making the sour cream in my disgusting chimichanga rise in my throat. However, considering this fine establishment we're dining at tonight, it's probably just the sour cream that's to blame.

Rafa had suggested Chili's. He said Dad's eyeballs might pop out of their sockets after one look at a menu where one *amuse-bouche* cost more than an entire meal in Honduras. A meal that would feed sixteen. I said that's just because the appetizer in question happened to be octopus carpaccio marinated in white truffle oil and served with lemon sorbet and micro lemongrass.

Then Rafa told me to get off my high horse and that I should know better than to talk white truffle oil and octopus carpaccio with someone who still remembers me playing with cheap plastic dolls dressed in old kitchen rags, and who'd shared a beat-up mattress with me back in the olden days when one room in a house was enough and two were a luxury.

I told him to go fuck himself.

Little brothers can be so exasperating.

But not as exasperating as parents who still talked to you like you were five and were oblivious to the fact that now, as an adult, you could see right through them.

Like how Dad wasn't always away when you were growing up shit poor because he was working hard to put rice and beans on the table but actually gambling a big percentage of that rice-and-beans money away. And that kid down the street who'd call you *hermanita* from afar before your mother shooed you away, a pissed-off look on her face, and told you not to talk to "that filth," that kid really was your bastard half brother. Apparently there were a few of them around town, but you didn't know that when you were five.

"What did the doctor say?" Rafa tries to catch Mom's eye to discern the truth. Because what comes out of that woman's mouth seldom is. It's not her fault, though. Life had dealt her a rough hand. Some women got a decent childhood, a cozy home, a somewhat loving husband, and at least one daughter who wasn't a complete and utter disappointment.

Mami got none of that, a fact she made sure to allude to every chance she got. But for all her failings, she had a good head on her shoulders, my *mami*. Instead of allowing my father to sneak into the States as an illegal fruit picker, or sidewalk paver, or high school janitor, or doing whatever the hell work he could get, and send back a pittance for his family to live on—if he sent anything back at all, that is—she summoned the little bit of backbone she still had in her after a lifetime of neglect and told *papi* off good. He could do whatever he wanted, but he couldn't break up the family. So off we went—me seven, Rafael four, and my parents. She even applied us for citizenship and everything, and we were lucky enough to get it. The fact that we were legal immigrants didn't make much of a difference on the playground, or anywhere else to be perfectly honest, we were still spics, weren't we? But we got used to it. We bonded with the rest of the illegals, but even that relationship wasn't too cozy—kids aren't stupid. They can piece together the concepts of "legal" and "illegal." The parts that matter, anyway. Not that I let that bother me too much. Because I was going places. And when I got there I wouldn't turn my back on *mi gente* like so many of my pseudocolleagues did. I wasn't going to pretend there was something better about me just because I'd been fortunate enough to slip through the politico crap and be deemed "legal." As if there could ever be such a thing as an "illegal" human being.

Please.

"There's nothing wrong with me, Rafaíto, *mi corazón*." She taps the back of his hand warmly, with that wistful look in her eye she gets when a Julio Iglesias song plays on the kitchen radio. "It was just a cyst, *mi vida,* nothing to worry about."

"Thank God for that," Rafa says, then glares at me as I continue to pick at the unidentifiable goo in front of me.

I just shrug in response. What—you expect me to play nice? After everything these people put me through? I had to fight—*fight, chica*—to be allowed to go to college. Not to mention pay every bit of the way. "What does a woman need with a college education?" *papi* would say when I talked about my dream of starting my own magazine one day. Right after he nearly laughed himself into a heart attack at the notion that a tiny little *hondureña* from a backwater shantytown with dark skin and a bad attitude would make it in a white man's world.

"This is America," I would reply, arms crossed across my sprouting chest, a hip jutted defiantly.

"There are two Americas, *m'hija*," he would say, in the few and far between tender moments when he would dignify my feeble hopes with an answer. "The one for people with money, and the one for people without money. Guess which one you're from, huh?"

Then he would say something about how money talks and

shit walks, and chuckle at his own stupid joke while my mother glared at him from the corners of her eyes, eyes that seemed to see through the back of her head sometimes but curiously chose to look past my father's multiple indiscretions.

Now I ask you, what do I owe these people?

"Will you be bringing a boy with you this year for *la navidad*?" my mother says kindly, wanting to dispel the awkwardness that often falls upon forced family gatherings, as mothers always do.

"No, *mamá*."

Another long silence, with a sound track of clanging forks and slurpy sips, and slicing of knives through fatty meat. Maybe that's why food and culture are so intertwined. How would family members not kill each other if food weren't involved? Even Chili's did the trick.

I haven't brought anyone to have Christmas dinner with my family for nine years. The woman has patience, you've got to give her that much. You must, I guess, to stay married to my father for nearly forty years. Who would I bring any-way? Joe? Ha! I can just see it—Joe's Alfa Romeo saddling up coolly to . . . Chili's.

Or the delicious *tigre* from the bar . . . double ha. Of course he'd have to cab it here, as his busboy salary doesn't leave enough on the side for something as luxurious as a car.

But my parents couldn't care less who I settled with as long as I settled and was off their conscience once and for all, but I wouldn't want to inflate the poor boy's hopes more than I already have.

He's delicious; did I mention that? Long, thick, curved-ever-so-sexily-at-the-ends black lashes. I say this because I've watched him sleep and couldn't help but notice. Just once, *chica,* don't get all excited. It's just that I haven't had a man actually sleep in my bed since . . . well, since ever. Plenty of men had stopped over for a quick tête-à-tête with my 400-thread-count Indian sheets over the years, but none cozied up to them.

Adam might have, one day, if he'd made it past the dating me when I was seventeen stage, when I finally had the cash to move out. But one fine morning on the eve of my seventeenth birthday, he had to knock me up.

And a month later when I found out, I was a mess. Panic at what *papi* would do to me set in, with the added despair of having lost my one opportunity of crawling out of poverty, and the emotional black hole of watching my life blowing up before my eyes in an inferno of thwarted dreams.

And yet feeling strangely maternal about the whole mess, thinking about how I loved Adam with my whole entire heart, and would it be so bad if we had a baby, and what would be the best way to tell him.

I never got the chance to. He broke it off a couple of days after I'd found out. We had been going together for a year, my senior year at high school, and it was prom time. His mother was beside herself at the thought of her son taking a shiksa—a poor, Hispanic shiksa no less—to the prom, when there were at least a half a dozen suitable Jewish girls at the corner synagogue.

That's right. My Adam was a Lifstein. He was also lean
and lanky and disheveled with that preppy cool look of an
Abercrombie & Fitch model, and he constantly spouted nonsense, which I bought by the bushel, about Simón Bolívar and
José Martí and the Peace Corps and how he'd love to take a
motorcycle—Che Guevara–style—across the Americas and
connect with people, the real people of the Earth, not the
airbrushed variety who roamed the streets of his affluent,
mostly Jewish, Miami neighborhood. And when Adam was
introduced to a distant cousin visiting from Israel, with long
dark lashes like my *tigre,* and creamy white skin and black hair
down to there, it seemed he thought Mom might be right.

I don't know if he eventually married his Israeli Snow
White, because after high school I never saw him again. I
told *mamá,* who cried and agreed we wouldn't tell *papi.* That
much I owed the woman. She'd loved Adam, though, with
all her heart, and so took the news especially hard.

Poor Mom. A ruined woman for a daughter, and a phi-
landerer for a husband. Can you blame her for loving the
hell out of Rafa? He's the only normal one in the family. A
software engineer with the same girlfriend for three years
and who I'm reasonably sure he's not cheating on. Nothing
at all like *papi,* my Rafa—maybe that's why Ma loves him so
much. She's a pretty little thing, too, this girlfriend. All
shiny blond and button-nosed, and wears horn-rimmed
glasses and off-white Uggs, presumably to give herself the
look of intellect and depth, like she's above consumerism or

whatever. I wonder what she'd say if I told her those hideous boots cost more than what my dad used to make in a week working under the table at the Miami docks.

"Adam sent me a Facebook message this week, Ma. *¿Imagínate?*"

Why not tell her? There's nothing else to talk about, and frankly, keeping the leftover shards of hurt and pain inside is getting to be too much. Maybe saying his name out loud might help. Rafa and *papi* don't know about the *incident*. It's okay.

She nearly drops her fork on the floor.

I can tell she's not quite sure what to make of this "Facebook" thing but that getting Adam's message is somehow momentous—like getting a phone call out of the blue, or having a long-lost loved one drop by. She also knows that when people pop back into your life for whatever reason, it's not always to declare their undying love for you, or to admit they tried to move on but simply couldn't—so she's predictably cautious in her enthusiasm, weighing her words carefully. But eyes don't lie. And hers are on fire.

¿Verdad?

"Yup. I kid you not. And Facebook is like e-mail, Ma."

"*Ah, bueno.*"

"What did he say?" she adds in Spanish, ever the hopeful one.

"That he has a wife and three kids, and wants to get together for playdates." I take a big bite out of what's left of the chimichanga.

I don't add that Adam mentioned his wife had left him.

I'm not exactly interested in becoming his go-to whore a second time around.

I wish I could see past the hurt look in my mother's eyes. Like somehow Adam's being a family man these days is somehow my fault. Or maybe a part of her thinks that if I hadn't gone out and got rid of the *thing*—I refuse to call it a baby—if I'd considered keeping it, *papi*'s wrath notwithstanding, then maybe now, at thirty-one, my life would not be a totality of failure. Women live for their kids, God knows she did, but no one, at least not anyone human, lives for their magazine.

I don't know why I do this to her; honestly I don't. What's worse is I have no idea what I could possibly do to make up for it.

"Rio? Rosario Vargas? Is that really you?"

Oh, no. Of all the depressing, cookie-cutter "family" restaurants in all the districts in all of Florida, she walks into mine.

"Wait—let me check to see if it's actually snowing in Miami, because after this I'll believe anything! Rio Vargas having dinner at Chili's. I'll be damned, *chica*."

Veronica. My size-zero, auburn-haired whip-sharp nemesis.

"You're here, too," I say in between the limpest, fakest handshake since Yitzhak Rabin met Yasir Arafat.

"That's because I have three kids, darling." She waves at them with her pointy chin. "These lovely people must be Mr. and Mrs. Vargas? And this . . . ." Her gaze falls upon the chiseled profile of Rafael's face, even more handsome with the scruffy five o'clock shadow and neat but longish sideburns.

"My brother, Rafa."

"Encantada." She looks him up and down like he was made out of solid Swiss chocolate. *Salivating.* I don't know why, but this gives me a tiny little jolt of smugness, as if I had anything to do whatsoever with Rafa's superior genes.

She greets my mother, who peers at her through a veil of shyness, awed as I'm sure she is by such polish as only the filthy rich can afford. A kind of gleam that shines through the ordinary and the banal. A Patrick Cox stiletto lost in a bin of Payless pumps.

At my father Veronica only nods curtly, and honestly I can't blame her, busy as he is at picking a piece of leftover mashed-up food stuck in his dental work and ogling her breasts as though they were coming up right after dessert. Can't take him anywhere, that man. For the thousandth time this evening, I thank my lucky stars for Rafa.

"So—what's your game plan?" Veronica says to me in a hushed tone, surveying the room as though someone might be watching. In Chili's? Are the diet pills messing with her head?

"If you're interested, we're always looking for talent at *María Mercedes.*" She winks—fakely, of course, which is the only way she knows how.

"What are you talking about?" I make no similar pretense at discretion as one of her tots starts pulling at her beige sweater set.

"*Ohmigod*—you don't know?" Her "oh my God" comes out in one unbroken breath. My stomach lurches a tiny bit. With that much glee in her wicked little face, it can't be anything good.

"No—what?"

"*Suéltate*'s been bought off." Most people might be a little uncomfortable with delivering bad news. Veronica, on the other hand, can barely hide her glee at being the bearer of ill tidings.

"It's being talked about as a possibility," I correct her, "but no decisions are being made before the redesigned issue comes out."

She pauses, as though weighing her words for maximum pulverizing effect.

"I'm afraid not, *m'hija*." She lays a hand on my arm. "One of the major media conglomerates," she leans in and whispers the name into my ear, "just made the announcement this afternoon. . . . They must have made a phenomenal offer for the deal to have gone down so quickly. . . ."

And there it is again. The swooping slice of impending loss.

I couldn't have felt it more if I was reliving that awful day all over again—the day they told me to lie back, lift my legs, and relax, and that it would be over in a minute. Except that it wasn't. I carried the emptiness of loss with me for years, nearly caving into its black depths. I'd barely made it out with a shred of self-worth and hope, and now what was left of me might be gone. For good.

Ranya

Dinner was lovely, and Joe well behaved. Which is great, seeing as I'm planning on telling him I don't ever want to see him anymore.

Here I thought I was indulging in some innocent fun, going on a real date for once in my life, a date with no strings attached, and what do I get? A man who unilaterally decides I'm his girlfriend. That's even how he introduced me to the dashing Cesar Sotomayor, a Brazilian son of a diplomat turned restaurateur. He'd started out at the ticket counter of Brazil's national carrier, earned a pilot's license, and somehow gotten it in his head that he wanted to launch splashy, fabulous "restaurant concepts," as opposed to mere places where people get together and eat. In other words, a guy right up Joe's alley. The two of them took off like a house on fire. Before dinner we toured the venue, which, to be honest, was more like a resort than a restaurant—dining areas festooned with gigantic, dripping-icicle-effect chandeliers, illuminated by a ferocious light play of reds and oranges and blues and greens, an "ultralounge" that I can only describe as Cubism meets Africa meets Paris Hilton, and a garden that boasted private wooden cabanas separated by little rivers—*rivers!* Georges hadn't been kidding about Miami's "unique personality."

In spite of the pretentiousness of the place and the food, I had fun playing Pretty Woman to Joe's dashing businessman. Cesar had a date, too, a Slovakian model, tall, dark, and not terribly interesting, which brought down the little bud of awe that burgeoned in me for this larger-than-life being after hearing Joe talk about him in the car. Still—I think he'd make an excellent profile for the magazine. I make a mental note to tell Rio about him.

"Listen, do you mind if we stop somewhere, love," Joe says on the drive home. "There's someone I'd like you to meet."

"Ugh—no, please, Joe. I'm exhausted." Plus I still had a few surreptitious phone calls to make, to faraway places in different time zones, and I had to stay up to make sure I caught them.

"It won't take long, I promise." He casts me a mock-pleading look that really becomes him. What had he convinced women to do over the years with that face?

"Does it really have to be tonight?" I say.

"No—but it would mean a lot to me."

Uh-oh. Maybe it would be a good idea to do this and then corner him for a "chat." The faster I put an end to this charade, the sooner I can start worrying about confronting Dodi and my family.

"Fine. Where are we going?"

"It's a surprise, but I'll give you a hint: I've never brought a woman here before. Ever."

My stomach lurches. What is he going to do to me? Is being here with him even safe? I quickly shake the negative thinking out of my head—this is Joe, Georges's brother, my boss's boss. He wouldn't be stupid enough to try anything again. And if he did, Georges would kill him.

Would he?

Where had that thought come from? I can't believe it—after everything I'd gone through, I was still unconsciously counting on a man to rescue me from my problems. Am I ever going to learn?

We drive on the expressway a while longer, and Joe eventually exits onto yet another Miami road running alongside the water. At first there isn't much to see, it's dark anyway, but houses start coming into view. Big houses. *Enormous* houses. More like estates. All Mediterranean-style and sprawling.

We wind around a few of these roads before Joe pulls

into what has to be the biggest driveway I've ever seen—two other cars, a Land Rover and a vintage Mustang, already lined up in it.

"Good. Fadi and Mike are home." He slaps my thigh playfully while I gape at him, to the house, and back at him again.

"Why are we here?" I blurt out.

"I want you to meet my mother."

"But I'm not . . . but I wasn't—"

"You look beautiful." He kisses my cheek with unusual, almost brotherly, tenderness, steps out of the car, and ambles over to my side, letting me out.

I am a jumbled mess of nerves when we cross the lavish gardens leading up to the porch. He rings the doorbell and a petite woman with a blond bob and severe features that remind me of Botoxed actresses opens the door.

The resemblance between them is striking—there's no doubt I am standing in front of Mrs. Mallouk.

For some reason I was expecting a butler.

"Good evening," I gush, already thinking of ways I could kill Joe for the ambush later on. "I'm really sorry to bother you at this hour."

"Bother me?" She leans over and wraps me in a hug. "I've been waiting to meet this wonderful girl Joseph has been going on about these past weeks."

I giggle nervously. What has Joe been saying about me?

"*Entrez, entrez!* Come in." She hurries us inside. "It's getting chilly out there."

The house is as impressive on the inside as it is from outside, all sprawling spaces and winding marble staircases, and yet oddly Lebanese. I follow Joe's mother, who introduces herself as Mylène, to the living room. And there it is—over the mantel is an oil portrait done up in the Arabic style of a man I presume is Joe's father. On the mantel itself is a gaudy shrine to the Virgin Mary, somewhat incongruous with the cold, straight-out-of-a-magazine décor of the rest of the living room.

We sit down, a young woman in a neat white-and-blue-striped uniform brings us miniature silver cups of tar black Turkish coffee, and Mylène starts asking me how I'm enjoying Miami.

"How long will you be here, *chérie*?"

"I . . . I'm not sure, auntie," I stutter, fumbling to come up with a halfway believable story.

I glare at Joe as the maid serves us dates and tea biscuits from an antique bronze tray. He responds with a peck on my nose.

"And what did you used to do in . . . Montreal, is it? Oh, that's such a romantic city! The Paris of North America. I was just up there last year visiting some old friends. We stayed at the Château Versailles . . . lovely place. Do you know it?"

"Yes, of course. I have a friend who threw her wedding reception there. So much more quaint and understated than the Ritz."

I latch on to that in the hopes it might distract Mylène

from her original line of questioning. Thankfully, her eyes light up at the mention of the Ritz.

"You're absolutely right, *ma chère,* the Ritz has gotten so . . . pedestrian, so . . . *vulgar,* lately, hasn't it? With all these nouveaux riches everywhere it's hard to know where to go anymore. Joseph—remember Grand Cayman?"

She clutches at her age-spotted chest. "We'd gone there with Georges to celebrate the building of a Mallouk shopping plaza, you see." Mylène leans over conspiratorially to my side. "We ended up staying in our suite most of the time for fear of braving the locals in the lobby night after night. It seems they'd let anybody in with enough money for a cocktail. Honestly. I don't think the Montreal Ritz is any better, what with those tasteless weddings they keep hosting there."

I'm not sure how to tell her my wedding had been one of those "tasteless" affairs she seems so distressed by, so I say nothing and smile instead.

"Tell your friend she has wonderful taste picking the Château." She winks.

"Montreal is lovely, great food and friendly people and all that, but Miami is just stunning! And the weather . . . it's heaven." I am anxious to move away from the Montreal topic and anything even remotely associated with it. Maybe I could ply Mylène with some talk about the latest protests in France I'd just read about this morning and how the French president should just forget about negotiations and pull out the water cannons instead. That ought to get her excited. I look from her, to her late husband's somber face on the wall, to Joe, who has yet to color even slightly at the absurdity of his mother, and wonder how Georges managed to be born out of this family.

"I'm glad you like it so much, dear, maybe it'll persuade you to stay instead of whisking Joe away from us."

What?

I ask about the portrait of the balding man above the mantel, with his steely, austere airs and droopy jowls. "That must be Mr. Mallouk."

"Georges Senior." Mylène nods wistfully. "He's the one who took his father's little supermarket chain and turned it into what it is today. Then he left us, much, much too early."

"I'm sorry." I pat her shoulder gently, thinking of what I'd do with my "aunties" back home.

She seems to appreciate it, taking my hand in return. *"Merci, ma chère."*

She takes a sip from the scalding little bronze cup on the coffee table. "Left Georges at the head of it, with a strict will that everything would always stay in the family. And he's done a wonderful job, really, for someone who's had to take on so much responsibility so young."

"Really?" I ask, suddenly very curious. "How old was Georges when Mr. Mallouk . . . passed away?"

"Barely twenty-one. I used to call him the boy-king." She laughs throatily, the garish rings on her long, withered fingers reflecting a confetti of shadows on the walls. "It wasn't easy for anybody, but it was particularly hard on

Georges. He was still a boy, his head full of silliness, like going off to Berkeley and vagabonding around Europe and Latin America like a penniless pauper—imagine, with his means. I just didn't understand it. But when his father passed on, well, he couldn't just entrust our livelihood to the hands of strangers. What if they made off with everything we had? My husband didn't trust many people in his lifetime, so Georgie didn't have much support, I'm afraid. He had no choice."

"Didn't any one of his brothers want that job?" I sneak a nasty glare in Joe's direction.

"Fadi was adamant about going into politics—not to mention he was twenty at the time and not in a much better position to head up a company than Georges was. Colette wasn't interested, and Michael and Joseph were just kids."

I hang my head filled with so much sadness. Life seemed so unfair all of a sudden—anyone who'd ever deserved good things just seemed to get the short end of the happiness stick time and time again.

"But Georges has a business degree from MIT. How did he manage?"

"Once he'd gotten in and learned the ropes, stabilized the company and put a few people he trusted in positions where they could watch over things for him, he did go back to finish his undergraduate degree. I think he was always a little bit ashamed around all these important, educated types with MBAs and CPAs and all sorts of other qualifications, when he hadn't even finished college. But he did, eventually."

I want to ask her how many passions had been crushed by this burden of responsibility, how many relationships had fallen by the wayside so he could pull together a family in crisis. And how much this family had appreciated the sacrifice it had exacted. Did they even know, Joe, the sister, the other brothers, even Mylène herself? Maybe she was happy to leave the fixing and the coping to her eldest, afraid reality might let the air out of her bubble of cushy lifestyle, and secure in the knowledge she had four other children to lavish her motherly attention on. *What did Georges get out of all of this?* I would like to ask her.

"Anyway," she turns to Joe after a contemplative silence, "aren't you going to show Ranya the rest of the house?"

I now understand why none of these Mallouk boys mind living at home with their mother. If you wanted to, you could spend months in the labyrinth of wings and "bachelors" and guesthouses and cabanas that make up the sprawling estate. Joe points out his brother Fadi's "room," which is to say palm-tree-shrouded cabana with a private terrace complete with daybed and personalized landscaping.

Around another bend stands a flamingo pink structure that—predictably—belonged to his sister, Colette, before she married and moved out. We also pass by Georges's little bachelor and my heart lurches at the off-chance that he might catch me sneaking around with his brother. I have to leave.

"Why did you bring me here?" I ask Joe when we finally make it to his corner of the compound, a studio cottage facing the pool and done entirely in spotless, clean white. The carpet, the leather daybed for two, and his gigantic king-size bed and what looks like a flattened polar bear resting atop the snow-white duvet.

"Can I get you some champagne?"

I see a dark green bottle rimmed with shiny gold paper chilling in a silver-plated ice bucket in the corner of the room. This is starting to feel eerily like a setup.

"No. Joe, seriously, why am I here?"

"Why wouldn't I bring you here? I'm serious about you, Ranya."

"That's the thing, I'm—"

Before I have a chance to finish, his lips are on mine, his hands holding my face in the most tender of kisses. I close my eyes for a second—just one second—and wonder if this might be what it's like to kiss Georges. But this isn't him.

"Get off me!" I shove Joe back with all the strength I can manage.

"That was too fast—I'm sorry."

"You should be!" I fume. "I can't believe you'd do that again after what happened in your car the last time!"

"I know, I know . . . that's just it."

"That's just what?"

"Ranya." He traps my face between his strong hands again. "Ranya." His breath is hot against my lips. "I'm not messing around here. I want to marry you."

Oh. My. God.

"Joe . . . wait . . . wait a second."

"I know this is fast, but I also know you're not the kind of girl you screw around with. I knew that from the first time I tried to kiss you—I couldn't believe how adamant you were. . . . You looked like you were going to kill me!"

That's because I was.

As I look at Joe's beseeching face, a little ping goes off in my brain.

Why am I getting a creeping sense of déjà vu?

"You barely know me," I say cautiously. "How do you know you love me?"

He chuckles cynically at this. "Come on, Ranya. That I would have expected from one of these foreign girls, these *ajaaneb.* Not from you."

"And what's that supposed to mean?" I pull away violently, scanning the room for something to hit him with. Something hard. But the room is spotless and utterly devoid of clutter.

Damn minimalism.

"Nothing—just that marriage is about more than just love. For God's sake, don't act like you're all shocked and innocent. Look—I like you. A lot. You're beautiful, and sexy, and I love the way you get all worked up and angry over things, and you were so great with my mom. A real lady."

Great with his mom. He likes how I get worked up over "things."

"What things?"

"Huh?"

"What things do I get worked up over?"

"Fucking Christ, Ranya. I don't know . . . this is supposed to be a romantic moment here, you want me to give you specific examples?"

Yes. Yes, I do.

The Madonna and the whore. He figured I am the former of the two.

Just like Dodi had. I could be his pristine little Madonna, a nice face to put out to the world, while he went whoring around with my decorator. Very convenient. And I was only too happy to oblige.

"Joe, you're nothing but a—"

A ring. A huge, massive, loose-chuck-of-meteorite-size rock of a diamond, princess cut, and sitting atop a stunningly simple platinum band. Just like my old ring.

I gasp. I can't help it. I don't care who you are, big shiny objects will do that to you. Big shiny objects being offered to you, just like that. And everything that goes along with them. Home. Stability. Never having to show up to a wedding or a funeral or a movie by yourself ever again. Saturday nights at fancy restaurants, summers in Italy or Spain or Buenos Aires. It's all right there in that gigantic little piece of shiny mineral.

"I'm married, Joe. I can't marry you, even if I wanted to, because I'm already married."

I'm looking at his feet when I say it, but when a moment passes by and he still hasn't said anything, I look up.

He has one of those half-grinning, half-frowning frozen

faces on, the kind you get when you suspect you might be the victim of a practical joke but aren't quite sure.

"That's fucking hilarious, Ranya. Is it the best you can do?"

"I'm serious."

I stare straight into his icy blue eyes with all the self-possession I can muster—not very easy when the man in front of you is taking on the look of a wild animal as you're watching him. He grips the edge of the mantel above his fake fireplace, his knuckles turning as white as the walls around us. He runs his other hand over his face, and I start to bite the corners of my lips, tasting what's left of my lipstick, running my tongue back and forth over the fragrant artificial flavor. He turns away from me and starts pacing.

I really need to get out of here.

Taking an audible breath, I start to move toward the door but cower down to the floor at the sound of something smashing just beside my head, my hands held tight against my ears, bits of broken champagne glass dust sprinkling over my hair.

"What's the matter with you?" I hear my own voice, barely above a whisper. I'm shaking. This isn't altogether un-familiar.

"The matter with me? *Me?*" he spits.

I want to crawl toward the front door, but he's blocking it, so I back into the corner instead. Where is everybody? Can't anyone hear him? Of course not. This place isn't enormous for nothing.

"You fucking two-timed me!"

Smash.

The second glass shatters several feet away from me—far enough that I know it wasn't aimed at me, but loud enough that I am shaking anyway.

Why is it that the worst liars are the ones who react the most terribly to being lied to in return?

I get up slowly, still shaking, but trying to get a grip.

"Joe," I say steadily, "that's enough. I'm leaving."

He actually looks ashen, remorseful.

"I'm sorry," he says as I try to get past. "I totally over-reacted. I was never going to hurt you. I would never hurt you, Ranya, seriously; *look at me!*"

He grabs my arm mid-bicep. Hard.

"Oww!"

"I'm sorry! I'm sorry. . . . Look, don't go, please."

"What is there left to say?" I try to break free.

"You can't be too happy if you're here . . . without him."

"That's none of your business."

"Ranya . . ."

His breath is hot on my face. Still smelling faintly of alcohol—what I'm not sure. Whiskey? Cognac? I can't remember what he drank at dinner tonight. I don't want to remember. I want to get out of here.

"Let me *go!*" I scream, and yank my hand away as violently as I can. The jolt of energy sends me careening back, hitting the wall with a loud, hollow bang.

The sobs start coming, fast and strong and unexpected. I can't see in front of me for the tears welling in my eyes and streaming down my cheeks in weak, fluid streams.

"What do you want from me? Why can't you just leave me alone?"

"What the hell is going on here . . . Joe?"

I lift my face, swollen pink and mascara stained.

Georges.

"What's going on?" He blinks wildly, as if not quite believing the images his eyes are projecting against the walls of his mind.

"Georges . . . ," I mutter feebly, and fly into his arms.

He holds me for one brief second, then tears past me, toward Joe.

"Look, it's not—"

Before Joe can say another word, Georges's fist smacks him square in the jaw. He falls back, knocking the ice bucket and champagne bottle in a wet, cold stain against the snow-white carpet, fading outward into wet, widening shadows of moisture.

Georges and I stand frozen in shock, the room quiet except for the croaking of cicadas and the heavy sound of our bewildered breaths.

"I'm bleeding, you asshole."

Scattered drops of red mingle with the dampness of spilled water on the carpet.

"Come, I'll take you home." Georges speaks to me without looking my way.

I scurry out the door and down the stony landscaped path, the comforting sounds of Georges's footsteps close behind me.

I don't look back, even though I know this is the first and last time I would ever get to see the Mallouk family home.

Thank you," I say, mostly to dispel the awkwardness that had descended upon us when we'd climbed into Georges's jet-black Audi. "But it really wasn't as bad as it looked."

He keeps his eyes focused straight ahead, at a point in the distance I can't see.

"I think he just got a little angry when, when . . ." I can't even bring myself to tell him. It's ridiculous enough that Joe could've gotten it in his head to propose, but to talk about it would be dignifying it. I'd rather just pretend it never happened, and after tonight I'm sure Joe will feel exactly the same way.

Still, Georges is as impassive as the hot, wet night engulfing us.

"I think maybe he thought . . . I felt a certain way . . . and was a little surprised when—"

"When were you going to tell me?"

His voice is steady, his eyes still fixed on the road, darting from turning signals to blind spots as if he hadn't just sent the dull hum of the car engine, the pine-scented, buttery cream leather interior, spinning all around me.

"Tell you what?"

How much did he overhear?

"Ranya." This time he looks at me, eyes brimming with . . . what? Disappointment? Sadness? Pain? It's not possible. "I know."

"I didn't mean . . ."

"You didn't mean not to tell me you're married?"

"No. That's not it. It's complicated." I'm aware of the hollowness of my words. "I was going to tell you the next time I saw you, but—"

"You don't owe me an explanation, Ranya. Don't worry about it."

No! Not like this!

"You're okay, right? Joe didn't . . . He didn't do anything . . . too bad, did he?"

"No, no, not at all." I can't look at him. If I do, I will lose it, and I've made enough of a fool out of myself for one night.

I say nothing for the rest of the short car ride. Neither does Georges.

Eventually he swerves off the highway, and suddenly we're double-parked in front of Zahra's building, the uniformed doorman already rushing to my side.

This is it? Is that all he's going to say?

The doorman is holding a hand out to me. I reach for it and swing one sandaled foot onto the gray asphalt.

"I'm really sorry." His hand barely skims the edge of my shoulder and yet I feel my entire body flush with heat.

What would have happened if I hadn't lied about Dodi? If I'd told Joe I wasn't interested right from the start? If I'd been honest with myself that I'd finally begun to understand what it was to fall in love with someone slowly, with your heart, not with your mind, because you admired a person for who they were, not what they could do for your life?

"Ranya." He stares down at the steering wheel.

I will the butterflies somersaulting in my stomach away. I'm going to tell him. I know he feels it, too. I have to tell him. It's either that or spend the rest of my life wondering *what if.*

"Look . . . don't take this the wrong way—there's all kinds of stuff going on right now, but . . ." He pauses for a deep, labored breath. "It might not be such a bad idea for you to start making plans to find another job."

Those same fluttering butterflies suddenly drop into a lump of misery slumped at the bottom of my gut. He wants nothing to do with me.

"Oh."

"I wish I could explain, but—"

"You really don't have to, Georges. You don't owe me an explanation. You have no idea how . . ." How no one had ever trusted me with anything important—anything meaningful—before. No one ever believed in me and you did. And you may not love me, but I know you cared, and that's all I need. "Thank you for the opportunity you gave me. I'm more grateful for it than you'll ever know."

"It was nothing—you could have done so much more. You can do so much more. I hope you know that."

"I do now." I smile, and swing the other foot onto the sidewalk. "Good night."

Rio

There was a message from Georges on my machine this morning. He didn't say much, just that he was coming in this morning at nine, which means it's his first meeting of the day, which means it's D-day.

And as if that weren't enough, he's bringing his Handmaiden of Death and Destruction, Zahra.

"Behnaz." I press my finger down on the conference button. "What have I got this morning?"

"Umm . . . ," her plaintive little voice comes whining over the crackling phone line, "Jaslene Gonzalez's people want to discuss a possible cover shoot. . . ."

No way. *María Mercedes* covered the *Top Model* winner last month, and I want to make it perfectly clear that *Suéltate*'s no second-fiddle publication. Of course, *Suéltate* may be nothing more than an old discarded pipe dream after this morning, but *chicas* from the 'hood don't become fearless leaders by indulging in negative thinking. Think like a champion, be a champion.

It's not too late. It can't be.

"Call them back, tell them to come to us first next time they're looking to push their C-list celebrities. Maybe then we could work something out. Next?"

I hear her scribbling frantically.

"I didn't see Ranya this morning, where is she?"

"She called to say she's researching a piece this morning and won't be in till the afternoon."

What? Who gave that prissy little *árabe* princess permission to write a piece before consulting me first, and time off for research? I swear, *chica,* you give some people an inch and they leave pointy little stiletto scars all over you. To think, I was contemplating giving the sex column to Behnaz (seriously—I don't know what I was thinking . . . that girl's dating half of straight Miami and probably a good chuck of bi Miami, too). I figured I might try Ranya on some meatier social topics, try to move away from those freelancers. Maybe the savings will get Zahra off my ass for a while. But who am I kidding? A bulldozer wouldn't make that chubby little Rottweiler leave me in peace.

"Tell her to come see me when she gets in."

"Okay. Edgar Ramirez is coming in for a photo shoot this morning. Are you going to sit in with the photographer?"

Ohhh . . . chica. Ever since I saw that chunk of hot Venezuelan booty jump Keira Knightley in that *Domino* desert scene, I had to get him in the magazine. I could tell he was going places. And then one day, who do I see playing opposite Matt Damon in *The Bourne Ultimatum* but my choice Latino pick for next hottest thing since skinny jeans? He had to play the bad guy, *claro*—it's Hollywood, what do you expect? But still.

"Tell Lazlo I'll be running a bit late, but I'll definitely be there. Clear anything else from my schedule."

"Sure thing, Rio."

I take my finger off the button and sigh.

What's going to happen to me after the magazine? It's my life. I have nothing else going on, as *mami* is so generous to keep pointing out.

I'm tired. Life just seems to be an endless cycle of frenzied work and smuggled play, as if I was always grasping at scraps of something just a little better than this. I'm exactly where I want to be. I made it. Against the odds. I can do anything. And no, I know what you're thinking; that . . . that *thing* . . . would not have made it all better. I made the right decision. I know I did. I just have no idea why nothing feels like it's ever enough.

There's a soft knock at the door. I glance at my watch—is it nine already?

"Rio?"

"Georges! Hi, come in." I shuffle some papers on my desk, messing it up a little. Messy desks signal lots of work and no time to lose cleaning up.

He steps in, more tired looking and frazzled than usual.

"How's everything?" he asks.

"Daria gave me the latest numbers. Newsstand is up, so is circulation. Ad sales are also looking up. Mari expanded the Procter & Gamble contract to include both English- *and* Spanish-language ads. She's also talking to the Target people. I'm moving Behnaz onto the sex and relationships for today's Latina column and looking at utilizing Ranya for features. What she lacks in experience she makes up for in enthusiasm." I pause, short of breath. "When she shows up on time."

"Impressive." He cocks an eyebrow.

"Apparently not impressive enough."

"You heard?"

He slumps into the chair across from my desk, looking miserable and defeated.

"It would have been nice to find out about this before the editor of our archrival publication, but whatever. Details, right?" I look him straight in the eye.

"Rio . . ."

"I thought you were going to wait, give me a chance to show you what we could do."

"We didn't go looking for this. They came to see us and made an offer."

"And?" I feel the sticky sweat. Everywhere. I feel my heart pumping out instructions to every pore on my body. Beads of sweat lining up in neat rows under my wispy side-swept bangs, cut just like our last "No-Stress Latina Hair" feature prescribed. Sweat soaking through the armholes of my banana yellow Etro bubble dress, a gift from Dillard's for our four-page spread. Sweat coating my palms, leaving little smudges of moisture over the ad proofs spread across my desk.

Just say it!

"Rio, I'm really sorry."

Fuck off. Fuck off, fuck off, fuck off, Georges.

Don't cry. Grown women don't cry. This is like handing it to those male macho bastards on a silver platter—why women don't belong in the office unless they're lowly eye-candy secretaries or mail girls or fucking professional blowjob givers. Leaders—fighters—don't melt into a puddle of sentimentality. Sentimentality is for suckers. Fighters fight.

"We couldn't pass up the offer—it wouldn't have made financial sense."

"We surpassed every one of our objectives," I say, doing my fucking damnest to keep my voice steady.

"I know." He speaks with soft, measured words. Like he knows I'm a ticking bomb, a lioness biding her time, set to pounce at his throat and shred it to pieces. If it were Joe delivering the blow, I just might have. Where is that *desgraciado* anyway? Too chickenshit to face me?

"It's not about that. You did an amazing job. And I'm going to make sure to tell the managing editor and the publisher when I meet with them."

"Why would you do that? Aren't these deals made at the top? You don't exactly talk small potatoes, Georges, I know you. Just take your money and leave."

He exhales slowly, his cheeks deflating like a pierced balloon.

"This is going to be different. I know what this magazine means to you and I'm going to make sure you get as much creative freedom as possible. Rio—they're offering a fantastic price. Mallouk Enterprises is making a killing on this sale. It's a testament to your abilities—it's all you."

And somehow it hadn't made a difference.

"When?"

"You've already got all the issues through March in the pipeline. April should be the last."

I feel punched. No—knifed. A combination of the wind being knocked out of you and a swift tear ripping through your vital organs.

I get one more issue. One that's all but put to bed at that. Enough room to slip in yummy Edgar Ramirez, maybe one last "Burst into Spring—Latina-Style!" feature, and something serious, weightier . . . but what? Where do you leave off your dream? What defines a legacy?

"This isn't the end, Rio. Just different management."

"Are you being deliberately naïve or just plain condescending?" I meet his stare, struggling to keep my contempt from bubbling over. "I made it into what it is and now someone else is going to be calling the shots. What if they don't agree with my vision? What if they make me compromise it? Tell me, Georges, how do I sit back and watch them do it?"

He doesn't take the bait. Just looks sadly into my anger-twisted face and says gently, "Not all bosses are going to be as easygoing as me, or as plain disinterested as Joe. You had a good run. Maybe it's time you think about doing your own thing. You've got passion, Rio—go for it."

Go for it.

Isn't that what I'd always told my girls when I channeled the thick-hipped, gray-haired fabulously fictitious Tía Elvira?

Then again, I'd never been too good at taking my own advice.

But we already covered that, didn't we?

Zahra

I have been hiding from her all day. Hiding in my own condo. My own house. Why does hiding seem like a recurring theme in my life?

I called Georges this morning to tell him I wouldn't be breaking the news to Rio. He would have to do it on his own. He's a big boy, though you wouldn't know it sometimes.

I've spent the morning pitter-pattering around the house, drinking tea out of big, chipped MIT Rocks mugs, and stuffing my face with cream cheese—slathered bagels from the kosher bakery downstairs with the Hebrew lettering in the window. One day I am going to greet the nosy, floral muumuu-wearing sixty-something-year-old shopkeeper with a "Good morning, and did you know that fat girl from 1310 you keep offering to set up is actually Palestinian vermin?" I wonder if that's enough to make her stop offering up her grandsons as conversation bait. Or maybe I should take her up on the offer, keep my Palestinianness to myself. It's not like I'm getting any younger, and the well of willing Rodrigos is bound to run dry soon.

I feel like shit. Rotting, stinking human manure.

It's not Ranya's fault Georges is a spineless mama's boy. Aren't they all mama's boys at heart? And again—maybe his mother wasn't the problem at all. Maybe he just didn't love me.

Not to mention this is all ancient history. How long is someone allowed to carry the torch of heartbreak before the cosmos rolls its eyes and scolds you to get over yourself already?

Is Waleed rolling his eyes at me now?

Daytime TV is terrible. No reality shows, not even *Blind Date*. Just crappy soap operas and pop psychobabble.

I decide to see how my mother is doing. It's been a while since we talked, and in my world a week without news could be deadly.

It rings once, twice, a third time. My heart lurches. Are they okay?

"*Na'am?*" my mother's voice crackles weakly from across oceans, across worlds.

"*Ahlan, mama,* it's Zahra."

"*Ahlan, ya binti.*"

I ask after my sisters, after Mirvat, who is expecting her third, after my father, still suffering apparently, and business is no good. Nothing new here.

"Will you visit this year?" she asks.

"I don't know," I say. It's hard. Things could always take a turn for the worse, I could get stuck there—or worse—and then where would everyone be?

"I'm thinking of leaving Miami," I say.

"Reema needs money for a new coat. She's been wearing this one for years and years; I can't patch it up anymore. Your father's car is in the shop again. Abu Kamal says it needs a lot of work. Can you send a little extra this month, Zahra *habibti*?" She sighs, the pain of an entire family on her shoulders.

What's a small depression when you can't afford a new coat? What's there to be depressed about anyway? It's nothing a little gourmet ice cream washed down with Pinot Noir can't fix.

"I'm not happy, Mama."

Silence.

I honestly don't know what I expect her to say. She's too old to care much for these things anymore; her daughters are grown, one is engaged, and between the three married ones they've given her nine grandchildren so far. Why should she care about the whining fifth daughter, one who's whoring herself on the other side of the world at that?

"What's the matter, *habibti*? Tell me."

I start to cry. A soft whimpering at first, and then long, loud, snotty sobs. I collapse against my stainless-steel fridge, cold, rocking back and forth, a lunatic.

"I'm all alone, Mama. I'm going to die like this. Alone." I hear the words through broken sobs, through labored intakes of air. I hear them as though they were coming from someplace else.

She sighs on the other end. And waits for my hysteria to subside. She is too burdened with sadness herself to be surprised.

"We all have to suffer, my daughter, this is our burden on this Earth. But God didn't leave us here alone. We will always be with you—you're one of us. Come home, it's time. We miss you."

"What about the money?" I stutter.

"What about it? We'll manage."

"Who's going to buy Reema her coat?"

"We'll manage," she says simply.

Mothers always have a way of putting things simply. Even the most complicated things.

"Mama? Why don't you ever ask me if I've met anyone?"

"Have you?"

"No, but still."

"I don't ask because I know that when you do you'll tell us. And we will be as happy and proud of you as we always are. Zahra—we're all very proud of you. Maybe we don't tell you enough. It's hard, but you must know this."

Of course I know. I know it's hard to talk feelings when one of your daughters needs a new coat and all you can do is ask your other daughter, the one who is all alone and a world away, for help. It's only that it's nice to be reminded every once in a while. Sometimes all you need is to be reminded.

"Are you okay, Zahra?"

"Yes, I'm fine. I just needed to cry a little."

"We all need to sometimes, *habibti*. You've always done right by us. Just remember to do what's right by you, too."

"I will, Mama."

I will.

Ranya

Are you on drugs? Did Joe make you do it?"

"This isn't a joke, Priya."

"I know—I'm not joking, either."

I hadn't gone to work this morning. I rushed to Madame Vilma's Beauty Spa instead and waited patiently for Priya's husband to drop her off at the door, and even waved politely at him when he glared at me, his bushy brows furrowed, through the half-open Honda Civic window.

Little did he know I had plans for his wife.

"And what's this nonsense about you going back home? To what?"

"To face Dodi. My ghosts. My family—I don't know. It's time."

I don't tell her I might have kept hiding just a little longer if I thought there was even the smallest chance a little bit of me had seeped under Georges's skin. But it was his idea I leave after all, wasn't it?

"This is a wonderful article, Ranya. How did you manage to interview all these women?"

We're sitting on the plush red cushions of the reception area, incense and sitar music wafting in the air around us. I'd handed her a copy of my yet-unfinished work, in the hopes she'll provide me with the missing link.

"I'd gone to school with some of them, others are friends of friends. It's amazing how much they opened up."

"People love to talk about themselves, even when they're naked from the bottom down and have their legs up in the air." She shakes her head.

"Priya, seriously, why don't we go down to Ocean Drive for lunch or something? We'll make it quick—no one has to know. . . ."

"Cities have eyes, dear. I can't do it. What if Rahim finds out? He'll say if I'm lying to him about closing up shop to go have lunch with girlfriends, what else am I lying to him about, and so on. . . . He'll never shut up."

"Don't you ever go out?"

"Only with Rahim-and-Vilma-approved women. I'm afraid that you, my darling, aren't going to make the cut."

"And why not?"

"Look at you, Miss Glamour Puss. All tan and glossy and sparkling. Are you sure you didn't do the nasty with Joe? I could swear something's different about you."

"I haven't done anything with Joe, nasty or otherwise," I say, anxious to change the subject. "I really think your story will help. . . . It'll help you, too, you know."

"Who told you I need help?" She tosses her head, her gold-speckled red scarf blazing behind her.

"You don't think it might be helpful to expose . . . ," this is harder than I thought it would be, ". . . to raise awareness that just as religion allows some women to flourish, it's sometimes used to mask ugly things. And that it isn't right to turn a blind eye because we're afraid to be critical." I drag my stare down to the hardened bits of wax on the floor, to tiny scraps of linen not yet swept away by Priya's broom, to the linoleum tiles. I had always assumed that just because I was free to flit around, free to take the veil or not, free to marry or not, it was exactly the same for everyone else. When people threw ugly statistics at me, I accused them of bigotry and turned away. Of course some of them were bigots, but here was Priya, and what had she done? Didn't she deserve to have her story told alongside the success stories, the Diana Shalhoubs, of the Muslim world?

"That's a brilliant idea. Just don't ask me to be a part of it."

"If not you, then who?" I plead.

"Anyone! The world is full of injustice. Maybe not your world, but trust me, it is. What about you?"

"What about me?"

"Did you ever think that the subconscious reason behind

you marrying a gay man was so you could finally get a bit of freedom in your life?"

Now she's gone and lost her mind.

"What I *think* is that all this incense is getting to your head."

"No, seriously . . . ," she continues. "You must have sensed the distance during the engagement, the subtle indifference, the lack of passionate emotions, one way or the other. You don't think that somewhere in those mysterious recesses of your brain where strange things we don't know about happen it occurred to you that here was a man who would stay out of your hair, give you a measure of free rein you never had before?" She nods her head knowingly, looking pretty proud of her bout of Freudian introspection. "I'll bet that if you went back to Montreal right now and proposed to go on with the charade in exchange for his letting you do whatever you wanted in private, he'd go for it in a heartbeat. And what a convenient arrangement that would be for a girl with your . . . *baggage*."

"My baggage?"

"That's right." She nods. "I told you I read a lot in my spare time."

I tilt my head and give Priya a once-over. "You're too smart for your own good."

"Don't I know it!"

"If I could get you a job at *Suéltate,* would you take it?"

"What, and leave all this?" She throws her hands up and laughs. "Rahim would kill me, darling. Actually, I think Vilma might get to it first. . . ."

"He couldn't because you'd have filed a restraining order against him, right?"

Priya glares at me under furrowed brows. "Stop putting
silly ideas into my head. Just because you're Miss Indepen-
dent now, you think I can just up and leave like you did?"

"I'm just saying . . . it's something to consider. Now
back to you and my article. . . ."

I try to let my plaintive eyes do the talking.

"Stop looking at me like that." She gets up and heads to the
back, returning a few minutes later with some piping chai tea.

"It's a slow day, isn't it?" She sighs.

"It's also a really beautiful day . . . sunny, not too
humid. . . ."

"You say it would be an anonymous profile?"

"Of course! Do you think I'm an idiot?"

"Well . . . you had a chance to finally give that embarrassing virginity of yours the boot and you didn't—"

"Priya!"

"And she still blushes! Honestly, when are you going to
grow up?" She giggles.

I might have. I just might have, if maybe he'd asked.

"Did you say you were buying lunch?"

"Aaahhhhhhh!!!!!" I leap into her lap and smother her in
a massive hug.

"I hope you know I don't come cheap." She gathers her
purse and flips over the Open/Closed sign.

"We'll go wherever you want—you say the word."

Rio

Ranya traipses into the office at one this afternoon. I am too devastated to care. I don't think I would have even noticed had she not sauntered in to see me as if she were floating on some sort of feel-good cloud, all bubbly and nauseatingly perky.

"What do you want?"

"Hello, Rio, I'm fine. How are you?"

Glare.

"Here's my feature," she flusters. "I know you didn't ask for it, but I thought you might like it."

"Just leave it in my in-tray." It's all I can manage to say right now.

The girl's face drops. Just drops, *chica*. Like I just told her her Louis Vuitton was a fake.

"I'll look at it later." I try to eke out a drop of humanity. It's not my fault, really.

"I put a lot of work into it. . . ."

"I'm sure you did. We all do, Ranya. We all put a lot of ourselves in every piece we write. That's how it's done. It's what we expect of you every time." I know it doesn't matter if I coach her or not, who knows if she'll stay on with *Suél-tate* after the buyout or not? I know I certainly won't be her boss, but hey, I'm sappy like that.

My firmness does nothing to wipe the doe-eyed look off her face. She spins on her too-high heels and storms out of my office. Great. Let her go run to Georgie and tell him how mean I was to her, how I hadn't fawned all over her just because she actually hunkered down and did some real work, like the rest of us.

But that's not entirely fair, is it? She'd turned out to be a lot better than I'd ever given her credit for. She hadn't gone complaining to Georges—not that I knew of anyway. He was the one who asked after her. She hadn't tried to steal Joe from me—he was just a two-timing asshole. It's not her fault my world is falling apart.

Zahra

After I hung up with my mother, I picked up the phone again and called *The Miami Herald*. Put an ad in the real estate section. The market isn't so hot here these days—I'm not going to sell. Besides—we Palestinians are peculiar about owning property. A bit of an obsession with us, something to do with displacement and all that perhaps. I'm just going to put it up for rent, and poor Ranya won't be able to afford it.

I will have to tell her.

It's going to be the hardest part. Harder even than telling Georges.

Weird, isn't it?

That I'd waited so long, unable to cut the cord, and then once I'd put it into my head things were going to change, it was suddenly so . . . so much less difficult than I thought. Not easy. Scary. Very scary. But doable.

Maybe it's because no matter how bad things are, some hope is always better than no hope. And as I was watching Georges pacing my living room, watching him run his fingers through his thick black hair, hair that had once lain on my chest, one night on a messy sofa in Boston long ago, hope had finally run completely dry.

It was time for new hope.

I reach for Baroque Christ, still hanging there on his wispy gold chain.

Hope.

After the paper and the real estate agent, I called some places in Boston. Not the old places, the ones I'd been pining over for years and that didn't want anything to do with me. International banks, investment houses, fund administrators. Places I never fit in before and would never fit in ever. Places where I didn't want to fit in.

But I didn't fit in Miami, either.

I'd cut out an article from the *Herald* once, a couple of years ago. It's now yellowed and curled at the corners, the paper frail and brittle, but still legible. I'd stuck it between the pages of a photo album that held pictures of my last trip to the Middle East. I'm not the kind of person who keeps Martha Stewart type boxes of "ideas" and "mementos" and "craft suggestions," an old photo album being the next best thing.

I pull the cheap plasticized album off my shelf—my mother had bought it at the neighborhood variety store in Bethlehem, and I'd never managed to part with it in favor of something a little more dignified—and flip to the pictures taken at the Dome of the Rock. Stuck to a picture of Reema and me, our arms wrapped around each other while pilgrims filed behind us, is another photo, this one of three confident women, in prim yet casual outfits—sweater sets; boxy blazers with jeans; a crisp white shirt with funky jewelry. One had once been a Wall Street investment banker who took in a few cool mil in bonuses alone every year, who had her own private chauffeur and personal chef, another had been a senior manager at a Chicago consulting firm, and the third used to be a partner at a major venture capital outfit. They'd all met at Harvard Business School and stayed friends throughout their sparkling careers. And each had eventually come to the same epiphany: "Time and time again, we would see capable women being turned down for investment capital because their business ideas weren't flashy enough, or they themselves weren't as overconfident as most of the male candidates who presented to us. My colleagues on the board—men—just didn't respond to the women's more restrained, self-effacing attitudes, no matter how solid or original their ideas were, and that's when we realized there was a hole in the venture capital business," the article quoted. "Combined with statistics that show women all over the world have a much higher loan payback ratio than men—well, we figured we had a winner."

They went on to boast about financing housewives with school-age children who'd started modest gourmet cookie ventures from their kitchens and turned them into companies with double-digit growth numbers, young women who exposed deficiencies in the hair-care service industry—and how they helped start a chain of "curl expert" salons that catered specifically to women who wanted to stay natural and resist the overprocessed, glossy, pin-straight look of Hollywood and the socialite cliques.

Men wouldn't understand about the dire need for "curl expert" salons on the market—especially not Wall Street and Harvard Business School men, and frankly, I'm not sure I did, either—but one thing I was very well acquainted with was how small women were made to feel in the world of big money. How much of themselves they had to hide, change, or give up altogether for a piece of the action.

I found the number for Athena Capital online and arranged for an interview. They were always interested in speaking with promising candidates, and my profile fit the bill.

For the first time in a long time, I am not paralyzed with fear at the prospect of another failed interview, more unfriendly faces gathered around a table, interrogation-style, waiting for me to slip up. I sense this will be different, that what Athena Capital is looking for is a very special profile, and for the first time in a long time, maybe even ever, I feel . . . confident.

I am ready.

I flit into the bathroom, a towel slung over my arm, my

step light and airy, but my heart heavy with the knowledge I will be leaving the scraps of a family I've built over the years to replace the one I left behind. And Ranya, who never tired of trying to take the place of the sisters I was wrenched away from. I decide that when she comes home, I will finally let her take me shopping—something she's been begging me to do since she moved in here, convinced that the right pair of jeans and accompanying handbag will take Ben & Jerry's place in my heart, and stand a better chance at landing me a date or two in the process.

I am about to turn on the hot-water tap when I hear someone at the door.

At first I'm sure it's a mistake—it's not even four yet; it's another few hours before Ranya comes home. But the knocking starts up again, insistent and unmistakable.

"Who is it?" I peer into the peephole.

A man. Tall. Dark haired, clean shaven, and wearing a neat, expensive-looking suit, a little bit like Georges's suits but . . . more fashionable maybe?

"Ranya?" He looks as if he might beat down the door with his naked fists.

"Who's asking?"

"Does she live here? Tell me, does Ranya Hayek live here?"

"If you don't tell me who you are, I'm calling the police." I try to give off my best intimidation vibes.

"It's her husband."

Oh, no. This can't be good.

Ranya

I don't bother to stay until five. What's the point? I'd like to
be responsible and everything, but seriously, it's not like
anyone here seems to care.

I've only been gone for two months, but it seems like
years.

Had I really not spoken to my parents—my husband—for
over two months now?

What kind of person am I? Am I even human?

I hop into a taxi—too defeated for public transportation
today—and give the driver instructions to go to Zahra's
place. I'm going to have to tell her I'm leaving. As soon as

possible. Maybe at the end of the week. Maybe even tomorrow.

Maybe I should tell my mother . . . assuming she'll even speak to me.

At the thought of my mother another thought creeps into my head—one decidedly less pleasant: the last e-mail she'd sent me, the one where she'd cursed the day she raised a daughter like me and practically disowned me.

Drip, drop.

My head droops; tears start falling onto my wrists, sliding off the sides of my hands in clear streaks.

Drip, drop.

I was becoming a miserable, emotional mess, crying at the drop of a hat. Whether it was about losing a man I'd never had in the first place, figuring out what to do with the man I *did* have but who happened to want nothing to do with me, reconciling myself to a future of idle boredom when I'd finally had the chance to do something meaningful, at least to me, or how I was going to smooth this whole sordid disaster out with my family. It didn't matter what direction I turned, all I seemed to be facing was shit.

"Everything all right, ma'am?"

"Sorry?" Oops. Seems I might have been getting a little more emotional than I'd intended.

"On second thought, could we stop at the Bal Harbour Shops instead?"

"Sure thing, ma'am."

What can I say? Old habits die hard.

I can't explain it, but I knew something was wrong the moment I stuck the key into the keyhole.

Maybe it was hearing Zahra rush to the door to greet me. An earthquake couldn't tear that one away from the E! network, but today, the one day I wasn't in a mood to talk to anyone, she pounces on me.

"Are you okay?" I ask.

"Yes—are you?"

"Why are you acting so strange?" She's tugging away at my carrier bags in an effort to help me bring them inside. I did go a little overboard today, using Dodi's credit cards for the first time since that bastard tried to get me arrested, but I wasn't too worried anymore. If he wanted to come after me, he could go right ahead. I dare him. I dare him to look me in the eye and tell me I couldn't have Kors and Dior and Lanvin and Armani when he'd had plenty of Paolo the decorator. In fact, I double dare him.

"Look, Ranya—"

I hear footsteps rushing behind Zahra.

"Is someone here?" Now that explains it! Was she on . . . *a date?* "Ohmigod, Zahra! You have company over. . . . You should have told me!"

"No, Ranya . . . no, stop jumping."

"I'm just going to leave these in the entry and I'm out of here. Don't worry, I won't come back till later . . . *much later!*"

"Ranya, stop it! Look at me; it's your—"

"Ranya?"

Time stops.

It does.

Time can do that sometimes, you know. Usually when stopping is the last thing you want it to do. When all you want is for it to skip to the next scene, the next day, the next episode, just as long as you didn't have to live the present in all its magnified glory.

God is in the details, they say. Or is it the devil? I don't know. I'm just not sure if Dodi's hairline seems higher on his forehead today because he'd really started balding since the last time I saw him or because Time had never squeezed me in its grip quite as chokingly as this before and forced me to notice. His suit is dark and dapper, and pressed. He hasn't flown into a fit of rage yet, even though several seconds of stony silence have already ticked by.

And just as time now seems snagged on this precise moment, so have big chunks of it dissolved into nothing—entire weeks I'd spent writing copy, answering phones, and gathering photo shoot samples at the magazine had melted into the ether. London. Georges. Joe. Georges and Joe together. The thin trickle of bright blood against the darkness of the night, the whiteness of the room. All of it gone, evaporated. *Poof!*

It's just Dodi and me, and a quantum eclipse between that day I saw something so awful that it had made me pack up my things and run into the arms of strangers and standing at Zahra's doorstep, looking into Dodi's pleading face and wondering how we'd managed to end up here.

Dodi and me and Zahra, that is.

"I . . . er, I need to pick up my dry cleaning . . . and maybe catch a movie or something. . . . Don't worry about me." Zahra weaves between the maze of limbs and carrier bags at the door frame and quietly disappears down the stairs, leaving me all alone with my husband.

"Is this where you live now?" He turns to the apartment. "It's nice."

Strangely, he doesn't come off sounding sarcastic. Or at least not like he's planning to hack me to pieces and FedEx the remains to my parents.

"Aren't you going to come in?" he says.

"How did you find me?" My voice cracks with fear and fatigue.

"Don't worry—I'm not going to hurt you. I just want to talk—I swear." He holds his hands up, his eyes still pleading and miserable.

I finally cull enough nerve to trudge through the door frame and collapse on the couch in the living room.

He breathes in deeply and sinks into the armchair across from me, careful to pull his trousers up a touch so they don't get too wrinkled. Funny how put together he is. I'm not sure what I had been expecting—that his life had fallen apart, that he had lost the business, the house, his family's respect, everything, just because he'd lost me?

"You look great." He manages to crack a smile.

"You, too. I like your shirt. Brooks Brothers?"

"Hugo Boss."

"Ah. Did Paolo pick it out?"

I shouldn't have said that. He goes ashen, then drops his head into his hands.

There it is again. Time. Ticking by and yet unmoving. He stays slumped over, not moving, until slowly, quietly, his shoulders start to heave, a low, steady moan escaping through the cracks in between his clasped fingers.

I can't watch him cry. I just can't do it. Before I know it we're both at it.

"I don't know what's wrong with me," he says.

"It's . . . not . . . you. . . ." I dry heave. "Rio bought a feature on this topic last month. . . . Did you know it's estimated that four million women in America are married to . . . to . . ."

I can't say it. Neither can he, apparently.

"Who's Rio?"

"My b-boss." I inhale deeply.

"Your boss? You got a job?"

"What do you think? I had to! You had our credit cards declared stolen!" Let's see him weasel himself out of *this*. "How could you do that to me? Your *wife*?"

"What about you? You'd told your mother those awful things about finding . . ." He pauses, his face a battlefield of emotions, and forces himself to go on. It hurts just to watch him. ". . . lewd e-mails and messages on my computer, and then she told my mother. . . . I felt like the whole world knew and was just looking at me, like they could see me naked or something. It was awful. . . . How could you do that?"

Suddenly I'm the one who's at a loss. How *could* I do that?

Oh right, I remember.

"You were cheating on me with our decorator. We weren't married a month yet."

"We could have talked about it. . . ."

"Could we? Could we *really,* Dodi?"

In the weeks leading up to my wedding, I had steeled myself against the possibility that domestic spats might flare up between Dodi and me after our honeymoon. We'd both been babied by our mothers for a third of our lives so far, and suddenly we were each expected to start fending not only for ourselves but for another person, too. It would be a challenge, to say the least. What I didn't expect, though, was that the fighting would start *during* the honeymoon.

Whereas once it was up to me where we ate, what we did, who we hung out with, and how late we stayed out, suddenly I was a wife and not a fiancée, and somehow that was supposed to have changed everything. There were gifts before the wedding—lots of them, some celebrating made-up anniversaries and cheesy holidays and others for no reason at all. Then one day I was told I spent too much, had too many clothes, too much makeup, an ungodly amount of shoes, and that I clearly had no appreciation for hard work and what went behind earning the money that streamed so readily between my fingers, feeding an insatiable monster with a bottomless appetite for frivolity.

Well. That might have been a little bit true.

I stare at the carrier bags strewn at my feet, by the coffee table, behind the couch, tracing a path of grotesque wastefulness all the way to the front door.

Okay, maybe it was more than a little true. But the point is we'd never talked about it like a husband and wife were meant to do. I was just told what to do, exactly as if I were the kid and Dodi was the parent.

"When did we ever talk about anything, Dodi? I mean seriously talk. Like adults talk to each other."

His gaze lifts to the huge portrait hanging above the console in Zahra's entry. He manages to crack a smile. "How the hell did you end up here?"

"How did *you*?"

"It's not that hard to find someone when you set your mind to it. There are people who get paid to do that."

"So you thought you could pay someone to find me and then you'd come down here and bring me back kicking and screaming? I have a life here, in case you haven't noticed. I have . . ." What did I have anymore? "I have a job!" *Not exactly.* . . . "Friends!" *Not really.* . . . "And did you think that just because you didn't love me, I wouldn't find someone who did?"

Did it matter that the only man I'd managed to attract in this city full of sizzling, hot, worldly men was someone who thought I'd get along nicely with his mother?

"I had no idea what I'd do when I found you, to tell you the truth, but I . . . I didn't expect this." He shifts his gaze from a spot on the carpet to me. "Look at you. I would have never thought . . . When you left I was sure you were hiding out at your parents', and when I found out you weren't, that you'd gone halfway around the world—by yourself—I figured you'd be gone a few days. A week at the most. For as long as your credit cards would carry you, which, let's be honest, no one thought would be very far. But then you stayed away . . . and now I find out you got yourself a job? I can't believe it. I can't believe you're the same spoiled little girl I married."

Now this was the last straw. I was *not,* under any circumstance, to feel flattered by anything Dodi said to me today. It's all a ploy. This is the man who expected me to iron his briefs because that's what his mother used to do, and who didn't think married women should stay out late with their girlfriends. Not the respectable variety anyway.

"That doesn't change the fact you don't like me, you like boys."

He clutches his head as if by blocking off any sound from breaking into his ego, he could somehow protect it from the ugliness of it all. The funniest thing is that I don't think there's anything uglier than the sham of our marriage. Because I never loved Dodi and he never even pretended to love me—not really anyway, that was supposed to come with time—I couldn't muster enough of a sense of loss. Certainly not for what we had when I left.

"It was such a lie, what we had," he says, so softly I think he's speaking to Zahra's Jesus picture.

"Yes, it was," I echo.

He slowly pulls himself off the sofa and crosses to my side, sinking into the luxurious cream softness beside me. I'd forgotten how much I liked the scent of him. It was a long time since I'd liked anything about him. But once upon a time I had, when our paths had first crossed at a mutual friend's engagement party and then again at a Christmas cocktail reception friends of my parents had thrown, and then when he finally worked up the nerve to sit next to me at a New Year's Eve gala a full six months after our first encounter.

Of course I'd remembered him from that very first time at Huda's party—it would have been hard not to notice the best-dressed, smooth-featured man in the room with the softest gray eyes and strong, husky build, like that of a soccer player, or someone who never missed a gym appointment.

All we had to do was blush and giggle ourselves through that one awkward evening before the usual behind-the-scenes inquiries were made and he asked me out on a very much anticipated first date. Of course I use the word "date" loosely. We went to an amusement park with eight other friends. Like a remake of *Grease* with thirty-something-year-old Arabs. Then Dodi and I started chatting on the phone, and before I knew it, he said the magic words I'd been waiting all my life to hear: "Can I ask your father for permission to marry you?"

Not exactly the stuff of Shakespeare, but I wanted so much to be married and he seemed perfectly suitable, and I knew I'd be the envy of half the Lebanese girls this side of the Atlantic.

"Why did you come here?"

"Because I want to make this work."

He takes my face into his hands, and I feel my resolve seep out of my skin, pooling into a puddle of humiliation at my feet.

I am so weak. After everything I'd been through, I hadn't learned a thing. It felt so good to be wanted, to be wrapped in a cocoon of safety, even if I knew there was nothing right about it.

"Dodi . . ." I place my hands over his, and lower them gently, laying them flat against my lap. "I don't want to sound like a bad American movie, but . . . you can't change who you are."

"You can when you don't have a choice. You changed. . . ."

"Yes, but that's hardly the s—"

"It *is* the same thing." His expression is steely, unwavering. "Can you imagine how hard things have been for me?"

"Yes, but—"

"Come back with me, Ranya. I'll change. Everything will change."

I've never seen him look so afraid. "But aren't you . . . aren't you happier with . . ."

He shakes his head, on the verge of tears. "I'm not with . . . I . . . I haven't done anything you think I have. I know I can't help how I feel sometimes, but I can help what

I do, and I don't want anything to do with that life. I don't. I won't let feelings I don't want choose what kind of life I live."

Strangely, the picture of Priya, bubbly and full of life yet trapped behind invisible bars, pops into my mind. There was nothing I could do for her, but here is a problem I could do something about. I could go back. I could choose to believe he could change, to help him, rather than condemn him to the pain of facing his family, to the ridicule of a society that just wouldn't understand or forgive.

But what about me?

What about me? There isn't anything left for me here anymore. Georges is absolutely right.

It doesn't really matter right now that I have no idea what the future holds for me. It's time I went home.

Rio

My last act as editor in chief is to slash a big red "NO" across the top of Ranya's article.

I do it for the same reason I didn't tell Adam Lifstein where to stick his ad campaign even though the pain of his leaving me and the ghost of a life that never was still lurks in the shadows of my consciousness. I am nothing if not a professional.

It didn't matter that as I flipped page after page of well-written, engrossing copy, I was enraptured by the stories—stories of women from as far away as Jordan to right here in Miami, who were living challenges to stereotypes on both sides of the world, East and West. A human rights

lawyer fighting to push through anti–honor killings legisla-
tion that affected the poorest and most desolate urban ghet-
tos and far-flung villages alike when she herself had
graduated from Oxford and had split her life between the
fringes of two cultures: a wealthy wife of a politician in
Amman and a mother who packed lunches every morning,
watched *Oprah,* and attended important parties in London
dressed in Gaultier coats and Galliano ball gowns. There
was the young woman with the long shiny chocolate hair
who'd spearheaded a sort of Arab version of *The View,* a
roundtable of women from all over the geography of the
Middle East and its cultural persuasions. Then there was the
young girl trapped in an unhappy arranged marriage, right
here in Miami.

It didn't matter that as I read profile after profile of these
highly exotic creatures whom Ranya had somehow ren-
dered into relatable, brave women, I felt a teeny little bit
ashamed of having made up my mind about her so early on.
Neither did it matter that I'd caught myself wondering, as I
read, if my editorial aspirations were starting to suffer from
the same tunnel vision I exhibited in the rest of my life.

What *does* matter is that the article didn't fit in with
Suéltate's image and mission. And frankly, neither does
Ranya. Not the *Suéltate* I had fashioned out of nothing at
all and turned into a plug into the Hispanic-American market, another vehicle for Procter & Gamble to sell more bottles of Pantene to Latinas or for Kraft to peddle its latest
salsa-flavored products.

Ay, mi niña.

Whatever I feel about Ranya or her work, or the way I sold her short, she just didn't fit in with what *Suéltate* had become. It's really too bad, because, I now realize, she's not a dimwit riding on the coattails of luck and privilege.

And I wonder now why I never bothered to mentor her—or anyone, really. All I'd done from the very beginning was build the magazine, build it so that it was everything I dreamed my magazine would be like. Short of being named after me, it *was* me.

The irony, however, is that Joe Mallouk had been right all along. *Suéltate* belongs to him, and now it's time for me to go. I can't really muster up enough indignation to hate him.

Now—what about the rest of the staff?

I drum my fingers on my desk for a few moments, then dial Daria's extension.

"Yes, Rio?"

"Can you come in here for a second?"

A sigh. "I've got a meeting with GM later this morning, can't it wait?"

"This won't take long."

She hangs up and a few minutes later is slumped in the chair across from me, arms crossed, left foot tapping impatient little thuds against the office upholstery.

"You've heard?" No sense beating around the bush.

"Who hasn't?" she says flatly.

"Good. Always on top of things. I knew you'd be right

for the job. You can go now." I nod and start shuffling papers on my desk.

"Er . . . What do you mean? What job?"

I stop what I'm doing, lean forward, and clasp my hands together.

"Oh, I'm sorry . . . you gave me the impression I was being redundant." I may not be editor in chief for much longer, but I'm editor in chief *now,* aren't I?

She blushes. "I'm sorry."

"No worries. I just thought I'd tell you ahead of time I'm planning to recommend you to the incoming owners and their team. As editor in chief."

She blinks a few incredulous moments away. "What about you?"

I shrug. "I think it's time I moved on to the next challenge. I'm not going to grow here. If anything, the fact that I'm the old boss is just going to spur the new leadership to push me out the first chance they get. But with you it's different. They'll want someone who can teach them the ropes, without giving them the attitude. Do you think you can handle that?"

"Of course." She smirks.

"Good."

I turn back to the memos carpeting my desk, the proposals, the photo shoot proofs. . . . I'm going to have to get started on clearing up this place for Daria. Or whoever else takes over.

"We're going to miss you." She loiters at my desk

awkwardly. "We would've all been out of a job a long time ago if it weren't for you. So thanks."

I'd never been too good with taking credit for anything good I'd ever done. Taking shit for all my mistakes—and there have been plenty of those along the road, trust me, *amiga*—that I'm a pro at. But this . . . it's . . . nice.

"Thanks, Daria, appreciate it."

She nods and practically floats out of the office on a cloud of self-importance.

It's okay—she'd earned it.

Before the door has a chance to snap shut behind her, Zahra barges in, in her usual dumpy, annoying fashion.

Now there's one person I'm not going to miss.

"You know, Zahra, I can understand why you must have given up on grooming altogether, but manners I think you should probably hang on to."

"Why are you such a bitch? Is it the country bumpkin in you that needs the ego boost, or is it just for the sake of being a bitch?"

Ouch. The social misfit has a backbone.

"Ranya's gone." She beseeches me as if I was the police commissioner or something.

"Like on vacation?" I hate people who don't get to the point. Which usually doesn't include Zahra.

"No, like *gone* gone. Her husband came and took her."

Her what?

"Husband?"

"She's married."

"You mean this whole time she was in Miami, while Joe was running after her, she'd been *married* all along?"

Zahra nods.

"Did you know?"

She doesn't need to say anything, she's as busted as a pulverized piñata.

"Does Georges know?"

Again I am met with a wall of silence, but this time she clenches her face into a little ball of mortification and nods almost imperceptibly.

"You *told* him? *Ay, Madonna.*"

"I didn't mean to—"

"Don't give me that, I know how you fucking feel about that *pendejo,* all dopey eyed and stupid. Now you're going to tell me you didn't mean it? Please! You probably planned the whole thing."

"*Me?* All dopey eyed for Georges?"

"Yes, you. Who else? Couldn't take it that he was the one going dopey eyed for *her.*"

For a moment I actually think Zahra might chase me around my desk, cartoon-style, and hit me. Her normally bland brown eyes blaze with the lights of a fireworks festival.

"And how did you feel when Joe asked her out? You know as well as I do he would have married her. How did you like *that?*"

I grasp the edges of my desk and pull myself to my feet. *"Puta de cabrona . . ."*

I shove the swivel chair back with one firm hip movement and take a step round the corner of the desk.

She backs away immediately so that we are almost running around in circles, like a pair of schoolkids. We are literally going crazy over a pair of men. Undeserving ones at that.

Zahra cracks first. "What's wrong with us?" She muffles the nascent burst of a fit of giggles behind her hand.

"We're nuts." I dissolve into laughter.

"So what are you going to do now?" Zahra says, wiping the wet corners of her eyes with her sleeve.

"About what?"

"The magazine. Joe."

Joe. It's funny how problems always seem to feel bigger, more insurmountable, for those stuck in the middle of them than people looking on calmly from the outside. A couple of weeks ago, I couldn't have shaken Joe off if he'd been a nasty case of fleas. Scraps of affection, moments of illicit attention—that was enough. Then I had to go cold turkey. And that's when it all changed.

Of course, having a *tigre caliente* keeping your sheets cozy every night didn't hurt, either.

Twenty-five years old, *chica,* and going on forty. Lightyears ahead of Joe. Wrong in every way, but oh-so-right. Hey—it's good enough for Demi, isn't it? *Mami* and *papi* don't have to understand. It's enough that I'm finding out what it's like to have a real conversation with a man who gives you a real opinion when you ask him which layout looks better and then makes love to you like you're the last woman on earth. Is it going to last? Who knows? But right now, it's real, which is more than I can say for Joe and Adam put together.

Tomorrow, we'll see.

"I'm quitting the magazine," I say casually.

"What? Why?"

"Come on, Zahra, out of all people I figured you'd understand. I can't be told what to do. Not when it comes to my baby."

"So you're throwing the towel in on your greatest achievement? That's the dumbest thing I've ever heard."

"Dumber than you moving all the way to Miami for a man who doesn't even know you exist?"

"It's not like that!"

"Then how is it?"

We're both still perched ridiculously on either side of the desk, ready to either bolt or pounce.

"So . . . what do we do about Ranya then?" she says cautiously.

"I think we should stay out of it," I say even as I am slightly revolted with myself for saying it.

Luckily, Zahra has the sense not to take me seriously. "Really, Rio? After everything we did to her?"

"We weren't so bad. . . ."

"We were horrible. She'd try to tell me how condescending you were to her at the office—"

"And how you ignored her every night at home. . . . Did the poor girl even make any friends here in Miami?"

"There was Georges . . . ," Zahra says, "and Joe, of course, and I think she was hanging out with an esthetician down on Lincoln Road. . . .

"We need to do something," she continues.

Yes, but what?

And then we look at each other.

Georges.

Montreal

Ranya

They said it would be the biggest engagement party of the decade, something I heard was said about my engagement party back in a time that was already beginning to look like ancient history, but this is a new day, and with it, a new engagement party of the decade.

"You look stunning—Vera Wang?"

"Elie Saab." I kiss Dodi gently on the cheek as we sashay into the grand living room of an estate up north, decorated in sumptuous white and worthy of the Queen of Jordan herself, at the future bride's family home.

Even as we try to keep our focus straight ahead, I can

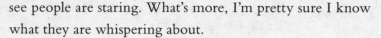

see people are staring. What's more, I'm pretty sure I know what they are whispering about.

Don't you know, that's the one who . . .

Gasp! No! And he took her back? Shame . . .

Sometimes it seemed like it didn't matter where I went on this earth, I would attract gossip like a putrid stench of garbage attracts scavenging dogs.

Coming home was the hardest thing I'd ever had to do. Harder even than running away. I didn't have much to show for myself after two months in Miami, and didn't think anyone with the possible exception of Priya would be bothered by my hasty departure. To her credit, she dealt my resolve a good blow when I stopped by her little place on the way to the airport.

"Have you gone completely crazy?" she said in a hushed tone after she gave Dodi a cursory smile and dragged me to the back. "It's not that I can't see the attraction," she leaned around me to throw him another admiring glance, "but there *is* one major problem, wouldn't you say?"

"I don't expect anyone else to understand, but I thought you might."

"What's there to understand? Just when you were finally moving on with your life! Then you go right back to square one. It's mind-boggling."

"He wants another chance, and I owe it to him to give him one."

"This isn't like he forgot to take out the garbage, Ranya,

or even that he was eyeing one of your friends. Well . . . actually, it *was* one of your friends, but let's not go there. You told me yourself, he wasn't even good to you!"

"I know I said that, and it's true . . . sort of. But he's not a bad person, Priya; I think he's actually a lot like me. Acting the way he thinks he should, cracking under the pressure, acting out because that's what you do when you've been kicked around your whole life."

"So that's the sob story he's fed you then?"

"It's not a sob story. If you'd met his father you'd know."

The quintessential man's man who likes his boys brutish and their women five steps behind. The kind of austere, authoritative jerk I only ever saw on bad Arabic soap operas anymore, a relic with a palpable disdain for something as effeminate and impractical as love, and who averages about five references per conversation to how things were done back in the Old Country. During the occasional getting-to-know-each-other dinners our families subjected themselves to, I would get the feeling, watching Dodi's father interact with his wife and sons, that the man lived in another time and place, wholly disconnected from my reality.

I went ahead with the wedding with nary a thought as to how this man's backward mentality might affect my marriage. For that I have no one to blame but myself.

I hugged Priya and she started to tear up. "You bust in here, start putting ideas about love and free will and self-respect in my head, and then you get up and leave," she said, wiping the corners of her eyes. "Fine, off with you. I hope for your sake that people really can change. Or at least become tolerable."

I squeezed her one last time, with a promise that we would never lose touch. There was nothing left to say after that.

Dodi had hired a black Town Car with tinted windows to bring us to the airport. When the quaint landscape of stout little Art Deco buildings with their pastel paint and curlicue embellishments gave way to causeways stretching across sprawls of cobalt waters, little islets of luxurious green and sand visible at the horizon, and then finally to the industrial, smoggy skyline of downtown Miami, I went into a mild panic attack. My heart beat like the wings on a hummingbird, my face, neck, and collarbone flashed hot and cold and then hot again. I turned to look at Dodi, staring quietly out the window.

"Are you sure?" I said.

He squeezed my hand and inhaled deeply.

My sentiments exactly.

Who was sure of anything in this world? But at least we'd face whatever came together. Still, I couldn't shrug off the pinch of leaving Miami behind, and the little nothings I'd achieved—laughable by most people's standards, but that were quite literally the world to me.

One business-class flight and several passport checks later, Dodi dropped me off at the foot of my parents' home. My old home. I'd traveled all over the world before my tenth birthday, and yet standing in front of those porch steps, taking in every crack and imperfection in the dark red bricks, peering into white-paneled windows to the soft light and curtained shadows peeking out from within, I'd never felt so far away. Like a time traveler reaching back into space, grasping at something steady, something enduring, my heart lurched for that house.

"Are you going to be okay?" Dodi asked gently.

"I'll be fine."

I felt anything but fine as I trudged up the front steps. What was awaiting me up there? I felt I'd already been hollowed out, my soul, steeped in shame and humiliation, eked out of me and lain out to dry.

Was I dead to them already? Were they already referring to me in the past tense? Had my old room been turned into a home gym?

I rang the doorbell knowing I would know the answers soon enough.

My mother didn't ask who was at the door when she cracked it open, which was probably a good thing. I mean really, what would I have said? Ungrateful and disobedient daughter come back to hide in family home after attempts at independence and adulthood were met with total and utter failure?

"Mama? . . . It's me. . . ."

I realized I was unconsciously holding my breath.

"Ranya?"

I met her wide-eyed stare with my own sheepish one.

"Mama, I know you have every right to hate me—"

I couldn't finish. No sooner had the first syllables escaped my lips than she was all outstretched arms and tears and wet kisses. We held each other and sobbed until the tears from more than two months of separation had run dry.

"Thank God you're back," was all she muttered over and over again, as though it were a prayer. Or maybe a prayer answered, I allowed myself to hope.

She ushered me inside where my father was sitting in the old armchair in the corner of his office, reading *The Economist* and having his evening Turkish coffee, the stifled air of the room laden with the familiar scents of cardamom mingled with jasmine and incense. More tears. More apologies, more sadness and relief and regret all at once.

Then, after the painful silence, it was as if a dam had cracked and fallen apart; torrents of stories and anecdotes, of news and gossip, gushed forward in an unorganized and frantic mess. What I'd done, who I'd met, how I'd lived, and where. I was careful not to mention what had happened with Joe, or talk about Georges too much. It wasn't time for that, and probably it would never be.

Then the dreaded question came—the mother of all horrifyingly embarrassing questions: Was it true?

I overreacted, I explained. I'd jumped to conclusions, I didn't give Dodi a chance to explain. That's what he and I had agreed would be best to say. It was at that point that the entire plan nearly derailed, so heartbroken was he over asking me to lie. But as bad as he felt over that, his fear of coming out was bigger.

Both my parents eyed me suspiciously.

"So you lied about the e-mail, the pictures, everything?"

I nodded, afraid of what might come out of my mouth if I opened it. My mother can read me like a fortune-teller can read an outstretched palm.

My father coughed and shook his head from side to side, got up, paced around, and sat back down again.

It occurred to me I might end up driving them crazy.

My mother was still staring intently into my face, squinting. "Your nose turns white when you lie, did you know that?"

Of course I did. I couldn't get anything past my mom when I was a kid, largely because of my nose. In fact, I placed the blame for a perfectly well-behaved childhood and adolescence squarely on the shoulders of that nose.

"It's the truth, Mom."

"Whatever you say," she sighed. "It's your life. What are you going to do now?"

"We're going to give it another shot," I replied stoically. I was feeling very proud of myself at that moment, very resolved and grown-up.

And then my mother took my hand and clasped it in between both of hers. "Whatever you decide to do, *ya binti,* we will support you. Even if you decide you don't want to stay here. Just please promise you won't ever run away like that again."

"I promise." I dissolved in tears, not feeling terribly grown-up at all anymore.

Do you think our wedding was this boring?" Dodi sneaks up behind me and grabs me by the waist. I can see his breath in the cool spring evening air.

To an onlooker we are the picture of perfect happiness and contentment, the poster pair for marriage and good, positive family values. But now I know better than to believe in poster anything.

Still, something had happened to Dodi and me when we came back from Miami together. There burgeoned between us the complicity of a secret and all the intimacy that comes part and parcel with it.

Just not *that* kind of intimacy.

In that regard we are no better off today than on our first ill-fated night together, when we were both so afraid of each other that we pretended to be asleep. At least we don't pretend anymore. To his credit, he tried once, but instead of anticipation and excitement, all I felt the moment he touched me under the covers was guilt and revulsion. Revulsion that anything this man did with me he was doing out of duty, and guilt because even though I am married to my husband, the only man who haunts my imagination is Georges.

It happens sometimes that the pain of loss keeps me awake at night, and that it robs my days of anything I ever found fun or meaningful, like spending time with my mother or hitting the art galleries.

But on most days I'm okay. Better than okay—Dodi and I have become a sort of Arab Will and Grace, except we're still too cowardly to admit to each other and to ourselves how much we want other people.

"Where are you two hiding?" a voice says from the direction of the house where the raucous laughter of rowdy men and the trills of jubilant women float above the steady drumbeat of the Arabic band.

Ikraam. Dodi's mother.

"People are asking about you," she says to Dodi. Ikraam still won't speak to me, except to bark orders, no matter how many times Dodi tells her we are trying to patch things up. It's almost as if she feels doubly wronged—once when I ran off and left her precious son in the most public, scandalous way possible, and a second time when Dodi took me back without punishing me enough for my treason.

Ikraam's gaze falls on Dodi's arm wrapped around my waist. She purses her lips.

Another thing she can't seem to stomach is Dodi's visible affection for me lately. "Behavior unbecoming of a man," she calls it. Effeminate.

"We're fine out here, Mom."

Instead of heeding the cue to leave, Ikraam stays glued to her spot, as if her heels were permanently lodged in the thin layer of snow on the ground.

"Your father wants to see you." She crosses her arms.

Dodi sighs and shoves his hands in his pockets. "Fine—we'll be right there."

We both follow Ikraam inside, and I wonder how long I will have to pay for my Miami adventure.

It's my in-laws' thirtieth wedding anniversary. Dodi and his siblings wanted to throw their parents a huge, catered, organized affair complete with a DJ, a band, and a belly dancer. His parents wouldn't hear of it. They wanted a nice intimate family dinner instead.

A two-hundred-person party worthy of a lavish wedding would have been easier to pull off than this. Because I am expected to cook for the brood of thirty-five. Two sets of parents, siblings, kids, and whatever cousins happened to be in town.

And should the whiff of the wrong kind of spice waft through my mother-in-law's nostrils, tipping her off that I had the event catered, it would follow that I don't have enough respect for my husband's parents to cook a decent meal for them, adding yet more fuel to the fire of Ikraam's loathing of me.

There's no use complaining. I knew this wouldn't be easy.

An hour before everyone is set to arrive, the lentil soup is simmering, the chickpeas boiling, the yogurt cooling, and the eggplant marinating in oil and spices. In the oven I'm baking kibbeh, which took me all morning to make, and in the fridge I've set aside a portion of the ground beef and cracked bulgur concoction that I will serve up raw as an appetizer, with rings of onion and red peppers. For the tabbouleh salad I have seven bunches of parsley laid flat to dry on the counter, and tomatoes, skinned, seeded, and chopped up into tiny cubes. I sent Dodi to get dessert from a bakery deep into Montreal's Lebanese neighborhood, *knafeh,* a sort of Arabic cheesecake soaked in syrup, and the only component of a traditional Arabic meal where it's deemed acceptable to go with something store-bought without coming off as a failed housewife.

My fingers are slick with olive oil from rolling vine leaves when the doorbell rings. Dodi must have forgotten his keys. Or else his hands are too full with sweets and groceries and maybe even a bottle of arak, my father-in-law's favorite kind of liquor, to manage the lock.

"Coming!" I trill, wiping my hands on my checkered apron. I check my reflection in the hall mirror just in case it's Dodi's parents. A new habit they seem to have picked up since my recent social debasement is dropping by either unannounced or ridiculously early, as if they're hoping they'll catch me in an act of something they can hold up to Dodi and my own family in the ultimate I-told-you-so moment.

Except for the cheesy apron—a present from Ikraam— that does nothing for the Roland Mouret tailored dress underneath, and the assorted food smudges on my face and arms, I look very prim and proper and worthy to be a well-to-do, respectable businessman's wife. If this doesn't make them happy, then I'm throwing in the *kuffiyeh.*

I swing the door open, huddling behind the heavy ebony from the chilly early spring winds blowing inside my entry.

"If this is spring, then what's winter like up here?"

"Georges?"

"Guilty," he says sheepishly.

"What .... how . . . Georges, what the hell are you doing here?"

"I should've called. . . . I just . . . Jesus, can I come in? I'm freezing!"

"No! They're going to be here any minute! What's the matter with you?"

"Ranya, please—I need to talk to you."

"Not now!"

"Then when?"

"Georges—this is my husband's home, don't you know that?"

I could have died then and there. A moment I wouldn't even let myself fantasize about for fear of depressing myself too much was right there in front of me, and I couldn't reach for it. After weeks of not seeing him, the details of his face, the exact curve of the twin ripples in his arms, precisely how much he towered over me, all these memories had begun to lose their sharpness. After that the small bits of fond memories would be next on the chopping board of time. How he defended me that day in London from the atrocious blonde in the frayed jeans and ugly sweater, the days at the magazine when he would call just to say hello, and that night with Joe.

Would those go, too? Where would I be then, robbed even of the memory of a time when a man cared that I was alive because he cared, not because he was duty bound to.

He hangs his head and shoves his hands deep inside his pockets.

"I was a complete moron," he says to his shoes.

"What are you talking about?"

"Priya told me. . . ."

Oh crap. The mortification makes my legs go numb. *What exactly did she say?*

"And even if she hadn't explained your . . . situation . . ."

Okay, now I am going to collapse.

"I still shouldn't have . . . reacted the way I did."

"I lied to you, Georges, you had every right to react however way you wanted."

Never mind that you shattered my heart to pieces in the process, but I deserved it.

"True, but . . . and here's the thing. . . . I think I love you."

He's not staring at his shoes anymore—sneakers that are perfectly inadequate for a Montreal early spring, which is to say winter for the rest of the world—he's staring straight at me.

He takes a step forward. I should back away. This is the moment you back away or else something really truly devastatingly horrible happens.

He breaches the small space between us, tilts my chin up to meet his face, gruff from a budding five o'clock shadow and slick with heat. I close my eyes and breathe him in. And then it happens. My shy, hesitant lips buckle under months of longing and despair, and the world around me, over me, and under my feet melts into nothingness.

"You have no idea how long I've been wanting to do that." He rests his forehead against mine.

I don't answer right away, still reeling from shock.

"What made you?" I finally manage, breathing in quick, short spurts of air.

"You'd be surprised how many friends you made down there. They wanted me to bring you back."

"What about you? What do you want?"

He lowers his lips toward mine, folding me in a cocoon of warmth.

"Ranya?"

Clunk. Smash. And splash, all over the sidewalk.

"What is this?" Dodi's mother is shaking from head to toe like a freshly shaven poodle in the middle of January. "What are you doing? May God curse the day we met you and your cursed family!" From her twisted mouth all the creative curses of the Arabic language spill out like lava from an outraged volcano. My father, my mother, my cousins, my entire genealogical tree are brought into the fray while Dodi stands helplessly behind her, shocked into numb silence.

"Get out of my house, you whore! You disgusting little—"

"Mother—"

"Shut up!" She reels at Dodi. "Shut up, shut up, shut up!

If you'd been enough of a man to control her in the first place she would never have dared do such a thing to you— to *us!*"

"And you . . ." Her wrath switches to Georges. "What are you still doing here? Out! Out or we call the police!"

Georges stands perfectly still for a few surreal moments. The corners of his mouth then start to curl up into a sardonic smile. His gaze skims the top of Ikraam's fake blond head and bores right into Dodi's terrified eyes.

"Don't you have something to say?"

Dodi's mouth gapes. He stares from one bemused face to my terrified one, and finally to his mother's indignant expression.

"Who is this man?" She juts her chin at Georges. "And what the hell is he talking about?"

Still, Dodi can't manage to utter a syllable. With his terrified eyes and ashen face he begs me for help.

"Dodi—what's going on? Did you know about this?" Ikraam rages on.

"I can't help you anymore, Dodi," I say. "I wish I could, but . . ." But it's his turn to fight his battles. All I could ever hope to do is to summon enough courage to fight mine. The charade is now well and truly over.

"How much time do you need?" Georges whispers to me.

"I won't be a minute. . . ."

I dash inside to the bedroom, and from the back of my closet I pull out the same duffel bag I'd packed the first time I ran away. The luggage tag with the MIA/YUL coding is still looped around the handle, tattered and smudged but there. This time as I haphazardly pull shirts and sweaters off racks and scour my drawers for whatever necessities I might need, I can't wipe the smile off my face. This time I'm not running away.

This time I'm going home.

Epilogue

"Ay, *papi!*"

I writhe and thrash and toss around until that familiar moment comes when everything inside my eyelids explodes into a firework display of lights and shadows and pure happiness. You could probably make solid bars out of this kind of happiness, *chica,* and bank on it.

"*¿Te gusta así?*" He slaps my toned derriere, though this year I've switched to interval training. You always need to switch things up, you know, shake things up, or else you don't grow.

Everyone knows that.

"Te amo, sabes." Diego sinks into the folds of my gorgeous Indian print sheets—those are probably due for a switch soon—and nestles his prickly chin into my neck.

"I love you, too," I say.

Okay, so this wasn't part of the plan, but as Tía Elvira might have counseled back in the day when there *was* a Tía Elvira, you've got to snatch love where you find it, *m'hija,* because it's rare and fleeting, and precious. I'm not talking about bullshit love. I'm talking about the cooks-for-you-when-you're-about-to-drop-dead-from-exhaustion, calls-you-just-for-the-hell-of-it, and asks-you-to-marry-him-twenty-five-thousand-times-a-day love. *That* kind of love.

Speaking of love in unexpected places, that *pendejo* Georges finally got his act together—with a little help from an unlikely pair—and was persuaded to see that life only throws so many opportunities at happiness your way. If you don't bite, life takes the hint. But, that being said, it's not easy to let go of old comforts. Even clinging to old pain sometimes feels better than risking fresh pain. Why else did I grab on to Joe for dear life? Why couldn't I shake Adam's shadow?

Who knows? I don't.

Diego stirs beside me. He's falling asleep. Pretty soon I know I'm going to be snoring as loud as he is (something he loves to point out to me on those occasions I happen to beat him to it). Calm people have a way of drawing you into their Zen orbit. I can't say I'm not enjoying all this "oneness with the universe," but I need to be sharp and on the ball if

I'm going to run my magazine with the same drive as I ran *Suéltate*.

That's right. *My* magazine. Not Joe's, not some big corporation's, not even Georges's, though I'm pretty sure he was a major investor. But I'll never know since he wasn't the one who cut me the check to start *Rio*.

Okay, so I named it after me. It wasn't out of some puffed-up sense of pride (okay—maybe just a little). "Rio" had a nice ring to it. It felt hopeful. Promising. Full of possibilities. Open. Plus, who am I kidding, that's my *name* up there, *chica*.

And if you're wondering why Zahra was the one to cut the check, it's because the girl's a major partner in Athena Capital these days, all the way up there in Boston. I say good for her. If misery had a face, I think it would have been Zahra's. She's different now, though. I went up there to make my pitch to the board, why I thought the market was ready for a magazine like *Rio,* and what my vision and mission was and all that jazz.

She'd lost weight, and her dumpiness wasn't so . . . well, it just wasn't that dumpy in the Boston context. I was the one who stuck out like a sore thumb, what with my white capris and bright peasant blouse with the wild print. People just don't *do* color up north, I swear. She says she's seeing someone now—imagine that. An NGO president or something. Next year they want to take some do-gooding trip to Africa together. This is Zahra's idea of romance. Is it any wonder we never got along? Still, it was about time she kicked her freaky Georges obsession. Good for her.

Claro, I recruited Ranya. She was freshly arrived from Montreal, all happy and bubbly and doe-eyed as ever. But this time brimming with confidence. Which was a nice change. With the confidence came a fair dose of stubbornness, but I still like the backboned version of her better. Tells me she's in the middle of divorce proceedings—¡qué escandaloso!—but if love could give people wings, she'd have made it to the moon by now. She even plucked that adorable Pakistani girl with her. Gave her her old job—waiting on me hand and foot. And though that article she wrote wouldn't have worked for *Suéltate,* it was a perfect fit for the more sophisticated, global outlook of *Rio.*

Diego stirs beside me, but this time I know he's not sleeping. He's very much awake.

Ay, chica.